SWINK

ADRIANA LOCKE

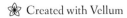

To everyone who has the courage to love who you love, even when people tell you not to.

And to Tiffany. For you.

ALSO BY ADRIANA LOCKE

The Exception Series

The Exception

The Connection

The Perception

The Landry Family Series

Sway

Swing

Switch

Swear

Swink

Sweet—coming soon

The Gibson Boys Series

Crank

Craft

Cross

Crave

Crazy

Dogwood Lane Series

Tumble

Tangle

Trouble

Restraint- Coming Soon

Standalone Novels

Sacrifice

Wherever It Leads

Written in the Scars

Lucky Number Eleven

Battle of Sexes

For an email every time Adriana has a new release, sign up for an alert here: http://bit.ly/AmazonAlertAddy or text the word adriana to 21000

SWINK

ONE

DOMINIC

I'm that guy.

Camilla Landry rustles against me, the silky fabric of her over-priced lingerie slipping along my bruised rib. The porcelain perfection of her skin is even more innocent against the colorful ink dotting my own. It's demure meets damaged, pampered meets punctured.

So, yeah, it's obvious I'm that guy. Dominic Hughes. Her attempt at rebellion. Her bid to see what the other side of the tracks feels like. I'm okay with being used, because from where I'm sitting, the other side of the tracks has never looked so good.

She lifts her head, her baby blue eyes finding the darker blues of my own. "What time is it, Dom?"

"Not sure. Around five, probably."

"I should get up and get ready to go."

"Yeah, you better. You'd hate to be late. Daddy wouldn't like that," I tease.

"It's not just my dad," she moans, smacking my stomach as she rises. "It's Ford's dinner party."

I start to give her shit, but the sight of her body dissolves the words before they can leave my mouth. She bends her five-two frame to pick up the panties I flung a few hours ago, her blonde hair hitting the curve of her hip.

She moves with ease, the result of finishing school and a stint in ballet that she claims to have hated. Even with her hair a mess from being wrapped around my fist and her cheeks flushed from the orgasms I expertly delivered, she still appears absolutely put together. Unaffected. Maybe even slightly aloof. That is, until she turns her head and catches me looking at her.

Just like the first time I saw her nearly a year ago, as soon as our eyes lock, everything changes. Her eyes hood, her lips parting ever-so-slightly. She bends again, slowly this time, her gaze never leaving mine.

With one arched brow, she scoops a pair of pink heels from the floor. The globes of her ass pop in the air and give me a glimpse of the sweet spot I enjoyed for the last couple of hours.

"Keep that shit up and you won't be going anywhere," I warn, not totally kidding.

"I have no idea what you're talking about. I'm just getting dressed." She turns away, her bare ass facing me, giving me a front row seat as she slips the lace up her legs.

The bedsprings groan as I leap off the bed and grab her around the waist before she can react with anything but a yelp. "Dom!" she giggles, her feet coming up off the floor as I lift her up and against me. Her chest rises and falls, the air rushing in and out of her lungs as she awaits my next move.

"You wanna fuck with me?" I whisper in her ear. Her body melts into mine as a spray of goosebumps spatters her skin. "I'm not sure how much more cock you can take today, pretty girl."

Letting her feet drop to the floor, I keep one arm wrapped tightly around her waist as I lean my body, nearly a foot taller, down with hers. My lips hover over the shell of her ear. The warmth of my breath against her skin causes her breathing to become even more rapid.

My free hand runs roughly down her body, starting just beneath her perky, full breasts and down the arch of her stomach to the tip of her pussy.

Her cheek is soft against my chest as she releases a loose, heavy breath.

"What do you want, Cam?"

"You."

The word is just one syllable, a barely audible rush of air. Yet, it's enough of a bucket of cold water, a dose of reality, to make me press a kiss to the back of her neck before stepping away.

"You better get dressed," I gruff, smacking her on the ass.

She glares at me over her shoulder. "I hate when you do this."

"Do what?"

There's no answer, but there doesn't have to be. Her point is clear and noted. For the record, I hate when I do this too. But it has to be done.

The bed squeaks again as I climb to the center and drop onto my side, wincing from the minor shot of pain in my rib. Propping my head up with one hand, I watch her sweep around the room, readying herself to leave.

I'd have no problem watching her move around my space all night. I'd actually love it, if I didn't have to feel the awkwardness that comes with her departure. I could just let it be, let her give me a weird look and walk out and leave it at that. Truth be told, I've let that happen with more girls than I care to count ... but not with Camilla.

Every time she leaves could be the last. And also unlike the girls before her, and most likely the girls that will come after, it would bother me to think the last time she was here ended on a sour note.

I'm a diversion in her life. I get it. So ideally she'll look back on it someday with nothing more than a smile and wet panties.

"So where are you going again?" I ask in a pathetic attempt to make small talk.

"To one of my brother's dinner parties," she says, buttoning up her shirt. "Ford and Ellie have some news about their baby, and they've invited us all over for dinner. Well, we're actually going to the Farm because Ellie realized how much of a production it is to have a dinner party with the entire Landry brood. So she caved and let Mom get catering from Hillary's House and we're just doing it at the family property."

"Sounds fun."

"You lie."

"Fine. It sounds boring as fuck," I grin.

"Trust me, it'll be anything but boring. When my four brothers and twin sister get together, it's always interesting."

"There's nothing remotely interesting about watching a bunch of yuppies have a dinner party," I point out. "And who calls it a 'dinner party,' anyway?"

"Normal people."

"Wrong answer, Ms. Landry. Yuppies. Yuppies call it a 'dinner party.'"

"Fine," she sighs, twisting her hair into a knot on the top of her head. "What would you call it?"

"Dinner with people. A barbecue. Supper. Dessert, if you're on the menu," I tease.

"You're impossible," she laughs, coming to the edge of the bed. "What are you doing tonight while I'm suppering with people?"

Rolling onto my back, I glance at her out of the corner of my eye. The light from the broken window causes a spray of color to dance across her features. Lifting my hand, I brush a lock of hair off her face, letting the pad of my thumb sweep against her forehead

"I'm meeting Bond at the gym in a little bit," I say carefully. "He's going to work out with me for a while."

"For the fight?"

"For the fight."

She sits on the edge of the mattress, but doesn't face me. She looks towards the doorway but her stare seems to go much farther. Her head is someplace else. Probably somewhere trying to decide whether or not to resurrect the argument we have every time my fights come up in conversation.

"I don't know why you do this, Dom," she says softly. "It's stupid."

"It's not stupid." I pull myself so I'm right behind her. I rest my hand on her shoulder. It covers her easily, her shoulders as narrow and delicate as the rest of her. "It's easy money. It's a couple of fights a year that land me a few grand. Besides, I like it."

"How can you like getting your head beat in for any amount of money?"

"I don't. That's why I don't let it happen."

"You say it like it's a fact," she says, twisting to look at me. "Like there's a chance you won't get hit."

"Oh, I'll get hit. I'll just hit him harder," I smirk.

She begins to protest, but I cover her mouth with mine. It takes a couple of seconds for her to give in and kiss me back. Her lips are soft and sweet, letting mine take the lead and guide her like one of those yoga sequences she does in the morning. When I finally pull back, I still see the fight in her eyes, but there's a smile on her lips.

"Don't you have somewhere to be?" I hint.

"Yes," she sighs, kissing me once more before standing. "I smell like you."

"If I've done my job you do."

"I'm going to have to go home and shower before I head to the Farm."

"There's a shower down the hallway, you know. But if you go getting naked—"

"I'll never leave," she finishes, giving me a little grin. "Call me later?"

"Yeah."

Kissing the tips of her fingers, she lays her hand towards me and blows. It's typical Cam—adorable on one hand, suggestively sexy on the other.

She doesn't look back as she leaves. As I hear the front door shut, a certain feeling settles over me, one that tells me this won't be the last time I see her.

I flop back on the bed with a smile of my own.

TWO

CAMILLA

I drop my purse on the sofa as quietly as I can, but it doesn't matter.

The Farm, which is actually an old plantation-style house on a few acres of land that my family has had for decades, is bustling with activity. The noise level makes one thing clear: my entire family is here. There are laughs ringing through the air, the sound of the television on some sports channel, and footsteps coming from every direction. As much as I hated leaving Dominic earlier, I love walking into this just as much.

My twin sister, Sienna, is sitting on a stool at the kitchen island watching our mother get things organized. The rest of the family dots the living room that's open to the kitchen. My brothers Barrett, Graham, Ford, and Lincoln are all discussing some business matter with our father. Lincoln holds his new son, Ryan, while his wife, Danielle, smiles adoringly through the window from the back porch.

Next to her outside is Barrett's wife, Alison, Ford's wife, Ellie, and Graham's girlfriend, Mallory. Mal is telling some story and Ellie is laughing, one hand on her pregnant belly.

A grin stretches across my face as I take them all in. Even though I'm the youngest, even younger than Sienna by two minutes, and am treated as such by everyone, there's nothing that makes me happier than being surrounded by them.

As I try to figure out how to assimilate and not draw attention to the fact I'm late—something the Landry's don't tolerate well—Barrett's son, Huxley, comes around the corner.

"Your dad was looking for you a few minutes ago," he whispers conspiratorially. "I told him I was pretty sure I saw you earlier."

"Thanks, Hux," I say, hitting the brim of his purple baseball cap.

My brother, Barrett, officially adopted Huxley a few weeks ago when he married Huxley's mother, Alison. I didn't really know the eleven-year-old very well until that night. When I woke up in the middle of the night for a drink, I found him at the kitchen island with a plate of cookies, glass of milk, and a lot of questions on his mind. We bonded over those cookies, both not completely sure—in our own ways—what the future held for us. We each knew what we wanted. The problem is, neither of us felt like we had any power over it. We were at the mercy of other people's decisions.

"Camilla Jane," my father's voice booms through the room. "Are you just getting here?"

"I've been here a while," I say, ignoring Huxley's red cheeks beside me. "I had a call I had to take outside."

Dad looks at me like he doesn't quite believe my story, but is redirected by something Ford says. When I look at my brother, he mouths "You're welcome."

While Sienna is closest to Lincoln, the youngest out of the boys, I'm closer with Ford. He and I both favor Mom a little more than Dad. We have a more compassionate side, and are maybe slightly less ambitious than our overachieving siblings. He's definitely the one I can go to for advice and won't just write me off as a pain in the butt.

"Let's go find your mama," Lincoln says to baby Ryan. He lifts off the couch and follows me as I head to the kitchen. "You have a hickey on your neck."

"What?" I almost yell, clapping a hand to the base of my throat.

My mind immediately goes back to Dom as I try to figure out when he did it.

Lincoln's laugh comes immediately. "I'm kidding. But a call? Really, Cam? Your lying game blows."

"I hate you," I say, trying to laugh but still feeling the panic. "That wasn't funny."

"No, it was. It was also very telling."

"Don't, Linc," I warn. "Don't go there."

"We're going to meet him sooner or later, you know."

"Maybe not," I shrug, ignoring his protest as I climb onto a stool beside my sister. "Hey, Sister. Hi, Mom."

"Hello, Camilla," Mom says from the sink. "Nice of you to bless us with your presence."

"I was ..." I start to give her the same story, but her quirked brow stops me. "I'm starving. When are we eating?"

Wiping her hands on a white towel, she faces me. Her eyes twinkle in a way that only happens when all of her kids, and now grandkids, are home. She's in her element, and by the way she's almost hopping on the balls of her feet, very excited to hear Ford and Ellie's news. "Let me grab Ellie and see if she's ready."

"Don't pressure her, Mom," Sienna laughs.

"I won't. I mean, I'll try not to."

As she heads out the sliding glass door, Sienna looks at me. "I take it you had a good day."

"I did, thank you very much."

"Should I ask?"

"Do you need to?"

She grins, swirling a straw in the tea in front of her. "No. You have that freshly-fucked look on your face. It's pretty, actually. Reminds me of the new blush I just bought."

"I'd rather get my blush from Dom."

"I can't say I blame you," she laughs. "How are things going with him?"

"They're going ..."

"Ellie was hoping you'd bring him tonight," Sienna says, choosing her words carefully.

I slump in my chair. "You know I can't bring him here."

"If you're going to keep seeing him, Cam, you're going to have to bring him around. You can't keep these parts of your life separate forever."

"And subject him to them?" I say, jabbing a thumb over my shoulder towards our brothers. "Who would rip into him first?"

"I think Dom can handle himself. Besides," she says, shoving the glass away, "haven't you met his family?"

"No. I mean, I've met Nate and Ryder, but that's it." I look at the marble counter, the gold flecks sparkling. "I don't know for sure how much family he has, really," I admit.

Sienna leans across the chair, her arms resting on the countertop. Her eyes, the exact same color blue as mine, narrow.

"It's not a normal relationship," I offer before she can start asking questions. "You know this."

"Because you don't want it or he doesn't?"

Hearing the door open behind us and my sister-in-laws' voices ringing through the air, I feel anxiety kick me in the gut. "It's not like we met online and courted each other," I hiss. "He showed up at my house to fix my air conditioning and—"

"Your air is broken?" Mom asks from behind me. "Have you called anyone?"

"Oh, she called someone," Sienna snorts as I elbow her in the side.

"It's fine now, Mom," I say, glaring at my sister. "What did Ellie say?"

Mom points across the room. I follow her gesture and see Ford and Ellie standing in the front of the living room, the same spot they were married in a few weeks ago. Ellie is snuggled under Ford's arm as they both wear massive grins.

"I believe my wife promised you all a little bit of news today," Ford teases.

"It's a girl, isn't it?" I ask, swiveling around in my seat. "Please, please, tell me it's a girl."

"We don't know," Ellie says. "That's not the surprise."

"It'll be a girl because Ford isn't quite the man I am to get a boy," Lincoln says, getting a jab in the side from Danielle. He pretend-winces, earning a disapproving glance from Dad.

"Want to do a little man vs. man?" Ford offers with a smirk. "I believe the last time I had you tapping out in three seconds."

"I just had a baby," Lincoln protests.

"Excuse me?" Danielle laughs. "I believe *I* had the baby."

"Enough," Mom interjects, holding her hands out. "Stay focused, children. Ellie, dear, would you like to please put me out of my misery and give us your news?"

Ellie smiles, still not quite sure what to do with the entire Landry clan at once. "Well, Mrs. Landry—"

"Vivian," Mom cuts her off. "For the hundredth time, it's Vivian. Or Mom. Or Grandma," she adds. "But not Mrs. Landry. That was my mother-in-law, God rest her soul."

"Vivian," Ellie starts again, "the news is ..." She looks around the room, fiddling with the hem of Ford's shirt. "The news is there are *two* Landry babies on their way."

"What?" I shout, jumping off my chair as the family erupts. Everyone talks at once, questions shouted from across the room, Sienna and I wearing the cheesiest smiles of our life. "You're having twins? Oh my God! This is fantastic!"

"Hey!" Ford laughs, motioning for us to settle down. Once we're quieted, he continues. "We aren't done."

"Don't tell me it's triplets!" Sienna squeals.

Barrett, his hand holding Alison's, shoves away from the wall and walks to the front of the room. He tries to hide the shit-eating grin on his face but fails. "Huxley! Come here, son," Barrett calls out.

Hux strides into the room like a peacock. He's changed out of his plaid button-up and is now wearing a white t-shirt with big, black letters: BIG BROTHER TO-BE.

"Barrett?" Mom says, her jaw dropping to the floor. "Alison?"

"Great," Graham groans from the sofa. "That leaves me as the only non-child-bearing Landry man." Mallory gives him a pointed look that makes us all laugh.

"Alison and I are expecting just a week after Ford and Ellie," Barrett announces. "We are having the second Landry baby."

Sienna and I race to Alison, swamping her with hugs and congratulations. She and Ellie both beam, their faces already hosting the glow of pregnancy, as my brothers stand by like they just won a gold medal.

"Congrats, Barrett," I say, giving him a hug.

"Thanks, Swink."

"You know you have to move back to Savannah, right? I need my little niece here to spoil rotten."

"Although it's a boy," Barrett laughs, "Alison and I have decided it's best I don't make a bid for the Presidency and we'll move back home after this term."

"Seriously? That's fantastic!"

"Where else should we be starting a family than with family, right? And with Ryan here and Ford's babies coming right around ours, it would be fun for them to grow up together."

"You're making me look bad," Graham says, coming up behind me and pulling Barrett in a half-hug. "Congrats, man. I wish you would've put it off a little longer, but I can't blame you."

"You need to get in on the action," I tell Graham. "We need a little mini-CEO around here to keep the next generation in line."

His brow pulls tight, his jaw clenching. "That's a conversation for a different day."

"Fine, fine," I say, holding my hands up. "No pressure."

Turning away, I intend to head to the kitchen, but find myself on the back patio. It's one of my favorite spots on the estate. The view over the lawn, the tree line, the edge of the lake that you can glimpse through the trees, is so peaceful. Climbing onto the porch swing, I feel the warm breeze against my face.

The ruckus in the house is still in full effect, the noise drifting through the windows and walls. An excitement races through my veins for my brothers and their wives, but a little dose of loneliness sits squarely in my chest.

All I've ever wanted to be in life is my mother. I've wanted a family, to work for charities, to have a fabulous husband and sweet, gorgeous children, and make dinners like you see on the covers of a magazine. As a little girl, I would play in front of my plastic kitchen for hours, making meals for my baby dolls.

I got a degree in liberal arts because my parents demanded we go to college but nothing felt right to me. Nursing, teaching, business—squeamish, cringes, yawns. College was just a filler, something to take the space from high school until I met the man that would sweep me off my feet.

Yet here I am. On a path that looks nothing like that.

Twenty-five years old. Dating—if you can call it that—a man that I have no future with, yet can't leave alone. The charity work I thought called my name is only semi-satisfying, and I'm left with major holes in what I thought I would be my life by now.

"You're so stupid," I say to myself as I pull out my phone. I scroll until I find his name and pull up my texts.

ME:HEY.

Dom:You suppering?

Me:Not yet. My brother is having a baby. Everyone is celebrating.

Dom:Didn't you know that?

Me:Another brother.

Dom:It's a fucking baby factory over there.

Me:I guess so. LOL

Dom:Shoot me a text when you make it home. K?

Me:Ok. Be careful.

Dom:Enjoy your dinner party.

Me:That was written with sarcasm. I can feel it.

Dom:I always make sure you feel it, babe.

WITH A LAUGH, I tuck my phone away. His statement is true—he does make me feel it. He makes me feel a whole hell of a lot more than I can afford to.

THREE

DOMINIC

The mats are cool and still a little damp from the cleaning agent Hannah used on them a little while ago. I sit, legs together, and bend forward, loosening my hamstrings.

Hannah's gaze is heavy on my back as I stretch. She's the gym equivalent of a lot lizard—the chick that's ready and willing to give you a whirl. Or a twirl. Hell, she'll give you whatever you request with an enthusiasm that's hard to match.

That's what girls like that do. They know how the game is played and they want their chance, their fifteen minutes of legs spread wide open, to see if they can sink you as you sink into them. This is especially true if you're the fighter the gym is known for. That either makes you extra special or extra targeted, depending on how you look at it.

It's easy to be persuaded by how crazy girls like that seem for you. I mean, enthusiasm is fifty-one percent of what makes a good fuck. It's hard to beat an eagerness to take your cock like it's her purpose in life. Think about it. A little zest for the best can make up for a lot of the rest. A lot, but not all.

Fifty-one percent might be a majority, but no one ever said that was a passing grade.

As I look over my shoulder and see her watching me from the desk, the conclusion I came to six months ago when she walked in the door is reconfirmed: extra targeted.

"How's your rib, Dom?" she asks.

"It's good."

"Bond was worried he broke it."

"I'm sure he was," I say.

Turning away from her, my hands flurry against a heavy bag. With each snap, my muscles ease a little of the tension I seem to have been born with. It's something I can never totally get rid of. It's a feeling that something is always either wrong or about to go sideways. The result, I suppose, of growing up with an alcoholic father and a mother too weak to tell him to go fuck himself.

"Yo, Dom!"

Stepping back and sucking in a quick breath of air, I glance towards the locker room.

"Hey, Nate," I say to my brother. "Didn't know you were here."

"Yeah, I just stopped to get a quick workout in before I head to the bar. My bartender called off tonight so I got Chrissy to watch Ryder."

"You still fucking her?"

He grins. "Not on the regular. But she wanted a little last night and I gave it to her like the giver I am. So she owed me one."

"I love how you convince her that you're doing her some kind of favor," I laugh.

"Hey, she likes my cock and my kid. What else could I ask for?"

"I'd put not trying to get herself knocked up on the list."

"Which is why," he says, drawing out the last syllable, "I'm not fucking her on the regular." He taps the side of his head. "I'm the one with the brains. Remember?"

My right hand smacks the side of the bag in a quick jab. "That's what you keep telling me."

He stands with his hands in the pockets of his jeans, watching me work. Nate is three years older, a little shorter, and a lot stockier. We look a lot alike besides our build with jet black hair, our mother's blue eyes, and a musculature that's proven to be the only good thing our father ever did for us.

"I got a call from the bank today."

My head snaps to Nate, the weight of those words hitting me like a perfectly delivered one-two. "What'd they say?"

"They said I got the loan."

Sighing in relief, I wrap an arm around the bag. "That's good news."

"It'll take sixty days or so to get the money, so I gotta figure out how to float until then. But, yeah, man, that has me breathing a little easier."

"You know it's bullshit," I spit. "They triple your property taxes on The Gold Room and expect you to just come up with that while doubling your fucking license fees?"

"I know. But what can I do?"

"Just pisses me off," I say, slamming a fist into the bag as my blood pressure picks up. "You got some silver-spoon-fed assholes sitting somewhere trying to figure out how they can give themselves a raise. What do they do? They charge you for it while you're busting ass day in and day out to feed Ryder."

Nate's serenity does what it's done since the day we were at the park and our mom came with tears streaking down her cheeks, telling us our oldest brother got hit by a car—it centers me.

No matter how bad life gets, Nate weathers it. He took the hits from our dad when he was drunk. He kept me calm when our world fell apart and the third piece of our brotherhood was killed. He didn't completely lose his shit either when Ryder's mom overdosed on heroin six months after the kid was born.

We're brothers, as strong as the DNA that binds us. But we're also completely different, and while he accepts the bureaucrats almost forcing him to close the doors on his bar, I'd be happy rolling some heads.

"It'll work out," Nate says, smacking me on the back. "It always does."

"My offer still stands."

"What offer is that?"

"You and Ryder move in with me. Just until the loan goes through. Between rent and utilities, man, you'd save a ton."

He rubs the toe of his shoe over the floor, nudging the edge of the mat.

"It makes sense, Nate."

"I don't want to go cramping your style," he laughs. "You don't know what it's like living with a four-year-old."

"Just don't bring that purple dinosaur video," I wince, "and it'll be fine. It's just for a few months, right?"

"Yeah." He looks me in the eye, the start of a smirk on his lips. "What about Cam?"

"She doesn't live with me."

"No shit. She wouldn't be caught dead living in that apartment," Nate laughs. "But I'm guessing she comes over for booty calls now and then."

My eyebrows wiggle as I think of her from a couple of hours ago. "God, that ass."

"You're gonna have a hard time letting that one go, huh?"

"Nah," I say, tapping at the bag again. "I know what time it is. I know how this goes."

"The one time I knew how it went, it almost made it harder not falling for her." He shoves his hands in his pockets again, watching me throw punches. "Of course, with me it was with a girl that set a new level of crazy. With you, it's with the princess of Savannah."

"What can I say?" I laugh.

"As much as I hate her brothers," he admits, "I kinda like her."

"You're just pissed they walked in your bar like they owned the place."

"Damn right I am. They probably could've pulled out their wallets and bought the place with their pocket change, and I find that downright offensive."

My laughter booms through the gym, getting the attention of the two guys sparring in the ring across the room. "So, you and Ryder gonna move in or what?"

"You sure it won't fuck up your love life?"

"Love life? Try fuck life, and no, it won't."

A wash of relief passes through his eyes and isn't missed by me. "Thanks, brother."

"Shut the fuck up and just don't ask me to help you move your shit." Circling the bag, I concentrate on my footwork and not the thoughts of Camilla that are wiggling their way in my mind.

"Bond's here, so I'm out," Nate growls. "Call me when you're done and we can work out the details."

"Okay." Over his shoulder, my gaze lands on Hannah's. She's talking to Bond, but watching me. Flipping my sight back to my brother, I laugh. "I think this will be a quick one."

"What? The workout or her?" he asks with a little nod to Hannah.

"I'm not touching that with a ten-foot pole."

"I never could count well," he says, heading for the door.

"And you say you're the smart one," I call after him.

"We all have our moments."

As Bond's voice trails through the air and makes its way to me, my eyes involuntarily roll to the back of my head.

Bond Grayson is a fantastic boxer, my height and weight, and aggressive. He's the perfect training partner—or he would be, if he could keep his mouth shut.

Outside the ring, he's the epitome of what I can't stand. Loud, arrogant, and impulsive—he's a dick. I can only barely tolerate him the time or two a week we meet up to train, and I wouldn't tolerate him then if I didn't need that prize money a couple of times a year.

My shoulders sag as the truth swirls around me.

I don't really need that money this year. God knows my ribs don't need the punishment either. But Nate and Ryder do.

With the curled smirk of Bond coming straight at me, I push aside what I really want to do—saying fuck it and going to find Cam— and prepare to bang it out with Bond.

FOUR

CAMILLA

"Hey," I say into the phone as my keys hit the little glass tray I keep by the door. "How was the gym?"

"You home yet?"

My brows furrow at his quick question. "I just walked in. Why?"

"No reason."

"I was going to call you in a second," I tell him. "I literally *just* walked in the door. Is everything okay?"

He blows out a breath. "I just, you know, it's getting late and I wanted to make sure you made it home."

A warmth unleashes in my chest and pulls the corners of my lips into an achingly wide grin. "Yeah, I'm home." I wait for him to say something else, but he doesn't. "So, how did it go with Bond?"

"He left holding his ribs tonight, so pretty damn good, if you ask me."

"Isn't training supposed to mean helping each other get better?" I ask, flipping on the light in the kitchen. "It sounds to me when you 'work out' with him, it's a little more serious than that."

"Any time two men are fighting, whether it's sparring or actually going at it, there's ego on the line. Factor in that it's him I'm in there with and there's a whole new dimension to consider."

As he rants about how much he dislikes Bond, I find a carton of chocolate frozen yogurt in the freezer and sit down at the table with a spoon. "I still think you should just stop fighting altogether."

"Not your choice."

Stabbing my spoon in the dessert with a little more gusto than necessary, I sigh. "I know it's not my choice. You've made it perfectly clear you don't want my opinion on the matter."

"If you know that's true, you'd think you'd stop throwing it out there left and right."

There's a moment of silence, one that worries me every time it happens. I find myself holding my breath, my chest burning, as I stare off into space and brace myself for him to give me a bullshit answer and end the call. One of these days, it's going to happen.

I'm surprised it hasn't yet. When I pulled my door open last summer, looking like a sweaty mess, I didn't expect to see him on the other side. I didn't expect to have my knees get all wobbly or my stomach turn to mush at the smile he sent my way.

There was no way to predict I would've been handing my phone number over to the air conditioner repair guy a few hours later or that I'd be enjoying a hamburger and French fry dinner with him the next evening. Least of all, there was absolutely no way in the world I would've believed I would see him again almost every day for the next ten months. But I have.

His presence in my life feels, in lots of ways, like I'm stuck in limbo. Moving on in any real way with Dom is unrealistic. I shouldn't even want it. But I do and I don't know where that puts me. Or him. Or us.

"Nate is moving in with me."

"Why?" I ask, caught off guard.

"He's behind on a bunch of payments and managed to get a loan, but it'll be a couple of months before it's processed or something. He and Ryder are going to shack up here until he gets things sorted."

"That's nice of you," I offer.

"Yeah, well, what am I supposed to do? It's family, right?"

"Of course. My family would do the same."

"Your family would just buy the other person a house," he laughs. "I bet two of you haven't lived together since you were kids."

"Not true," I say, taking a bite of my froyo. "Sienna and I lived together until she moved to LA."

He laughs again. "And she managed to stay away from you for how long?"

"She was there for four years, actually. She still kind of lives there. I think," I consider, spooning in another glob of yogurt.

"She's been in Savannah the whole time I've known you. She doesn't live in LA, sweetheart."

"She still has an apartment there," I counter.

"Sienna lives in LA as much as I do, and I've never even been there."

Giggling at his analogy, I lick the spoon. "Yeah, that's probably true. She's thinking of moving to Illinois now anyway."

"Must be nice."

Jamming my spoon back in the carton, I sit back in my chair. "What's that supposed to mean?"

"Nothing."

"No, say it."

"Say what?"

I can hear the smirk in his voice, the level of amusement I'm providing thick in his tone. It annoys me that he doesn't take me seriously. That he thinks my life is some kind of charmed existence that doesn't have a lot of substance.

He's never said that, not to my face, anyway. I see it hidden in the depths of his sapphire-colored eyes sometimes.

He doesn't have a problem with the volunteer work I do. He just thinks I should be doing something else, something that matters specifically to me. That pushes me. That drives me. And I don't know how I feel about that.

"Don't laugh at me, Dominic Hughes," I warn.

"Or what, Camilla Landry? What will you do?"

I pause. "I don't know."

He just laughs harder. "I'm not laughing at you, babe. I'm laughing at how your sweet little voice tries so hard to break into a roar soon as you're mad, but it can't quite get there."

"I'm not mad."

"Then what are you?"

"I don't know."

"No, you *do* know," he goads. "I hit a nerve. Say it, Cam. Tell me how you really feel."

"You didn't hit a nerve—"

"One of these days, you're going to blow the fuck up, and I'm going to laugh my ass off."

"What if I blow up at you?" I tease. "You won't be laughing then."

"Yeah, I will, and I can't wait to see it. You're all prim and proper, and then—boom! Here she comes."

"I wish I was *coming*," I hint, kicking off my shoes. "My body is so *tight*. I could use a good workout."

A low rumble rolls through the line. The gravelly sound floods my veins like the lit end of a stick of dynamite. The fire scorches, burning up the fuse as it hits the center of my thighs. "Dom," I whisper, clenching my legs together. "Stop it."

"I didn't say a word."

"You didn't have to."

The line might be quiet, but it's not still. It's filled with an anticipation, a feeling that one of us might jump to action. With bated breath, I stare at the shaker of cinnamon on the counter that I forgot to put away at breakfast and wait for his next move.

"If I didn't have to get up so damn early in the morning and head up north for a job, I'd be on my way over," he promises.

"What would you do when you got here?"

It's a loaded question, one that will only make it harder that he's not here tonight. Not that he would be here all night anyway. He doesn't sleep here. He won't. He'll come over, but I always wake up in my bed alone.

"I'd hope you'd be wearing that yellow silk robe that isn't long enough to cover your ass," he says, a grit to his voice that's as smooth as it is rough. It reminds me of his hands—soft enough to caress, yet coarse enough to cause my body to fire on all cylinders. "I'd find you standing in the kitchen, watching porn on your phone."

"No, you wouldn't!" I giggle. "I don't watch porn on my phone."

"This is my little fantasy," he teases. "Don't interrupt."

"Fine. Continue on," I say, propping one leg up on a neighboring chair.

"I'd walk in behind you and almost lose it when I see you with your hand between your legs. Your head would fall back just a little as you moan like you do when you're turned on. I'd wrap your hair, still wet from a shower, around my fist and tug your head back just a little more so I can bury my face in the crook of your neck."

The whimper that passes my lips isn't intentional, but I couldn't deny it if I wanted to. The thought of his hands on my skin, his breath against my cheek, his cock rock hard and long against the small of my back, has me shifting in my seat.

Lifting the hem of my floral-print dress, I move aside the lace of my panties and feel the heat and wetness radiating from between my legs.

"I'd kiss you right behind the ear just so I could feel you shiver against me," he breathes. "Smelling your vanilla perfume mixed with the scent of you all turned on would make me so fucking hard."

"And me so wet," I whisper.

"I lay my hand over yours," he continues, "my fingers holding yours in place. You breathe in, the top of your robe falling open so I can see those big, round titties swollen for me, wanting my mouth on them."

"God, Dom," I groan, spreading my legs a little wider. Flicking at my engorged clit, the sensation makes me gush a breath of pure need.

"What are you doing right now?" he whispers.

"Ah," is my response as I roll the nub with my thumb, my eyes squeezed closed imagining it is Dominic's hand on me and not mine.

"Are you touching yourself, Camilla?"

"Yes."

"Fuck," he hisses. "Do you wish it were me?"

"Yes."

"I'd shove your robe up, bend you over the table, and bury myself inside you so deep you almost can't take it. Would you like that?"

"Yes," I almost moan. My back is now arched, my breathing heavy and panting, as I replay two days ago when his words tonight were almost a play-by-play.

"I love the way you squeeze around me. Your little pussy almost milks my cock, begs for it. Do you know that?"

My eyelids clench together harder, almost painfully hard, as I touch myself in just the right way. The burn begins low in my stomach, the rumble getting louder with each and every movement of my hand.

The lace of my panties causes friction against the back of my hand, just another bit of sensation that sends me on a spiral higher and higher.

"Think of how good it feels when I hit that spot in the back of your pussy," he coaxes. "The way you let loose. How your legs shake as you flood my cock with so much fucking juice that it almost shoves me out of you."

"Dom," I utter through clenched teeth as the tremors of my orgasm hit me full-on.

"You coming, baby? You coming thinking of me buried inside you?"

"Yessssss."

My body hums at the imagery he's painted for me, the thought of him doing all of those things sending me on a high that could only be topped if it *were* him doing them.

Sucking in a breath, I hear him follow suit, as I whimper at the aftershocks of my climax. My legs relax, the riot in my stomach eases, as I let my head fall back with a contented, satisfied sigh.

"Damn, lady," Dom says just as I'm piecing myself back together. "That was ridiculously sexy."

My cheeks heat as I drop my hand to the side, my body now spent. Embarrassment rears its ugly head as I realize, without an orgasm-needing brain, what just happened.

"Cam?"

"Yeah?"

"Don't."

"Don't what?" I ask, trying to keep my tone light.

"Don't be embarrassed."

"I'm not."

"Yes, you are. I hear it in your voice and you're a terrible liar."

"That's the second time I've been told that today," I laugh.

"Who else you lying to?"

"Lincoln, but I wasn't really lying to him. He was just being an ass."

Dominic takes a deep breath before blowing it out slowly. "Did that conversation have anything to do with me?"

"Why would it? They don't know what I'm doing."

"You mean slumming it?"

"Stop it, Dominic."

He chuckles through the phone. "I'm kidding."

"Do you want to meet them?" I ask with hesitation. It would be a bloodbath, most likely, and my family would definitely have reservations. And questions. And issues. Still, I can't deny the leap in my chest that maybe his reaction is because we're *there*. To the point where he does want to admit to being serious. To—

"Hell, no."

My spirits fall like a piece of confetti out of a sixty-story building. "I didn't think so." I stand up and get my skirt smoothed back down. "My froyo is melting on the table."

"That could be fun."

"What?"

"Melted ice cream. If I would've known that was happening, I could've added it into my little fantasy."

Still reeling from the hopes of a few seconds ago, I watch the chocolate treat create a little puddle on the white tabletop. "You should remember that next time."

"Noted. But, in the meantime, I'm gonna get off of here so I can go get myself off. That little show you just put on has my cock so hard it's ready to explode."

"If you came over here, I'd help you out with that."

"I bet you would." I hear him groan and he moves. "You have any plans for tomorrow?"

"I'm having lunch with my mom, Sienna, and a couple of my brothers' wives. There's a charity thing they want to put together and I volunteered to head the effort. What about you?"

"Working then heading to the gym straight after. Maybe we can hook up late?"

"I'd like that."

He pauses. "Me too, Cam. Talk to you tomorrow."

"Okay."

"Later." And just like that, the line goes dead.

I pad down the hall and into the master bathroom, washing my hands, teeth, and face. Dressing in the yellow robe that I know now is Dom's favorite, I climb into bed.

Looking around the white walls, white carpet, and pale pink furnishings, I think back to last night. This time yesterday I was snuggled up in Dom's bed. His ratty blue comforter, eighties-style wood paneling, and grey shag carpeting that I wouldn't wish on my worst enemy is almost preferable right now to lying here alone.

Without him.

"Come on, Cam," I admonish myself, burrowing in the down blankets. "You can't expect anything. Not from him."

And I shouldn't expect anything from him. Worse, I shouldn't want anything from him. He's not what I need.

I need stability. I need a five-year plan. I need someone that can raise a family and give me and my future babies a solid foundation. He's none of that. I'm not even sure he's capable of it. Worst of all, he's made it obvious he doesn't want it.

He doesn't even want to integrate me into his life or be interwoven into mine. He doesn't want me at the gym, at Nate's bar, and he's not about to go to the Farm for Sunday dinner. As wonderful as he is when we're together, he has a way of making it clear there's a line between my world and his, and that line will remain. I'm an interesting addition to his collection of women, and while I know he likes being with me, I also know there's nothing between us that will last forever.

It can't. All of those dreams I want to come true aren't possible with him.

"Uh," I grumble, trying to get comfortable.

My stomach sours as I imagine working him into my life. Explaining to my family the man I love fights for a living. Can barely pay his rent. Is related to Nolan—the man that tried to ruin Barrett's entire career.

Closing my eyes, it's the memory of his face that greets me. I imagine he's behind me, his chin resting on my head the way he does when he's waiting for me to fall asleep. It's this feeling, this warmth, that makes me want to blur the line he so carefully creates so I don't have to eventually let it go.

FIVE

DOMINIC

Climbing out the shower and wrapping a towel around my waist, I rub the fog off the bathroom mirror. There's a small cut over my right eye that shouldn't look too bad by morning. My face lights up in the glass as I picture Camilla's reaction to the scrape if she were here.

She hates me fighting. It seems barbaric to her on some level. She can't imagine someone being so down and out that they would willingly go into a brawl to get a payday. I tried to explain it to her the first time it came up in conversation, but that was the last time I wasted my effort. She won't get it. How could she? She just swipes a card if she wants something or asks her brother for the money from her trust fund if it's over a certain amount.

That's what *I* can't imagine—letting someone else control my shit. They control everything about her from where her money goes to who she dates to what she does with her afternoons. It's wild.

It's also one of the reasons why this little thing we have going on is temporary. It's carried on a little longer than I expected it to, but that doesn't mean an expiration date isn't stamped on it somewhere. Her world isn't just the other side of the tracks; it may as well be the other side of the fucking universe. My side? It's no place for a girl like her, a girl that not only nails that fifty-one percent, but aces the other forty-nine. A girl that's way outta my league.

My phone rings in the bedroom and I shut the light off behind me before heading across the hallway. It's buzzing on my nightstand when I pick it up.

A little drop of disappointment hits me when I realize it's not Cam. "Hey, Nate," I say, sitting on the edge of the bed. "What's up?"

"Just got Ryder to bed. Chrissy let him have way too much sugar tonight and he wouldn't settle down. It was rough, man. I pulled out all the stops, even singing that twinkle star song." He laughs. "Hell, before it was over, I was singing the old Oscar Meyer hot dog commercial theme."

"What a way to spend a night," I laugh.

"Yeah, but fuck it, Dom. I mean, what else is there, really? I had three chicks on the bar tonight, basically doing a strip show by the time we closed. Juicy asses, big titties, lips carved to wrap around a cock. There was a time in my life when that was the end to a great day. Now, I just wanted to get home before Ryder went to sleep."

"I get that. He's your boy."

"Yeah," he sighs through the phone. "I don't know. It's more than that. It's ... Remember Dad not being home? Hell, half the time Mom wasn't either? We'd let ourselves in after school and pour some shredded cheese on some stale tortilla chips and watch television? I want to give him something more, something better than what we had growing up."

"You're doing that," I say, running a hand over my damp hair. "He never has to worry about where his next meal is coming from. That's more than we had a lot of the time."

"I was thinking ... maybe when the loan goes through, and I get everything caught up, maybe I can start thinking about changing the atmosphere in The Gold Room."

"To what?"

"Something more respectable, I guess."

"You're going yuppie on me, aren't you?"

He barks a fit of laughter through the phone. "Fuck, no. I just mean clean the place up some. Change our reputation a little. Maybe pull in a different group of customers, ones that have more money than Joe and Copper."

"So you mean ones that have any money?"

"Basically, yeah."

"Joe ever paid his tab?"

"Nope."

"Did you stop letting him charge?"

"Nope." Before I can respond, he keeps going. "Sometimes that ham sandwich is all he eats all day. How do I cut him off, Dom? He doesn't ask for much. A drink and a sandwich sometimes. And he pays when he can."

My heart tugs at the predicament. The hollowness in my stomach -- from being hungry and scared and not seeing a clear way out after Mom's death came a year after Dad's -- is never too far away. "I feel ya. Maybe think it through some between now and the loan going through and get a plan in place."

"That's what I'm thinking. This is either going to have to be a long-term, successful thing or a really expensive headache."

His words spark something in my brain that I've been toying with for the past few months. Maybe it's time to start looking at the HVAC job as a career, that I might be at the point in life where things just are the way they are. Go in all the way because ... this is it.

I've always felt like something was going to change, that if I peddled along, busted my ass, kept going for long enough, eventually there would be a turning point. That things would get easier. That I'd get the stability and straightforward life I'd always craved.

Maybe that's not true.

Maybe it's always a struggle. Realization is starting to set in that maybe this life *is* my life. Whatever hopes I had of rising above my current situation, of starting my own business, of making something out of myself, isn't really going to happen. Maybe the stars were just stacked against me from the night my inebriated father fucked my mother.

I've been considering I need to accept all this and move forward accordingly, being real with myself about what's what. Before that can work its way into my psyche, my brother groans.

"Ryder is moving around. Shit."

"So I have that to look forward to," I say, half-kidding.

"You still want us? Look, Dom, if not it's no big deal. We'll figure—"

"Damn it. If I didn't want you to come, I wouldn't have offered."

"You know I appreciate it, right?" he says. The relief is evident, lingering on the last note. "I'll help out with the rent. With groceries. Whatever you want."

"We'll figure it out." I look across the hall into the dark bathroom. "There's a bed in the guest room. If you want to bring his kid bed with you, you can fit it in there. Or one of you can take the couch."

"Don't worry about it. I'll get it all sorted." He heaves another breath. "Did you mention it to Cam?"

Her face pops up in my mind and I fall back on my sheets, wishing she was lying a few inches over and waiting on me to end the call and curl up next to her to listen to her lecture me about the cut above my eye. "Yeah, I told her."

"She okay with it?"

"It's not her decision."

"So that's a no?"

"It's a 'I didn't ask her opinion,'" I tell him. "Why would I? I fuck her sometimes. That's it."

"Oh, that's it, huh?" His laugh makes me cringe. "I think not, little brother."

"Okay. I fuck her often. Better?"

"Sure. If that makes you happy, I don't give a shit. But I think it's a little deeper than that."

He waits for me to respond, but I don't. Not immediately. I think about his question and how I can navigate these waters. Was my assessment of my relationship with Camilla accurate? Fuck no. But should it be? Definitely.

It's my fault I see her so damn much. I can't help myself. And as much as I'd like it to be just for the sex, even I know it's not. That's what fucks me—the non-fucking. That's where I'm going to get so burned I'm afraid I'll be unrecognizable.

"You know, it's okay to actually feel something for someone, Dominic."

"You're using my whole name now. Is that some kind of hint that you mean business?"

"That's my way of telling you to listen to me before you go messing up a lot of shit," he sighs.

My abs strain as I sit back up, my eye starting to pulse like it's swelling. "Look at me," I laugh, "and look at her. I'm sitting here with the taste of blood in my mouth from the cut inside my lip, and she's lying on some thread-count bullshit I don't even understand. You don't think this isn't already messed up?"

"No. I don't."

"And you claim to be the smart one," I joke. "Look, I'm okay with this as-is. I see it for what it is. But don't go telling me, 'It's okay to have feelings for someone, Dominic,'" I mock, "because it ain't real. You don't have feelings for something that's gonna be busted in the days to come."

"You've been with her almost a year," he tosses out like he's some kind of genius.

"Okay. Fine. You wanna go with me to meet her family? I mean, let's just do the family-to-family thing. You've already made friends with her brothers, yeah?"

"Fuck them," he growls.

"My point. That's before they even know our uncle is the guy that almost tanked Barrett's campaign. How's that gonna look in their press release in the next election cycle?" I point out. "Look, I hate Nolan too. But that doesn't matter. It's all about appearances with these people, Nate. This would be a PR nightmare, and they're all about avoiding the problem."

"Again, fuck them."

I shrug, even though he can't see me. "And then the shit about—"

"Don't tell me you're going there. Our piece-of-shit father has nothing to do with anything."

"But he does."

"But *he doesn't*," he hisses. "Use whatever reasoning you want for not locking that girl down, but don't let that motherfucker play a part. That's not fair to her or you."

"Fair or not, it's life," I say, feeling defeated.

He yawns through the line, saying something I can't make out.

"I'm guessing you said you'll see me tomorrow," I say, glancing at the clock. "I gotta try to get some sleep."

"Me too. I'll start moving our stuff in tomorrow?"

"Sounds good. I'll be working up north, but you have a key, right?"

"Yeah. Thanks again, Dom."

"No problem. See ya tomorrow."

"Bye."

Dropping the phone to the blankets, I lie back again. My head feels foggy like it usually does after a sparring session.

Closing my eyes, I see Camilla's face. The fact that I'm beginning to associate her with my life—that she's what I envision when I have six seconds of quiet or how I automatically hope to see her in my bed —worries me a little. No, it worries me a lot.

I get why. She's the full one-hundred percent. The problem? I'm not.

SIX

CAMILLA

"Camilla, would you wait a moment, please?" My mother gives me her best no-nonsense look over her clasped hands.

"Sure." I fight the anxiety in my chest as I say goodbye to my sisters-in-law and watch them walk out of Picante, a restaurant nestled inside a ritzy hotel downtown. We had lunch and discussed a charity launch the family is putting together through Landry Holdings. It's been a nice afternoon ... until now.

I know the look on her face. This isn't Mom wanting to get pedicures tomorrow. This is her wanting to *talk*. Real talk. The kind I've been avoiding.

Smoothing out my dress, I retake my seat. "What's up?"

"I wanted to see how you were, sweetie."

"I'm fine," I say, furrowing my brow. "Why would you ask?"

It's a rhetorical question. There's no doubt why she's asking. The only thing I'm unsure about is why she hasn't done this before now. Still, I'm not offering information freely. If she wants something, she's going to have to ask for it.

She gives me a knowing smile. "It's nice to see you in love."

"What are you talking about?" I scoff, feeling my cheeks heat.

Her laugh makes me feel like a little girl called out on a white lie. "Darling, I'm not blind. Or deaf," she sighs, rolling her eyes. "Your brothers—"

"It was Lincoln, wasn't it?"

"No," she giggles. "It wasn't."

"Then it was Graham."

"Camilla, stop it."

"They're overbearing, Mother," I hiss. "They won't leave it be. I don't have to parade whoever I'm seeing in front of the family if I don't want to. Shit."

"Camilla Jane!" Her jaw drops open. "That's no way for a lady to talk."

"This is also no way to be treated," I volley back.

"They're just worried about their little sister. You can't blame them."

"Oh, I can."

She sits back in her seat, getting a new strategy together. It's the look in her eye, the way the greens flare through the blues that has me forcing a swallow.

"I had a chat with Ford yesterday after the baby announcement. He's worried, Camilla."

"I give up," I say, throwing my hands in the air. "I see now why Sienna wants to move to Illinois."

"That isn't nice."

"This isn't nice either! Don't you see?"

She ignores me. "Ford hinted that the boys want to call up Nick Parker—"

"The private investigator?" I cry, recognizing the name from Barrett's campaign. "Mother!"

"I told him not to," she promises. "I said that was a step too far."

"You think?"

"But, honey, you're going to have to let us meet him."

She sips her water, the lemon a bright spot as it gets flipped below the ice. I focus on that and not the impending doom that's burrowing in my gut, making the Cobb salad I just ate threaten to come back up.

"I want you to know," Mom says, wiping her lips with a linen cloth, "that I trust your judgement. If you like this man, then I'm sure he's an admirable person."

"I do like him."

"Do you love him?"

It's easier to ponder this question in the privacy of your own mind. There, you can answer or not, tell the truth or not, shove it off to the side if you prefer while you go do something else. It's impossible to consider this question sitting across from the one person that can read you like a book.

"Camilla?"

"I don't know."

"Then you don't," she says simply. "If you love someone, you know it."

"It's more complicated than that, Mom."

"Honey," she says, her bracelets jingling off the tabletop as she leans forward, "love is always complicated."

"I said I didn't know. You said that means I don't."

She smiles. "Can I give you some advice?"

"You're going to anyway."

"Your brothers are overbearing. I know that. Your father can be too. But don't let them sway you to or from someone that makes you happy. Okay?"

My eyes drop to the table, my stomach churning. "What if ... what if no one will like him? What if they even hate him or don't understand him?"

"Is he nice to you?"

"Yes," I say immediately, looking up at her.

"Does he make you smile?"

My lips turn up. "Yes."

"Is he respectful? Is he loyal?"

"Yes."

"Then your brothers will come around," she says. "And if they don't, you'll have to tell your mom. I hear she has some pull. Most of them have wives now too that can help keep them in line."

Although I'm still not sure this helps anything or only confuses me more, I stand and walk around the table. Wrapping my arms around her, I squeeze. She smells of expensive perfume and the warmth of home. "Thank you," I say against her cheek.

She pats my arm. "I do want you to think about introducing him to someone. Me, Ford, Graham—"

"Graham?" I say, pulling back. "Let's just ask for his tax returns and background check while we're at it. He'll make him think it's an interview for a job!"

Mom laughs, pushing away from the table. "It is, in a way. If he's serious about stepping into your life, your brothers ... *and your father and I,*" she says pointedly, "will expect a certain level of responsibility."

We gather our things and head for the elevator. I admire the way she almost glides through the room, waving discreetly at certain acquaintances.

"Mom?"

"What, Camilla?"

I rest my head on her shoulder as we stand behind a handful of people for the elevator waiting for the button to ding. "Why couldn't you have had Sienna and I first?"

"We had to save the best for last." She turns her head until she's looking at me and winks.

"Good point."

**

The Gold Room sits in front of me in all its non-glory. I didn't mean to come here specifically. When I left Mom in the parking lot of Picante, I didn't want to go home. I didn't want to call my friend Joy and see if she wanted to head to yoga or go shopping. All I wanted was to see Dominic. Maybe I even needed to see him, but the thought of that makes me lightheaded.

Now I'm here. Biting my lip. Fighting the rumble in my gut.

If needing to see him makes me lightheaded, seeing him here, at the bar, makes me downright dizzy.

Looking from the half-lit sign to my phone, wondering if I should call him first and warn him or just walk in, I refuse to bite my freshly painted nails even though I want to gnaw them off.

It could very well be counterproductive to think showing up here will satisfy the craving I have for him. The Gold Room is off-limits to me. Yet, here I am.

"You're stupid," I mutter to myself, grabbing my purse off the passenger seat and locking the car door behind me. I garner a whistle and a lewd offer before I can get to the heavy front doors. It takes a little more effort than it should to pull them open and step inside.

The bar was probably the place to be at some point before I was born. There are traces of its past elegance in the trim, the molding, the layout of the space. It's almost regal, like some of the old restaurants my parents frequent. This is just less cared for. It smells salty, kind of like body odor but not quite as offensive, and could use a good "air out," as my mother would say.

"Who the hell is that?" A man at the end of the bar slams his drink down, looking at me with a wobbling swagger.

"That's a broken jaw if you don't check yourself," Nate says, coming around the corner. With a thump on the counter in front of the man, making him jump, he calms me with his bright, wide smile. "What are you doing here, Priss?"

His nickname for me, short for Prissy, bothered me when he first began using it. Now it's almost a term of endearment. If he stopped calling me Priss, I might be offended.

"Oh, just in the neighborhood," I say, sighing for effect. "Is Dom around?"

Nate's lips press together as he tries to hide a grin. "Is he supposed to be?"

"He said he was coming by," I shrug, chewing my bottom lip.

"I'm guessing he doesn't know you're here," he smirks.

"You would guess right, sir."

Nate runs his hands through his dark hair that's the exact color of Dom's, but cut closer to the scalp. He shakes his head, clearly amused that I'm standing in his bar. He heaves a breath and blows it out slowly.

"Are you going to help me or not?" I laugh.

"Fine," he sighs. "Dom's in the back."

"What's he doing?"

"He's just looking over some papers for me."

"Papers, huh?" I prod. "You don't know how to read or what?"

His eyes light up as I poke at him, the easiness of our semi-friendship making my nerves settle just a bit. Nate and I have gotten along since the day he showed up with his little boy unexpectedly at Dominic's. He's a handful in a lot of ways—loud and a little sharp sometimes—but he's kind. And when he's with Ryder, he's downright amazing.

"I don't know how to read this shit," he blushes. "I got some papers from the bank on a loan and he's making sure nothing looks off to him. They speak a complete other language in the banking world."

My heart drops as I realize what he's saying. "Dom told me you were going through a rough patch. Can I help?"

"You sure can. Let him finish looking at those papers before you wind him up," he winks.

"I'm serious," I say, shoving him playfully. "If there's anything I can do, tell me. I'd love to help."

"I'll keep that in mind."

He says that, but the look on his face says differently.

"I mean it, Nate. If you and Ryder need anything, please don't hesitate to reach out."

"That's sweet of you, Priss," he says softly, "but we're gonna be fine. This is life. We're tough."

"Of that I have little doubt," I smile. "Dom said you guys are moving in with him."

"Just for a while. I'm getting a loan for ten grand, but it'll take a couple of months to go through. Until then, I'm just eliminating a few bills that I can."

"The ten grand will bail you out?" I ask.

"And then some. I know how to manage money. I just got hit with a few big unexpected expenses," he tells me. "Plus, I want to make this place nice again. Build something Ryder can be proud of his old man for one day. Something my brother won't go nuts about when he sees you're here," he says, making a face as he takes a step, then two, backwards towards his customers. "Speaking of, head on back to the office. You know where it is, right?"

"Yup."

"I'll watch you from here." He leans against the bar, cocking his head towards the man he threatened earlier. "Hurry up before I have to break Joe's neck here."

With a little wave, I ignore the stares of the patrons lined up on stools like drunken ducks and make my way to the back. A door is tucked away with a gold plate that has lost the lettering that once embellished it. I knock gently, but can't hear Dom's voice on the other side over the sound of some classic rock song from the jukebox.

"Dom?" I say, twisting the knob and pushing the door open. "Oh. I'm sorry."

My face burns in part embarrassment, part anger at the sight before me. Dom is sitting with a pile of papers in his hand and his feet kicked up on a rickety wooden desk. He's not looking at the papers though. His attention is on a red-headed girl sitting on a love seat that's looking at him like he just stepped out of the heavens.

"What are you doing here?" His head snaps to me as he sits up, the papers splashing across the desk. The lines that mar his forehead tell me everything I need to know.

This was, as I feared, counterproductive.

"I, um," I stammer, clearing my throat, "I thought I'd drop by. I didn't know you'd be busy."

Glancing to my right, I see Red with the corner of her lips curling into a bitchy smirk. If I knew how to throw a punch, I'd land one in the middle of her too-pink pucker.

"I'm not busy." Dominic leans forward, his elbows resting on his knees. "I just didn't expect you. Here."

He's unhurried, like he doesn't even realize Red's here. Like it's not bothering me at all that another woman was alone with him and I just walked in. That annoys me. *Big time.* But if there's one thing I learned from my mother, it's not to let them see you sweat.

Growing up, lots of girls weren't nice to me and Sienna. Our sophomore year, in particular, was rough. We learned to say everything with a smile, to act unaffected. It takes the wind out of their sails. That or it makes them react and look like idiots.

"You know what, I should've called. How thoughtless of me," I say, pasting on a grin. Turning to Red, I extend a hand. "I'm Camilla Landry. It's nice to meet you."

She pulls her drawn-on brows together and looks quickly at Dom before returning her gaze to me. "I'm Hannah. Nice to meet you?"

We shake in an awkward maneuver before I adjust my purse and look at Dom again. Plastering on as pleasant of a smile as I can, I turn away. "I have some errands to run. You can call me later if you want."

"Cam."

"Yeah?" I say, looking at him over my shoulder.

"Stay." He looks at Hannah. "Wait for him out there."

"Nate said I could wait in here."

"And I just told you to wait out there."

"But ..."

He gives her a look I haven't seen him give a woman before, just men that think they're going to make him jump when he doesn't want to jump. The blues in his irises darken, his lips pressing together. "Go on."

"Fine." She looks at me with a smirk before turning to Dom. "See you at the gym tomorrow."

I keep the bored look on my face as she walks by and out the door. I don't turn to look at Dominic for a moment, needing a few seconds to process this ... that this girl can spend time with him here and while he trains. And I can't.

I wait for him to say something, to tell me she wasn't here for him, but he remains quiet. Finally, I turn around. "Should I have called?"

"No," he growls. "You shouldn't be here."

"Did I interrupt something between you and Red?"

The question eases some of the tension in his face. "'Red'?" he asks, fighting a laugh.

"Yeah. Red."

"Okay. Red it is." He leans back in his chair and takes me in. His dark hair is mussed from the gym, the front of his grey t-shirt stained from sweat. It's sexy as hell and if I wasn't borderline angry, I'd straddle him. "No, you weren't interrupting anything. She was waiting on Nate because he's fucking around with her."

"But not you."

"No, not me," he grins. "Does that bother you?"

"What?"

"The thought of me fucking around with her?"

"No," I lie, fidgeting with my purse on my shoulder again. "You can do whatever you want." He just sits there, leaning back in his chair, his muscled thighs tensing beneath the jersey of his red gym shorts, and doesn't say a word. "You can do whatever you want, just like I can."

This gets his attention.

His eyes swirl ferociously, his jaw pulsing as he works it back and forth. "What's that supposed to mean?"

"It's not supposed to *mean* anything. Just stating facts. We're free to do whatever we want."

He nods, uncrossing his arms from over his chest. "Come here."

Tossing my purse where Red was sitting, I take the few steps to him. He spreads his feet wider, allowing me to stand between his knees. As soon as I'm in his personal space, I breathe a sigh of relief. This is what I wanted. What I needed. To feel the comfort that I only find when I'm with him.

My shoulders sag, the expectations I've faced all day to be me, Camilla Jane Landry, are gone. I'm here, with him, and that's enough. There's no need to remember exquisite table manners or to choose my words thoughtfully. No need to remember the impact of my behavior on my family's business or my brother's campaigns. Dom doesn't care about all that. If anything, he tries to provoke me to act out, which I resist but find entertaining.

He looks up, assessing me. "You know I don't like you coming down here," he says, his gaze narrowed.

"Why?"

"You know why, Cam. This is no place for a girl like you."

"Red is here," I point out, narrowing my own gaze. "Apparently she gets to be with you everywhere I don't. You don't have a problem with that."

"Let me reiterate what I just said: this is no place for a girl like *you*. And Red is in all these places because she's fucking everyone ... but me."

He has to notice the way my shoulders fall just slightly at his statement. He sits up, his knees pulling together and resting against the outside of my thighs. I can smell the sweet sweat on his skin and notice a small cut just above his eye that I want to inspect, but don't.

"I'm a big girl, Dominic," I say, letting the last syllable click on my tongue. "I've been here before and nothing bad has happened to me. Hell, nothing bad has ever even happened in front of me here. It makes me wonder if there are ulterior motives for you not wanting me around."

"Damn it." His palms rest against the backs of my legs, his hands splaying out against my skin. They're extra coarse from the boxing gloves he's undoubtedly been wearing and make me break out into goosebumps as he strokes up and down my thighs. "There is no ulterior motive. The reason I'm asking you not to show up here is self-explanatory. Look around," he chuckles. "Why in the hell would you even want to come to this shit hole?"

"I wanted to see you," I say softly, draping my arms over his shoulders. "And you were here."

His face rests against my stomach. He nudges me towards him, pulling me tight against him.

Leaning down, I press a kiss to the top of his head. My heart swells in this moment, in a way that I haven't gotten to experience too many times with him. He doesn't give in often. He's not one for showing too much softness, and when it happens, it strikes some instinct in me to want to protect him from the world.

"I thought about you today," he says, still tucked against me. "I wondered how your lunching went."

"My *luncheon* went well." I smile as I enunciate the proper word. "Too much food, but it was nice being with my family."

He squeezes me. "I want to spend some time with you tonight."

"I'm here."

"But not here." He pulls away and looks me in the eye. "Nate's working for a while, I think. Meet me at my place?"

"Or we can go to mine," I offer.

"I need to go to mine anyway, and I don't want to spend an extra thirty minutes going back and forth. I need to glance at this one more time, and then I'll meet you there."

"Have you eaten?" I ask, brushing a damp lock of hair off his forehead.

He smiles. "No."

"I'll get you some food and then meet you at your place in a little bit." Bending down, I cup his face in my hands and press a kiss against his swollen lips. "And I'm icing you down when we get there."

He rolls his eyes, but I can tell he likes it. "Get outta here."

We walk to the door. He whistles loudly through the bar, getting Nate's attention. Without a word, they exchange directions. Dom squeezes my hip before disappearing into the office again.

An exasperated sigh escapes my lips as I side-step a broken piece of linoleum on the floor. Making my way to the entrance, I feel Nate's eyes on me every step of the way.

I almost look up at him and roll my eyes, their overprotective nature a little out of control. The fact that Red is sitting at the bar, facing me but trying to keep Nate's attention, is what stops me.

"Hey, Nate," I say as I get close. "Can I talk to you for a minute?"

As expected, he turns away from her and rounds the corner to me. "Ya leaving, Priss?"

"Yeah, Dom kicked me out."

"Like you didn't know that was coming," he laughs, then lowers his voice. "I didn't know Hannah was with him or I would've warned you."

"Would've been nice."

He grins. "Like you'd think he's up to something with *her*," he scoffs. "Dom is a dumb motherfucker sometimes, but even he's not dumb enough to risk *you* for *that*."

"Oh, Nate. You have such a way with words," I joke, laying a hand on my heart. "But, really, thanks for saying that. It makes me feel a little better."

"Better about what?"

I shrug, not really wanting to get into it with Red sitting a few feet away. "Are you staying at Dom's tonight?"

"Yeah. But I don't want to cause you guys any problems."

"You won't," I say. "I have a house, you know."

"I heard. A nice one if the word on the street is right."

"And because it's mine, I can go there anytime I want," I point out. "So, again, you being at Dom's won't cause any problems in my life. Besides, Ryder will give me someone to play with while you guys watch sports."

A thought crosses my mind and I try to shake it off, but it comes back full-force. I picture Ryder's little face capped with the same dark hair as his father and uncle, and I wonder how much of his life resembles theirs. And how different it is from mine.

A spark begins to take root in my stomach and the feeling of being absolutely right floods me. Lifting up on my tiptoes, I place my lips right against Nate's ear. "I want to do something."

"I won't tell Dom. I swear," he cracks, getting a swat from me. This makes him laugh harder. "Kidding."

"Sure you are," I giggle, dropping back to my feet. "But, seriously. I want to do something for you."

"What are we talking here? Homemade lasagna?"

Forcing a swallow, I look him straight in the eye. I give myself a moment to reconsider, to go with the lasagna, but that option falters to the wayside. Bracing myself for his reaction, I take a deep breath. "Nate, let me loan you the ten grand."

All humor erases from his face. "What?" he blanches.

"I about killed myself in a hole back there," I say hurriedly, trying to make him agree before we can establish a solid argument. "Someone could trip and sue you for more than that before the loan goes through."

"Priss, no," he says, waving his hands in front of him. "I can't do that. No way."

"And why not? I can have it wired to you tomorrow and you can start your renovations or whatever it is. Plus," I say, cutting off his rebuttal, "you'll get the money to pay me back in sixty days."

"No."

"Nate," I sigh. "Please let me do this for you."

His eyes fill with an unnamed emotion that makes my heart melt. "Is this you trying to get me out of Dom's house sooner? Because I already terminated my lease. I'm stuck there for the time being."

"Shut up," I laugh. "This is to help you get on your feet."

"I ... I just ... Wow, Camilla. I don't know what to say."

"Say yes."

"Dominic would kill me."

"You said you wouldn't tell him," I tease. "Besides, why would he care? It's not like it's a gift. You're paying me back in two months. It's not a big deal."

"You've rendered me speechless."

"Good. I like you Hughes boys better when you don't talk," I wink. "Text me your bank account number when you get off, before you get *her* off," I say, rolling my eyes and jabbing a thumb towards Red at the bar, "and I'll do it tomorrow. Just pay me back when you get the loan. Easy peasy."

"Are you sure?" he asks, still looking unconvinced. "That's a lot of money."

"I wouldn't loan it to just anyone. I'm not dumb."

There is no response.

"Look," I continue, "I may dislike business but I've heard enough conversations to know risk versus reward. This is a no-brainer in that sense. Plus, it appeals to the 'do-gooder' in me, as your brother calls it. Just say yes so I can get out of here before Dom sees me or Red glares me to death."

The features on his face smooth, his eyes beginning to twinkle. "I can't believe you offered me this. I owe you one."

"No. You owe me ten thousand," I laugh, swinging my purse at my side. "Now I'm going to get some food and meet up with Dom."

I get to the door before I hear Nate's voice again. "Priss?"

"Yeah?" I say, looking over my shoulder.

"Thank you."

My cheeks hurt from smiling, my chest filled with the sensation of doing something good. Of, like my mother says, making a difference in someone's life. "You are very welcome."

SEVEN

CAMILLA

Dom's car, a black-on-black Camaro, is sitting in the parking lot when I pull up to his apartment. The paint, although matte in finish, shines in the early evening sunlight.

I've never been a big fan of cars, but this one is almost as sexy as Dominic. It sits low to the ground and sounds ferocious when he presses the gas and lets it roar down the road. Sometimes we take long, pointless drives out of the city, and I settle back in the leather seats and enjoy being wrapped up in so much power with him at the wheel.

It's also why I love being in his arms.

No one has ever made me feel so safe and so reckless at the same time. From our first date, not once have I considered he'd ever make a decision that wasn't for my benefit. As much as I hate being chastised for showing up at the bar or the gym, I know it's because of some fear that something will happen to me. Even though I feel like a child sometimes when he calls me before I can text him that I made it home, I know it's because he's concerned.

This is the same man that will have me in the passenger seat as we hit a hundred and ten miles per hour on the interstate or that has me naked on the hood of his car on a bluff that overlooks the sea.

He's wild and uncivilized, but disciplined and thoughtful too. Being with him is like the real world doesn't exist. It's like there aren't societal rules with stupid expectations. With Dom, I can do what I want. I can be whatever I want. It's a crazy, exciting life.

As I climb out of my Audi, my laughter dances through the breeze. Never in a million years did I think I'd be walking up a broken sidewalk to an apartment on this side of town to see a man. Not only am I walking up it tonight, my feet can't get me there quick enough.

After letting myself in the building and taking the stairs to the third floor, I try not to breathe in the smoke at the top of the stairwell. Making my way down the hall, grumbling that there's no elevator, I balance the takeout bag and my purse in one hand and knock with the other.

It flies open before I even pull my hand away.

He's standing in the doorway, one hand on the sweatpants that hang just below his chiseled hips and the other leans on the frame. The tattoos that mark his flesh are vivid against his bare skin, making the blues of his eyes shine.

He flashes a lopsided smile my way. "Took you long enough."

"I don't drive like a bat out of hell," I laugh, stepping past him. "Did you shower already?"

"Yeah. I smelled like gym floors."

"As long as you don't smell like gym whores," I say, setting the bags on the table in the kitchen.

His laugh is contagious and I feel myself smiling. A set of arms cage me in from behind, grasping the table on both sides of me. My skin breaks out in a shiver as his lips find the sensitive spot behind my ear.

His face buries in the crook of my neck and he takes a long, leisurely breath. "You smell so good."

"Keep doing that," I say, relaxing my head onto his chest.

"What?"

"Talking with your mouth against me."

"You like this?" he asks all breathily so that each word whispers across my skin.

My eyes fall closed as I relish in this moment of nothing but him. "No, I love this."

"Can I tell you a little secret?"

"As long as you keep talking, you can tell me whatever you want."

He chuckles, dotting kisses up and down my neck. "I love this too, feeling your body give up the fight of the day and let me take over." He turns me in his arms so I'm facing him. "I love that you trust me enough to let your shoulders sink out of that perfect posture you walk around with."

As he reaches up and undoes the elastic in my hair, I watch his features soften. He moves carefully, unwrapping the tie from the twisted mess in my locks, careful not to pull.

"There," he says, cupping the back of my head through my long tresses, "that's better."

"You don't like my hair up?"

"Not like you had it. You look to lunching-y," he says, wrinkling his nose.

"Lunching-y?"

"Yes," he grins.

"You are too cute."

"You are too fucking sexy."

Reaching up, I swipe the pad of my thumb over the cut above his eye. He flinches, but just for a second. "What happened?"

"Bond's right hand."

"I hate him."

"So do I," he snickers.

"Let's get some ice for it."

He leans in, his brows tugging together. "Let's not." His eyes hood as he takes me in, his tongue darting out and wetting his lips. My knees weaken, my body humming with delight at his reaction.

"I want to take care of you," I whisper, although that's really on the backburner now. "Let me baby you."

Instead, he lifts me up and places me on the table. My stomach clenches as he positions himself between my thighs, my sundress curling at my waist. I ring my legs around him, pulling him so close that the soft cotton of his sweatpants rubs against my opening.

He looks down. "You aren't wearing panties."

"Nope."

When his gaze flips back to my eyes, it's so heated I think he's going to combust. "You've run around all day like this?"

"Maybe."

"Damn it, Camilla," he growls, placing his hand in between us. A finger slides through my slit easily, dragging the wetness around my opening. "Tell me you're fucking with me."

"What's it matter?" I moan, letting my arms dangle off his sculpted shoulders.

"Cam."

"Fine. I took them off in my car and shoved them in my purse when I got here. I wanted to be ready for you."

He sinks a finger, then two, inside. A gush of breath escapes my throat, a soft moan on its tail. Pulling them out, he thrusts them inside me again. "You're ready for me. There's no doubt about that."

"Dom?"

"What, beautiful?"

"I need you inside me."

Smirking, he works his fingers in a torturously slow circle. "Now?"

"Yes, fucking now," I pant.

My eyes are closed as I place my hands behind me and lean back, giving him as much access as he wants. His thumb sits heavily on my clit, putting gentle pressure as he works me into a heated frenzy.

"Dominic," I groan before yelping as he slides his long, hard cock into me. "God!"

"Is that what you want? Now?" he laughs, slowly withdrawing

before pushing hard inside once more, until he hits the wall of my vagina. "You want this now?"

"Yes," I hiss. "No, actually I don't. I don't want this. I want you to fuck me."

He growls, the intensity of his actions building steadily. "Say it again."

"Fuck me, Dom."

My hair swishes against the table, my legs burning with an orgasm that's been waiting to release since I saw him at the bar. His hands are all over me—cupping my breasts, holding my shoulders, squeezing my hips—as he finds the rhythm we both love.

When I open my eyes, he's watching me with an expression I can't quite put my finger on. He smiles.

"Harder, please," I say, the words bouncing with every thrust.

His smile widens, grows cocky, and pushes me that much closer to the edge. "Your pussy can't handle my cock. Feel that? That's me hitting the back." He slams into me, his girth stretching me so far it almost burns. "You're. So. Damn. Tight."

With each thrust, I'm brought to the brink of undoing. Every grin, every whiff of his cologne brings me closer and closer to the climax I crave.

I lean forward and grip his arms, his biceps sweaty and flexing under my touch. He growls, his Adam's apple bobbing as he swirls his hips as he's deep inside me.

"Either we stop or I'm gonna be done," he says through gritted teeth. "You have about two seconds to decide."

"Come," I say, letting my legs fall to the sides and drop onto the puddled tabletop. "Ah," I shout as he drives mind-numbingly hard into my pussy. "Dominic!"

"Cam," he mutters, powering into me one final, heavy time as I topple around him.

My nails bite into his skin, his back flexing against my hands as I yell out his name. My thighs tremble as I run my hands to his ass, feeling it tense as he spills himself inside me.

Every muscle in my body contracts, quivering from the orgasm that catapults its way through every piece of my being. I can't focus on anything but the intense sensation that starts in my belly and soars through my veins.

I sag as I come back to my senses, totally spent from both the physical and emotional rush. He guides my back to the table and I lie on the spot where we eat breakfast, my dress shoved to my chest.

He braces himself on the table, panting as hard as I am. "That was worth the wait."

"The wait?" I giggle, completely sated. "It took you like three minutes from when I walked in the door."

"I've waited on this a lot longer than that." He takes my hand and pulls me up. "Now make me a sandwich."

"Go to hell," I say, kissing his lips. "You make me a sandwich."

He nips my bottom lip, making me yelp. "How about this? You go get cleaned up and I'll stick the food in the microwave. Then you can get it out."

"That's a messed up compromise," I laugh.

"But a compromise no less." He smacks my butt as I head towards the bathroom. "You better hustle or I'll haul your ass off to bed."

Instead of hurrying, I pull my dress up to my waist and sway my hips back and forth as I walk across the room. "So not like th —Dominic!"

I don't get the words out before I'm hauled over his shoulder, one hand cupping my ass as he holds me in place and carries me down the hall as promised.

EIGHT

DOMINIC

The paper-thin walls of the apartment make it clear Nate is home. The door squeaks open and latches, the locks twisting, before I hear him shuffle down the hallway. He's shushing what I guess is a sleeping Ryder before the door to the guest room down the hall pulls closed.

Releasing a breath, I try to close my eyes but they pop open again. Sleep isn't my friend on a good night. I've battled with insomnia my entire life. I can remember lying in bed and listening to my parents fight it out upstairs above me. The walls would shake before a thud would hit the ceiling. I'd squeeze my eyes and hope my dad wasn't hurting my mom.

Of course he was. Her eye would be black, sometimes her lip cut, in the morning. She'd make up some bullshit excuse and pour our cereal and laugh it off, a cigarette dangling from her cracked lips.

The older I got, the more often it happened. I'd wait up and listen, wondering if that would be the night hell would break loose and he'd end up killing her. I'd go to bed with a knot in my gut, and by the time the sun came up, I was just drifting off to sleep.

It's a habit I can't break. When the sun goes down, those demons wake up and begin their ritual of torturing me with all the bad that can happen ... and all the bad I've done.

"Shh ..." I whisper to Camilla as she stirs next to me.

The shower kicks on, the pipes squalling in the walls, and I squeeze her tighter. My palm sinks in her curves, her breath hitching as I run my hand down her side, over her hip, and onto her thigh. She squirms closer, her head resting on the spot where my arm meets my shoulder with a little contented sigh.

Watching her asleep next to me puts thoughts in my head—crazy, unwarranted ideas that I have zero business toying with. The longer this little charade goes on between us, the harder it is to separate fantasy from reality.

Fantasy is this. Reality is what tomorrow morning will bring. She'll go home and take a bath or go shopping and I'll put in my eight hours, see if I can get some overtime, before putting in a few more at the bar.

Lying here in the darkness makes me think about coming home to a wife, falling asleep with her every night. When Cam cuddles up with me like I could defend her from the world, it fills me with the best feeling I've ever had. Like I matter to her. Like I'm capable of one thing that counts. Sometimes I don't even try to go to sleep. I just hold her and watch her and think ... and pretend this could be, and should be, real.

If she'd just fucking get this out of her system and move along, I could move on. But God knows I won't be able to walk away from her.

"Why do you do this, Cam?" I whisper.

"Do what?"

I flinch, startled that she answered. "I thought you were asleep."

"I was," she whispers, but doesn't open her eyes. "Why do I do what?"

For a split second, I consider telling her to go back to sleep. But something about the shroud of darkness gives me the courage to repeat my question. "Why do you do *this*?"

"Because you won't stay at my house."

I rest my lips on the top of her head. "Go back to sleep."

"Why do *you* do this, Dom?"

Leaving my lips touching her hair, I don't move. I don't answer her either. Instead, I concentrate on the way the fan moves the air across my foot that sticks out the side of the blankets.

"The answer was yes," she breathes. "When you asked me earlier tonight if it made me jealous to see you with Red—the answer is yes. I wanted to punch her in the face."

The grin that tickles my lips can't be stopped.

"Even now," she continues, "thinking about her smug face sitting in that office so close to you, I get mad. Thinking about her getting time with you I don't drives me bananas."

"I like it."

She pulls her head back and looks at me. In the dim glow of the streetlight streaming through the broken blinds, I can see her face. Her eyes are heavy, her face flushed from the heat of my body as a slow grin spreads across her cheeks. "You like that I'm mad?"

"Hell, yeah. There's nothing sexier than a woman claiming her property."

The insinuation dawns on me as the words leave my mouth. We pick up on it at the same time. She watches me, her breathing shallow, as she tries to decipher my reaction.

I just walked into a minefield and know I'm going to get my legs blown off.

I don't react. Looking her in the eye, I wait for hers.

"Are you?" she asks.

"Am I what?"

"Mine."

"You don't want me," I scoff with a burn in my chest. Tugging her down so she's lying next to me again, I look at the ceiling.

The silence feels thick in the little room, the only noise that of Nate leaving the bathroom. My stomach knots, a familiar anxiety coiling up in my gut. It's like being a kid again—my brother in the next room as I lie awake, waiting on the world to come caving in.

"Do you remember the first time you came to my house?" she asks.

"Of course."

"You were late. I was told someone would be there between eight and noon and you got there around four."

"It was hot as hell and everyone's A/C units were messing up," I recall. "My first job that day put me behind." My hand runs up and down her arm, causing her to loosen up some against me.

"I opened the door," she says, "ready to give someone a speech about time management and then I saw you."

"You were so hot ... literally and figuratively," I chuckle. "You were every repairman's dream in your little shorts and cutoff shirt."

I feel her smile against my side. "I've never been as instantly attracted to someone before. I didn't even know whether I should let you in or not," she giggles.

"Oh, you let me in all right ..."

Her hand hits my chest and I jolt, making her laugh. We settle back down, a little tension having drifted away.

"I think," she says, forcing a swallow, "I think when I first started seeing you, it was just lust."

"I hope it's still lust," I counter, reaching around and cupping her full tit in my hand. "God knows I still lust after you."

"To ease your concerns, I plan on sitting on your cock in a few minutes and riding it until I come."

"Can we skip to that part now?" I ask, twisting her nipple between two fingers.

"No," she says, stifling a moan but not stopping me. "As I was saying, at first I think that was the extent of my reaction to you."

"So you wanted my cock? That's it."

"At first," she laughs. "Maybe. But then something happened. I got to know you."

"It's amazing you're still here."

"Dominic. Stop." She struggles against me, fighting against my arm that's holding her to me. Eventually, I let go and she sits up. She gives me a look that I've only seen a few times, but one I think she must've learned from her mother. "You know what's amazing?"

Assuming that this is a rhetorical question, I don't answer. Instead, I focus on not pulling her mouth to mine and kissing the hell out of her. This time, not even because of lust. This time, because of how she's looking at me.

Moments like this scare the fuck out of me with Cam. I worry that maybe she's getting in too deep with me, even though I do my best to keep her at semi-arm's length. I try not to encourage her infatuation with me, to not let her entwine herself in my day-to-day as much as possible. When she looks at me like this, like I could be something to her, I falter.

There are things about me that she doesn't know. I don't want to tell her, afraid she'll see me differently. Yet, it's a burden I carry on my shoulders because sooner or later, if she doesn't walk away for another reason, it'll come up.

"The way you help your brother is amazing," she says.

"Do you know how many times he's helped me?" I lift a brow.

"You always say that, but I see you giving way more than him."

I bite back my next words. My throat squeezes closed, my annoyance at her perceived understanding of my relationship with Nate making it hard to breathe. As I watch her face shadow with the realization that there might be more between my brother and I than she comprehends, I war with whether to bring up the past.

If I don't, I'll continue to have this worry in the pit of my stomach. If I do, it could be the end of all this like the flip of a switch. I don't know what will happen when she sees all of me.

"I like your brother. I do. A lot, actually. But you shortchange yourself when it comes to him. If he asked you to give him this apartment, you would. And that's awesome of you, Dom," she says, placing a hand on my chest. "It's one of the reasons I like you."

Her palm flexes over my heart and she looks at me so earnestly, so tenderly, that I know I have to tell her. Now. Before I lose the courage. If she walks, at least she does it before she gets in any deeper.

Shifting under the blankets, I move so I'm sitting upright. "When I was sixteen," I say, clearing my throat, "my father beat the shit out of my mother."

She gasps, her hand flying to her mouth. "Why would he do that?"

"Because it was a Thursday," I say, emotionless. "Because we had ham sandwiches for dinner. I don't fucking know. But it happened a lot and this particular night in June, it was really bad."

"Did he hurt her?"

"Most nights he did. Usually a few bruises, a few chunks of hair missing, things that became almost normal to us. Isn't that sick?"

Her eyes fill with tears as she watches me recant my childhood.

"Then, one night, things were different." Forcing a swallow, I take her wrist in my hand and hold it. She slips it down so our fingers interlock and lays them, together, on my stomach. "I was in bed, my room just below my parents and it began. It was almost predictable, which is crazy. It started with yelling, then crying, then he'd throw her around until he was done."

"You had to hear that?"

Ignoring her question and the tears slipping down her cheeks, I stare at the glow of the television power switch across the room. "It got bad. And it didn't end. And I heard her cries turn to screams ..."

Camilla squeezes my hand so hard it almost hurts.

"I went up the stairs, seeing Nate behind me at the foot of the stairs when I got to the top. He came up as I opened the door to my parents' room."

"What happened?" she asks quietly.

"The sick fuck had her on her back, on the bed, a gun pressed against her temple," I say as calmly as I can. "I, um, I was afraid to move. Afraid to speak. Afraid that something would cause him to pull the trigger and shoot her in the head. She looked at me, her hand sort of halfway reaching out in an attempt to keep me back."

"Oh my God."

"He had a hand around her neck, holding her there. He must've heard me because he turned and I remember his eyes were like he'd been possessed or something. They almost glowed," I recount, shaking my head. "He was demonic."

"He told me to stay back," I continue, "rattling off how my mom was a whore, all this bullshit. It ended with the gun being pointed at me."

"Dominic!" The panic in her voice only feeds the frenzy in my body as I recall the scariest few minutes I've ever experienced.

I don't bother giving her the details about how he called Nate and I the biggest regrets of his life. That he blamed us for his bottle-a-day vodka habit or told us we'd grow up to be just like him. There's no point in going through all the movements of the next few minutes that only seemed like seconds. None of that matters.

"The gun eventually went off," I say, still looking at the television button. "It was supposed to fire at my mom, but the bullet hit the wall instead. I can still hear the wood splinter, the pictures that hung near the spot dropping to the floor and the glass shattering everywhere. Nate and I lunged towards him. Nate tried to hold him down and I worked on getting the gun away. His breath burned with cheap vodka ..."

Tearing my gaze away from the television and to Camilla, I see the tears dotting her face. Reaching up, I brush them away. "The second bullet went through his neck. It was supposed to hit Nate, but I moved his arm just a micrometer to the left and it got him instead."

Cam rests her forehead on mine, her body shaking as she cries. I hold her to me, reassuring her that it's all okay. Maybe me too.

"My prints were on the gun," I say, more clearly now. "We were afraid we'd go to jail for killing our father. Nate was going to take the rap for it. He was in my face, telling me what to do, what to say. We were so scared. We sat there, blood pooling around us, our mom sobbing, crying over this asshole until she was covered in his blood too. Then, you know," I gulp, "we had this feeling of almost relief."

"What happened?" she sniffles, pulling away.

"I wasn't letting him take the fall. It was an accident. So when a neighbor called the police, I told them I did it. I wasn't letting Nate take the fall."

"Did they believe you?"

"Yeah, I mean it was investigated, but with mom's injuries they ended up letting it go. It was self-defense."

She stills, absorbing what I've just thrown on her. I hold her, finding some comfort in the feel of her body against mine as I wait for her reaction.

"Dom," she chokes, pulling away. "Why didn't you tell me this before?"

Holding my breath, I try to steady my heart. "Why would I?"

She searches my face, but without the suspicion I expect. In its place is a look of resolution, of consideration, that steals my voice.

"Then why did you tell me now?"

I squeeze a swallow down my throat, wondering the same thing. "I don't know. I guess it felt like the right time." Looking at the floor, I feel a burst of panic. "It was an accident, Cam. I know it—"

She reaches out, her fingers cupping the sides of my face and halting my words. Her touch is so tender that I don't really know how to react. I wait for some outburst or question or a shove to get more answers, but none of that comes. Instead, her eyes fill with tears as she strokes my cheeks.

"I can't believe that happened to you," she breathes. "I'm so, so sorry."

"It's fine."

"It's not fine. There's nothing fine about this," she fires back, getting situated beside me. "How dare you have had to go through that. How dare he do that to you!"

"He's dead," I point out.

"And you have to live with it."

Her consideration for me, that her first thought is of me, sends a warmth shooting over my entire body. I don't even feel the pain in my side, nor the headache I've battled all evening. It's all numbed from this relief.

"Babe, Ryder's asleep down the hall," I say, a smile gracing my lips. "Keep your voice down."

She blushes, taking my face in her hands. "This is why we should stay at my house. I need to talk to you and I need to be able to express myself."

"It's one in the morning. We can talk tomorrow," I yawn, pulling her down beside me.

As she nuzzles under my chin, I feel like a weight has been lifted from my shoulders.

"Dom?"

"Yeah?"

"You were wrong when you said I don't want you."

We lie in the quiet, the fan swirling above us.

"Cam?"

"Yeah?"

"You were wrong when you said we're free to do whatever we want."

My cheeks break into a smile as I say the words because I'm mostly sure she'll still be here in the morning. Maybe even next week. And when she curls her leg around mine and crushes her body against me, I close my eyes and fall into the best sleep of my life.

NINE

CAMILLA

"You can tell Nate lives here," I laugh, peering into the refrigerator. "You have eggs, ham, some vegetables. There's even juice!"

"I have food," Dominic sighs, pouring a cup of coffee. "You act like there was nothing here before."

I look at him over the refrigerator door. "A pound of bacon and a bag of cheese fries doesn't count as food, babe."

"I happen to really enjoy a good cheese fry." He tips some creamer in his mug and settles at the table.

"That's a snack," I say, pulling out the eggs and ham. "Not a meal."

I work around the kitchen, preparing breakfast. I thought for sure he was supposed to be at the gym this morning, but he hasn't said anything. He doesn't even seem rushed, which is odd for him when he has to train. It makes him antsy and irritable, but today he's as calm as can be.

Looking up, I catch him watching me. Sticking my tongue out, I shake my knife at him. He laughs easily, happily, and picks up a magazine and leafs through it.

I cut the ham and beat the eggs, all the while keeping an eye on him. He seems different today. The lines on his face seem less carved and there's a softness to his frame that is unusual for him straight out of bed when he's still mentally going through his day.

It's a good look on him, one that tugs at my heartstrings. I imagine this is what he would be like if he was in college and just getting up in the morning for class and not the laborer-turned-fighter. Or is it the other way around? Did he take up fighting as a coping mechanism for his father's death or did he learn to fight because of his dad?

My knife clamors against the counter.

"You okay?" he asks as I scurry to pick it up

"Yeah. Sorry. I dazed off."

His brows furrow, but he doesn't call me out on it. Instead, he looks towards the door as Nate walks in with Ryder on his shoulders.

"Look who's here, Ry!" Nate looks at me and grins.

"Camilla!" He holds his arms out to me, his little blue eyes sparkling.

"Hey, Ryder," I say, wiping my hands on a towel. Lifting him off his father's shoulders, he wraps his arms around my neck. "How are you, buddy?"

"Hungry."

"I'm making breakfast. Want to help?"

"Yes. I missed you," he says, pulling his face away from mine. "You're so pretty."

"Easy there, Ry," Dominic says. "That's my girl."

"My girl," he says, burying his face in my neck again.

"Looks like you have some competition," I wink, carrying the boy to the kitchen counter. I sit him next to the cutting board, hand him a strip of ham, and go back to preparing breakfast.

Nate walks behind me, lowering his voice so only I can hear. "I had a deposit pending in my account today, Priss. Seriously. Thank you."

"Shhh," I say, keeping my head down. "You're welcome."

"You're welcome for what?" Dom asks, looking at us over the top of the magazine.

"For not beating his door down last night," I say. "Did you hear him snoring?"

A small smile crosses Dominic's face. "No. I slept. Strangely."

"Well, he snores. Prepare yourself." I look at Ryder. "How do you sleep with him sounding like he's sucking in the house like that?"

Ryder giggles, holding the half-eaten ham in the air. "He is loud!"

"You little snitch," Nate laughs, picking up his son. "Let's get you in the bath while we wait on breakfast."

They trample off down the hallway, Ryder's laughter making the apartment seem so much brighter. I watch them until they're out of sight. When I look back at Dominic, he's watching me.

"What are you thinking?" he asks, setting the magazine down.

"I don't know. Just what a little piece of sunshine that boy is." I pick up the knife again. "I love how happy he is to see me. It makes my day."

"Everyone is happy to see you."

My cheeks flush. "Can I ask you something?"

"Yeah. I might not answer, but you can ask."

"Jerk," I laugh. "Were you supposed to go to the gym this morning?"

"Why?"

"Just curious."

He kicks back in his seat, the sunlight highlighting the ridges in his stomach and the lines on his arms as he grips the back of his seat. "I was gonna go. Yeah. But I changed my mind."

Looking down, I pour the beaten eggs in a skillet and arrange the ham in another. I don't want him to see the smile drawn deeply across my lips.

"Does that surprise you?" he asks.

"Kind of. You usually go on Saturdays."

"Maybe I needed a break."

"Maybe I'm glad you took one."

The air between us changes. The levity from Nate and Ryder are gone, as is the easiness of the morning before their arrival. Now we're sitting a few feet from one another, albeit on opposite ends of the smallish kitchen, waiting out the other's next move.

The story he told me has been on my mind since the moment he delved into the tragic events of that night. Even after he fell asleep, which was odd in and of itself, it was me that laid awake. I rolled away from him and cried. Then I moved towards him and held him tight, hoping some of my energy would pass into him as he slept.

I couldn't tell him that it was him, not Nate, that snored. I've barely seen Dominic sleep, much less that deeply. But last night, he did. And I held him, prayed for him, wondered how much that devastating night impacted the man that has turned from an easy date to something that might be so special it scares me.

"You know, sometimes when I'm sleepy, I say shit I don't mean." His voice cuts through the air like a sharpened knife.

"Okay." Forcing a swallow, I keep my back to him. Running a spatula along the bottom of the egg pan, I watch them puff up into golden pillows. "You didn't talk in your sleep, if that's what you're asking."

"That's not what I'm saying."

Flipping off the burners, I turn to face him. His features are pressed together as he surveys my reaction.

"Then what *are* you saying, Dom?"

"Last night, I told you a story."

"I remember."

"And afterwards, you said in a roundabout way that you meant it when you said you wanted me."

"Yes," I say, pulling in a lungful of air. "I did."

He drops his arms to his sides and lets them hang towards the floor. "How did you mean that?"

There's a hope infused in his voice that turns me to mush. It's not that much different than listening to Huxley ask Lincoln if he's really going to play catch or Ryder asking me if he can really have another popsicle. It both warms and breaks my heart.

Coming around the counter, I stand in front of him. He looks up at me all delicious with his tousled bed hair and morning stubble scruffing his face.

"When I said I wanted you, I meant ... I meant I don't want to stop seeing you," I admit. "I sort of wait every day for you to move on, and if I'm honest with myself, I don't want you to."

Not a muscle moves, but his eyes sparkle. "You mean that?"

"Of course I do."

"Even after knowing ..."

I take his hand and press it against my cheek. "Dom, what happened to you was horrible, but if you think I'm going to look at you differently because of what you had to do to survive, to save your mother, your brother, you're crazy. If anything, I think more of you."

He stands, towering over me. Twisting his hand, he laces our fingers together. "I don't want to taint your life with mine."

"How could you think that?"

He snorts, rolling his eyes. "Your family would cut you off if they knew you were fucking the help."

I jerk my hand away. "For one, you are not 'the help.' And for two, fuck you for even saying that."

"It's true."

"For three, if you think all we're doing is fucking, then we should stop," I say, biting back tears. "Because it sure doesn't feel like just fucking to me."

I barely get the words out of my mouth before his arms are wrapped around me. I don't cry, but my heart squeezes so hard that I can't breathe.

Those are words I've wanted to say for months now but never could find the spot to say them. If I would've thought about it a few moments ago, I would've held back. But I didn't, and while I'm partially terrified of what he might say, I'm also relieved.

"At least I got you pissed off," he jokes, stroking my back.

"Not funny," I sniffle.

"No, it's not. You're right." He rests his head on top of mine. "It's a huge fear that my life will poison yours. You have everything going for you, lady. I feel like I'll hold you back, even if I'm pushing you along."

"Why don't you let me be the judge of that?"

"Because I can't let that happen."

He finally lets me go. We stand inches from one another, both of us clawing at the proverbial cliff we're about to go over, not sure if we want to fall together or just cling to where we are.

Clinging is safer. Falling could be amazing or could destroy everything.

"Will you do me a favor?" I ask, working to keep my hands from shaking. I've gone this far—I might as well push.

"Depends on what it is."

"Will you go to lunch with me and one of my brothers?"

"Hell, no," he laughs, sitting again. "Why would I do that?"

Sighing, I put a hand on my hip. "You know how you feel about not letting me ruin my life?"

"Yeah."

"They feel the same way."

"Exactly," he breathes. "They think I'm going to ruin your life and you want me to sit there and take it?"

"It won't be like that."

"Yes, it will." He shakes his head. "Besides, what am I going to do? Pretend to have something to talk about with them? Play make-believe that we have anything in common? For what, Cam?"

"Because it would mean a lot to me," I whisper. "It would take so much pressure off my plate. If we are going to keep *just fucking* or whatever this is for much longer," I gulp, "I'm going to tell them about you."

"Even knowing what you know, even having Nolan be my uncle, you'd still tell them?"

"Yes."

He considers this, to my surprise.

"They don't think anything about you because they don't know you. I'm not asking you to meet my entire family—"

"Good."

I roll my eyes. "I'm just asking to meet ... an emissary, of sorts," I offer, thinking immediately of Ford. "Just meet one of them so they can tell the rest of my family I'm not fucking some serial killer or bank robber. Okay?"

"You do realize I've killed someone. This may not work out in your favor."

"You didn't kill someone," I say softly. "You protected your family. The same thing my family is trying to do for me, just in a different way."

A flash of understanding flickers across his face as his brother's voice comes down the hallway. He looks at me, his big, blue eyes wide and worrisome. "This matters to you?"

"Yes. So much."

"It's just to make things easier on the home front?"

"Yes, Dom," I sigh again. "I won't take this meeting as meaning that you—"

"Fine." He cuts me off, his chest rising fast and hard. "Fine. I'll meet one of them to make things easier for you."

"Thank you," I say, not entirely sure if this is a win or a loss.

TEN

DOMINIC

A bag of groceries in each hand, I kick the door closed behind me. There's water running in the bathroom but the apartment is quiet otherwise.

Walking into the kitchen, I grin around the keys I stuck in my mouth. Camilla's mark is on everything. The salt and pepper are sitting on the middle of the stove, not jammed in a cabinet like I leave them. There's a towel folded next to the sink that's empty.

The bags hit the counter with a thud.

The scent of Cam's perfume lingers in the air, despite the fact that she left hours ago. I've worked out, showered, and grabbed a list of things Nate asked me to pick up from the market since she went home early this afternoon. Still, I can feel her here. And I miss her.

Taking out the items one by one, I ignore the growing sensation in my chest. It's a nagging feeling, one that digs at you until you're spurred to action. I've trained my brain to think of anything else in times like this. Like it's supposed to, my mind flickers through punching combinations, mixed drinks, random television trivia, but none of it works. None of it can distract me from her.

Not that this is an unusual development. I think of her all damn day. Today was different, though. More specific.

Instead of imagining her tight pussy or hearing her laugh at some stupid joke, today I've thought of the look she had in her eyes last night. It was devoid of judgement. There was no fear, which was my fear. It was just the look of a woman caring about ... *me*. The real me. The me that has all this dirt and garbage and not-so-nice things. Me. Dominic Hughes, born April 8, 1989.

It's like she sees me as someone worth seeing.

"Shit," I say, blowing out a breath.

Taking out the last item, a jar of smooth peanut butter, I walk to the pantry and place it inside. I turn towards the kitchen table when I see a piece of white paper on the floor next to Nate's shoes.

Lifting the folded piece of paper that looked like it had fallen to the spot where it was lying, I open it. The top has the logo of the bank Nate and I use. Beneath that is his name and a figure much larger than it should be.

"What the fuck?"

Bringing it closer to my face and ignoring the vomit that swirls at the base of my throat, I see that it's a notice of a money transfer. My body slumps, realizing he must've gotten the loan fast-tracked. I make a note to give him hell about moving out and start to drop it onto the counter. Before it falls from my fingers, I snatch it up again.

Camilla Jane Landry is listed at the bottom as the sender.

"What?" I hiss. The paper rasps as I shake it straight again. "What the absolute *fuck* is this?"

The lines blur as a heavy dose of adrenaline kicks in. The numbers don't make sense and it sure as hell doesn't make sense to see Cam's name on a bank receipt with Nate's name attached.

The rush of blood to my head causes me to wince, my jaw clenching so hard it throbs. A million thoughts roar through my mind, searching for a logical explanation to a situation I can't make sense of. Because there is no sense to make of it.

"Did you get the ..." Nate's voice drops off as he rounds the corner and stops in his tracks. He takes a quick look at my face, then to the paper, then to my face again. His eyes widen. The hand that's holding the towel he was using to dry his hair falls limp at his side. "Dom ..."

"First question, where's Ryder?"

"With Chrissy. Why?"

"I don't want him to hear this conversation," I state, the paper quivering in my hand.

"What's going on?"

"I'm torn here, Nate," I bark, twisting the paper around in my hand so he can see it. He blanches. "You're my brother, so I'm like, 'Yeah, there's a logical explanation to this.' Then I look again and, you know what? There's no logical explanation to this."

His head shakes, his chin dropping to the floor. "Look, Dom, I can explain."

"Oh, I hope you can," I growl. "And you better fucking start right now."

"Camilla offered to lend me the money—"

"And you fucking let her?" I shout, the muscles in my face straining as the words eject from my mouth. "You fucking let my girlfriend loan you ten. Thousand. Dollars?"

"I'm going to pay her back."

My laugh isn't from amusement. It shakes with a fury I haven't felt in years. Nate picks up on it because he takes a half-step backwards. "This isn't about you paying her back, cocksucker. This is about you taking the *motherfucking money!*"

Each word amps up my anger, each syllable getting a little louder until I'm almost screaming. My temples throb. The veins in my throat threaten to burst as I rip into him. Still, there's so much fury fighting to get out that it doesn't help.

"You know how this shit works. What the fuck are you thinking?" I step to him, my eyes glued on his. "What in God's name made you think this was okay? What made you think you could do this and not even fucking ask me?"

We're toe-to-toe, only inches separating us. Just like in the ring, I can taste his fear—sense his trepidation that I may close the distance between us with my fist faster than he can see it coming.

My chest rises and falls, nearly touching his on the uptake. If he wasn't my brother, I'd lay him out. If I wasn't his brother, he wouldn't let me get away with this either.

"You need to calm down, Dom."

"You have about ten seconds to explain or I'm going to assume there's not a good reason keeping me from knocking you the fuck out."

"I'll get the loan. I've been approved. I'll just transfer it back to her. This isn't a big deal."

"You paying her interest?" I spit.

"I don't know."

"Of course you don't fucking know," I roar, turning away before I topple over the edge. "You don't fucking know because you didn't think it through!"

Before I think better of it, I grab the edge of the table and slam it into the wall. A picture of a set of praying hands that hangs on the adjacent wall slams to the floor. I stand, staring at the mess, my breathing completely erratic. It occurs to me I might pass out.

"Dom, man, I didn't think it was that big of a deal. She was just helping me out."

I don't answer. I don't even look at him. I can't. If I turn around, I'm going to do and say things I'll regret. I'm self-aware enough to know that.

"I'm sorry."

"That doesn't cut it, Nate," I grimace. "Not this time."

He blows out a breath. His steps patter the floor behind me as he moves across the kitchen. "What do you want me to do? Want me to give it back to her?"

"I don't know what to do now. You've already taken it."

"What's it hurt? For real?"

Spinning on my heels, I face him. "What does it hurt? What you did was complete disrespect."

"To who?"

"To me," I seethe. "To my girl."

"How am I disrespecting Cam? *She offered it*," he reiterates, bewildered. "Maybe you I can see. But her? Fuck that. She offered it. She can afford it."

Waiting until I can semi-compose myself, I watch him. He opens his mouth and closes it a few times as I glare at him. The longer I wait to respond, the longer his words have to soak into my brain ... and piss me off worse.

"Is that what you think of her?" I ask, my heartbeat racing once more. "You think she's some kind of credit card?"

"Of course not."

"How's she gonna feel about this in a couple of days? You think she won't feel like you just cashed her out? Like you used her for a buck? No, ten goddamn thousand of them?"

"It's not like that."

"But what if it is?" I say, balling my fist at my sides. "And what about her family? Her brothers? You don't think they'll know there's money missing from her account?"

"Why would they? She's an adult."

"Because that's how shit works with them," I say through clenched teeth. "What's that make her look like?"

All he can do is shrug.

"I'll tell you what it makes her look like. It makes her look like she needs monitored like a baby and she doesn't," I boil. "Who goes around loaning ten grand to someone they just met?"

"It's not like that."

"It doesn't matter. You just gave them every reason in the world to think the worst about her, you fucking idiot."

"I—"

"They already treat her that way," I say, cutting him off. "They coddle her and treat her like a baby, and she's fighting to get out from under that. Then here you go taking advantage of her." I tug at my hair, the roots threatening to give as I yank on the locks. "If you were anyone else, I would kill you for doing this."

"For taking a loan?"

Dropping my hands to my sides, I look at him like he's the dumbest person I know. Maybe he is. "No. For putting her in this position. You took advantage of her kindness without thinking about how it might affect her."

His shoulders sag.

"Is there anything else I should know?" I sigh. "Anything else you've done or taken or discussed that I'm going to be hit with coming up?"

"Of course not."

Shoving my hands in my pockets, my fists burning from being clenched, I look at my brother. "Things were just maybe starting to go right, Nate. And then you go and fucking do this at the worst possible time."

"What time is that? How is it any different than yesterday or tomorrow?"

"I'm supposed to go to dinner with her and one of her brothers tomorrow night."

His brows lift. "Oh. That is a little different."

"Yeah," I nod, feeling the weight of the world sitting square in the center of my chest. "It is."

"What brought that on?"

I force a swallow. "I don't know. A moment of weakness, I guess. But I was hoping to go into it with a game plan. Of trying to make myself out to not look like the no-good asshole I am, see if there was a chance to maybe do something with this thing with Cam despite every indication there isn't. Then you go pull this fucking stunt."

"So don't go."

"No, I *have* to go now," I scoff. "If I don't, I'm suddenly the no-good that also managed to con ten grand from her and bailed."

"You didn't—"

"The one brother you talked to at the bar. The one you hated. What was his name?"

"Lincoln."

"Lincoln," I repeat. "Okay. Were the rest of them as bad?"

He shrugs. "I don't know. I just hated that cocky son of a bitch."

"But you lumped them all together because you didn't like Lincoln. Right?"

A look of understanding flashes before his eyes.

"So whether or not this had anything to do with me at all, I'm guilty by association. By blood." I shake my head, the anger starting to surge again. "You know what? Fuck you."

Swiping my keys off the counter, I glare at him as I march by.

***

Camilla

"I liked the one with watercolors, but not so much the primary tones," I say, balancing the phone on my shoulder as I wipe off the countertop. Tossing the sponge in the sink, I lean against the counter. "The reds and blues are too much for the design. Too heavy. Lighten it up some."

Sienna laughs through the line. "Since when did you have an eye for design?"

"I don't," I giggle. "I just know what I like."

"You have good taste because I think you're right."

"So my taste is good because it matches yours? What if I liked it in reverse? Then would my taste suck?"

"It would be less on-point, yes," she teases me. "Good call though. I'll keep playing with these."

Her keyboard clacks faintly in the distance. I imagine a pencil between her teeth, her hair in a messy ponytail, like she used to do when we were growing up and she was working on an essay for Mrs. Podaski's class.

"Sienna?"

"What?"

"Are you serious about moving to Illinois?"

"Yeah," she admits on a sigh. "I think it's a great opportunity for me, Cam. I have a feeling about it. It's the opening I've been waiting on."

"Then you should take it. I just don't know why you can't stay here and do things."

"If I stay here, I'll do what I've done for the last however many months I've been home. Nothing. I just ... I can't be happy volunteering and organizing things and being Mom," she laughs. "I know you love that and I'm proud of you for doing it. The world needs more selfless people. I'm just selfish, I guess."

"You are not," I object.

"Maybe not. I don't feel like I am. I just want to see the world. Meet people. Try different things. See what's out there, you know? I know what's here and it's wonderful. I'm not knocking it at all. I just want more experiences."

"You have wanderlust."

"I have wanderlust," she agrees.

"I can appreciate that. I think it sounds fun to not be tied down to one place."

"WANT TO COME WITH ME?"

"No."

"You answered that pretty quickly."

"Yeah, well ..." My voice trails off into a smile. "I'm happy here right now."

"Because of Dom?"

"Yeah." Fiddling with the drawstring of the workout pants I put on earlier, I take a deep breath. "He's having lunch with Ford and I tomorrow afternoon."

She gasps. "What? You're serious? Cam. That's ... that's wow."

"I know."

"Give me a minute here. Just ... *wow*."

Pacing through the kitchen, I remember Ford's voice as he accepted my offer. He's the only one I could ask, besides Sienna. The others would be too overbearing. Too judgmental. Too illogical. Still, I'm not convinced beyond a reasonable doubt this will end up in a good place with Ford either.

I can't blame them. I've always looked at their interest to keep me safe as an asset. There's a level of comfort knowing you have a family that loves you as much as mine does me. It's never bothered me at all ... until lately.

"You know what? It's not their call who I date," I insist, more to placate myself than Sienna. "If I want to see Dominic, then I will. This is not up for Ford's approval. This is an olive branch so they'll get off my back."

"This is totally up for Ford's approval or you wouldn't be doing it." She sighs again. "If it matters what I think, and of course it does because I'm your twin sister, I think you're doing the right thing."

I stop pacing. "You do?"

"Of course I do. You know I like Dom. Yes, maybe he's not what our parents expect, but I don't think it's going to be that big of a deal."

"What about the Nolan part?"

"Yeahhhh ... That might be a little tricky. But it's not like he had anything to do with Nolan trying to sabotage Barrett. He doesn't even know his uncle, right? Not really?"

"No, not really. But Nolan really fucked Barrett over. I'll never forget that night when Lincoln found the evidence on the computer of Nolan trying to undermine Barrett's campaign."

Sienna clicks her tongue in agreement. "I still think you're fine. They rallied around Alison and she was, like, investigated before she moved here. Remember that? Wasn't it for assault or something?"

I sink against the table, Dom's painful past weighing heavily on my heart. "What if Dom *has* done something? But there was a reason for it?"

"Cam ..."

A thunderous bang hits my front door, making me jump. It's followed by the doorbell ringing once, twice, three times. "Sienna, let me call you back."

"I want to finish this conversation."

"It's fine."

"Are *you* fine?"

"Yes," I laugh, peeking through the peephole. "Dom's here. Let me call you back."

"Fine, fine. Have fun with the man."

I end the call and pull open the door. "Hey, babe." My smile falters as I see the look on his face. "Dom, what's wrong?"

His jaw is set, his eyes cold, as he storms in past me. He's on the verge of exploding, barely containing the energy that's threatening to boil over. I can see it. Feel it. Take a step backwards because of it.

"Dom?" I ask again, shutting the door. My stomach flips as I wait for some kind of inkling as to what's happening. "What's going on?"

With his eyes trained on a spot across the room, he speaks. "If you have something you want to tell me, now would be the time."

"What are you talking about?"

"Now, Cam."

"I have nothing to tell you," I say, bewildered. "Why ... what ... I'm so confused."

At the pace of a snail, he pivots on his heel. His glare is a mixture of anger and resentment as it settles on me. "Did you loan money to Nate?"

The look in his eye has a new meaning and I feel my hands tremble. "Yes," I say, clearing my throat. "I did."

"Goddamn it," he growls, running a hand through his hair. "Why in the hell did you do that?"

"He's going to pay me back."

"Don't you get it?" he says, laughing through his teeth. "It isn't about whether he pays you back or not, because he will. *I* know that. *You* know that. *He* knows that."

There are too many words on the tip of my tongue to get one out. I just look up at him as he towers over me, his shoulders set back so he's at full height, and try to wrap my brain around this.

"Then what's the problem?" I ask, choosing my words with care. "He needed it. I have it. So what?"

"So what?" he asks, raising a brow. "It's never occurred to you how abnormal it looks to just wire someone ten thousand dollars?"

"No. I just helped your brother out. I—"

"Listen to me," he says, taking a step my way, "you didn't just help my brother out. You fucked *yourself* over."

"What?" I stammer. "I ... This is crazy. You're crazy."

Giving him a glare of my own, I push by him and head into the kitchen. The light is bright, streaming in from the window that overlooks the golf course behind my house. The sponge I just tossed in the sink still lies there and I wonder if there is a way to rewind the last few minutes and go back to talking to Sienna.

Instead, his footsteps ring through the hallway and into the room behind me. With a final look at the serenity outside, I turn to face him. He's standing by the island watching me. His jaw is a little less clenched, but there's no smile on his handsome face.

"I'm so mad right now ..." He blows out a breath, his hand shaking as he runs it through his hair. "I shouldn't even be here. I'm just gonna go."

"No, wait," I say as he turns away. "Stay. Please."

"This isn't something your little smile can fix."

"But I don't understand. What did I do that was so wrong?"

Looking at the ceiling, his Adam's apple bobs in his throat. His chest is rising and falling so quickly, I know he's trying to calm himself. I've seen him like this one time before when a guy said something disgusting to me at The Gold Room. If it weren't for Nate, I'm not sure he wouldn't have ended up in jail that night.

"You just proved them right," he says simply. I wait for more, but that's it. That's all he says.

"I proved who right?"

"Everyone." His arms stretch to the sides, his eyes blazing. "You proved them all fucking right. Except, you know what? They *aren't* fucking right."

"What?" I shake my head, trying to make sense of this insanity as he just stares at me like he's going to shoot fireballs my way. "What does being right and them—whoever they are—and my loan to Nate have to do with each other?"

"You're not stupid. Think about it."

"Um ..."

He forces a smile, but it's lethal. "If you'd given him a thousand, two, five—I would've been annoyed but not pissed. *It's ten thousand dollars*, Cam. Is this normal behavior for you? To just shoot large sums of money to someone else's account?"

"Of course not," I huff.

He takes a deep, haggard breath before looking at me again. Blinking back tears, I stand immobilized in the kitchen and watch him struggle to find the words he wants to say.

"I know you think your family will hate me."

"That's not true," I say, although it's not completely false either.

"Nah, it is. That's just the truth." He looks around the kitchen before settling his gaze on me again. "I can't say I blame you for thinking that or them for feeling that way. Look at me. Look at you."

"I am looking at you," I gulp. "And I know that even if they don't ... even if it takes a second for some of them to accept the idea, it won't be because of *you*, Dominic."

He nods. "I agree with that. It'll be because of everything else. Of shit like this—of appearances and assumptions."

Forcing a swallow, I watch the depth of the blues of his eyes swirl together. They're a tidal wave of unnamed emotions that I could lose myself in ... in more ways than one.

"When did you start caring about assumptions?" I ask through the dryness of my throat.

My question does nothing to stop the intensity etching his face or the way his eyes are dead-set on mine. "When I agreed to go with you to meet your brother."

As the words come out, his hands go through his hair, lifting the silky locks and tugging them in frustration. It's like he knows he's opened a can of worms and now he has no choice but to take off the lid and let the contents spill, no matter how painful.

"I thought if I went that maybe, you know, this thing between us could ..."

"What, Dom?"

"I don't know. Maybe it was going to be something for a while. Maybe I wasn't going to wake up one morning and see you'd realized you're better off without me."

I can't even respond to that. My heart tightens, physically paining me that he ever even considered that, while I'm speechless at the realization that maybe he'd hoped for that too.

Then reality hits. That was all in past tense.

"Do you still hope for that?" I ask, biting back a rush of emotion that will only complicate things.

"Can I? Really?" His shoulders lift, almost touching his ears, before falling. "Your family is everything to you. Here I am, about to meet them, and look at what I'm walking in to. They say you can't make a first impression twice. You've just taken my ability to make a decent one."

"No, I didn't."

"Yes, you did," he insists. "You've linked my fate with Nate's. If something happens with that loan ..."

My fingers itch to hug him, to wrap around his middle and press my face against his chest. To stop the anger that's flowing back to the surface before it spills over.

"As soon as they find out, and they will, their perception of me *and you*, will be linked with Nate," he gruffs. "They'll assume I'm from a family of freeloaders and tell you to get the fuck away before I really damage you."

"That's not true," I sniffle. "Besides, I'll do whatever and whoever I want."

For that, I get another half-smile. "That's not true. You do whatever they tell you, whenever they tell you to do it. You don't do jack shit without them telling you it's okay."

"I do you, don't I?" I fire back.

He clenches his teeth once more. "Careful," he warns. After a pointed glance, he takes a step back. "You stay in this little box they've put you in and go through the motions of your life. I think doing me is the first thing you've ever done that's against status quo. You've hidden me to the point that you have to—"

"I haven't hidden you!" I interject. "And you haven't wanted to meet them. You've been downright against it, so don't even shove that all on me."

The burn is quick and hot as it uncurls from the base of my throat. The tears I blink back are scalding and he sees them. It forces him to look away.

"Okay. That's true." When he speaks again, his voice is a touch softer. "You are so capable, Camilla. You're ridiculously smart, stunningly beautiful, the sweetest heart. It drives me insane watching you jump through hoops they've set for you. You do the charity work you think you should do but don't love—"

"That's not true! I love working with the Landry Holdings charities."

He lifts brow. "You love it? You jump out of bed in the morning raring to go? When is the last time you found something you loved to do? And I don't mean shopping or skiing. I mean something *for you*. Like what fighting is for me—when I'm doing it, I feel like me. Nothing else feels that way."

I don't respond.

"Answer me, Cam."

"I don't know."

Heaving a breath, he paces a circle, knotting his hands through his hair again. "The point is, you're gonna have a mess on your hands."

"Well, I guess it's my mess, isn't it?"

"Oh, it's your mess. It's just not contained to you."

A heaviness descends on me, and suddenly, I feel exhausted. My head hurts, my eyes are blurry, and my legs just want to collapse me into a chair.

"Are you going to tell them about the money?" he asks.

"It's none of their business."

"While I agree with that probably more than you even do, that's not going to keep them from finding out."

My hands go to my hips. "Aren't you the one that tells me I need to start standing on my own two feet?"

"*Sweetheart*," he says with more saltiness than sweetness, "you're the one that's set the precedent that they can look in your accounts and monitor your every movement. If you think that's going to miraculously not happen with this, you're wrong."

"Doesn't mean I have to explain it."

"Nah, you're right. Just let them think you handle money like a child and I'm some kind of low life that just wants you for your cash. If that's the case, I can't even blame them this time."

I grab a piece of paper towel and pat under my eyes. It comes back black, stained with the mascara I applied so carefully in case I saw Dominic again today. I just didn't expect it to come off like this.

"Cam ..." His voice is lower now, the tenderness I'm used to most days buried not quite as deep as before.

"Shut up."

"I won't shut up." He stalks around the island, his eyes set firmly on mine. "This is why I don't want you at the bar. This is the reason I tell you to stay away from the gym."

"Because I might loan everyone money?" I crack, feeling my moxie dissipate as he reaches me.

He almost smiles. "No, because you're too ... you're too nice for your own good." He touches my chin and tips my head back so I'm looking up at him. The anger in his eyes fades and in its place is a concern that makes me want to burrow my head in his chest. "Your family has fucked you over by sheltering you so much."

"They've given me a giver's heart."

"What they've given you is a rose-colored version of the real world and have been there to scoop you up from every problem you've ever had," he sighs. "You rest on your laurels. You absolutely could walk into a room and take care of yourself, but you don't. And that drives me insane. You've let them make you weak, when all I see when I look at you is a damn strong woman."

A smile tickles my lips. As he takes it in, his posture softens.

"You don't bother to analyze things sometimes, because it'll all be okay because it always is," he says. "You know what? Sometimes it's not."

"This will be."

"It will be," he acknowledges. "But you have to start being the woman I know you are all the time, not just some of the time, Cam. You just see the good in everything and I'm afraid ..."

"What?" I whisper.

"The world isn't like the gated community you've lived in your whole life. My world specifically isn't the one you're used to. If something happened to you because of me ..." He reaches for me. I'm in his arms before he even gets them extended.

Nuzzling my face in his white t-shirt, I breathe in the smell of linen mixed with cedar—something so unique and so Dom.

His hands run up and down my back, his cheek pressed against the top of my head. We stand in the kitchen, holding one another.

"Are you still going to go with me tomorrow?" I ask, my voice crackling.

"I have to now. If I don't, they'll think we took the money and ran."

"They will not."

He pulls away, his eyes now brimming with an anxiety that is contagious. "I'll be honest with you. If this was anyone else, I'd call it quits right now. I'd be looking at this like it's a fight between two different weight classes."

My hand trembles as I play with my earring, trying to hold on to the *if this was anyone else* part.

"I gotta go. I'm working a shift at the bar tonight for Nate."

"I'll call Ford and tell him we won't meet for lunch tomorrow."

"No, you won't," he says, shaking his head. "We're going."

"Why?"

"Because if he's going to judge me, I'd at least like him to have met me once. I don't want my complete reputation with Ford to be based on two interactions with my brother."

Looking at me over his shoulder, he heads to the front door. With his hand over the knob, he gives me a sad smile. Sunlight pours in the room when he pulls the door open and steps onto the porch. "I'll pick you up at eleven. See ya, Cam."

For moments longer than I should, I stand in the foyer and look at the closed door. I wait for him to come back in and kiss me goodbye. Then I hear the Camaro fire up in the driveway and my heart sinks.

With tears flooding my cheeks, I hope beyond all hope he's wrong. That this isn't the start to the end of us.

ELEVEN

CAMILLA

I observe my watch moving another minute forward, making it seven after eleven. That's seven minutes after the time Dom said he would be here today to pick me up. Dom's never late, not without calling.

For some reason, I didn't call Sienna after he left yesterday. I sent Joy to voicemail and poured a glass of wine and sat on the sofa alone. Having someone around would only have made it worse, made Dominic's absence that much more obvious.

He sent one text really late saying goodnight. It was a quick, simple few words that at least let me know he was thinking about me. I returned many more words than he sent, but there was no follow-up. I waited for almost an hour for a reply that never came.

I curled up in one of his t-shirts with the phone to my chest like it brought me closer to him somehow and fell asleep with tearstains on my pillow.

Just when I thought things were turning for us, moving to something more solid, this happens. Usually things like this are just a misunderstanding or something dumb that can be fixed. This is not. I can feel it. This is a harbinger of what we've both feared: that we're too different to work.

It's a conversation we've had many times, a case-in-point that's made over and over again. It's why he hasn't met my family. It's the reason he doesn't want me at the gym or bar. This is why we argue over who pays for dinner when we go out—when I know he's tight on money and he refuses to let me pick up the bill—and why I don't understand why he thinks fighting is an acceptable job. He also can't fathom how my family is so entwined.

We're entirely different. It's something we've always known. Maybe we both thought it would end before it mattered, but it didn't. And now it does.

A separate, equally intricate knot has twisted itself in my stomach that I can't loosen. When I think of Dominic and our argument, I think of Nate. My stomach rolls every time I consider I may have put a wedge between them. If anyone knows the importance and preciousness of a sibling bond, it's me. To think I might've chipped away at that makes me want to die.

NOW, eight minutes past eleven, I wonder if he didn't stay up pondering the same questions, coming to the same realizations ... leaving me sitting here this morning for nothing.

A knock sounds against the door and my heart leaps with the doorbell. I'm halfway there before I have to go back to the sofa, swipe up my purse, and then almost jog down the foyer again.

Taking a deep breath, I pause and try to remember the little positive mantra Mallory teaches at yoga. But after a few seconds of nothing, I can't resist seeing him any longer and yank open the door.

A crisp blue and white striped shirt covers his chest, a pair of khakis I didn't know he owned span his long, lean legs. His hair is styled to the side like he only does when he takes me out to dinner. He pulls his sunglasses off and I see a little puffiness beneath his blue orbs reminiscent of mine.

"Hey," I say, forcing a swallow.

"Hi." His eyes drift easily down my yellow dress, pausing at my espadrille sandals, before roaming back up my body again. "You ready?"

"Yeah. Let me lock up."

He waits patiently while I fiddle with the locks and I hold my breath as I turn around. Any other day, my hand would find his as we make our way down the sidewalk. Today, his palm finds the small of my back and guides me towards his Camaro instead.

His hand is heavy against the thin fabric of my dress. I can smell his body wash, a clean, cedar scent lingering under the spice of his cologne. Breathing it in, I let it dawdle on my senses, giving me the comfort I've craved for hours.

Without a word, he pops open the passenger door and watches me climb inside. He closes it softly before moving around the front of the car and slipping in the seat beside me.

Our gazes meet somewhere over the console and a million things are said, but none of them involve words spoken.

The engine roars to life, the tires semi-squealing as he moves us out into the street of my neighborhood, through the gates, and out onto the main road.

"I didn't think you were coming," I admit as we wait at a stoplight. Turning to look at him, he's watching me with a furrowed brow.

"I told you I would."

"I know. I just thought ..."

"At least you're thinking now. That's a plus." He shifts into first gear and charges the car forward. It zips through traffic and hits another red light. "I'm really trying to not be mad about this. I'm trying to be logical."

"I appreciate that."

The corner of his mouth lifts, but it's not quite a smile. "I know your intentions were good."

"Dom, I didn't mean to cause a problem with this. I—"

I'm silenced by the bark of the tires and a lurching of the car as we propel forward. My heart thumping in my chest, my back is pressed into the leather as we speed down the next block to the next light.

"Have you told Ford about the loan?" he asks, looking forward.

"No."

He rolls his thick, muscled neck around his shoulders. "All right then." He accelerates once more and we take a sharp right.

"Can I ask you something?" I ask.

"Sure."

"Are you and Nate fighting?"

His jaw tenses, but he looks at me out of the corner of his eye. "No. I've decided you two are adults. I'll let you handle your own business."

It can't be that easy. My stomach drops. "Dom?"

"What?"

"You know what," I sigh, "I've worried about this all night. Tell me you two aren't into it because of me."

"Not because of you, sweetheart. Because he didn't have the respect for either of us.

I grab the door handle as he gasses it again, the car roaring beneath me, and then whips a quick left. "Ford is bringing Lincoln," I tell him.

"Great."

"I know Nate didn't really hit it off with Lincoln, but he's not a bad guy," I insist. "He's funny and loves sports and really is a big kid. I think you'd like him if you gave him a chance."

"I bet I'll love him," he says, the sarcasm unmistakable. "And two against one should be a blast."

I roll my eyes. "He's just coming because they are going golfing afterwards right near the restaurant. This isn't a big conspiracy or something."

"Tell you the truth," he says, piloting the Camaro into the parking lot, "I'm fairly certain I could take the both of them. I'm not really worried."

"Hey, now," I say, "my brothers are no joke! Ford is a legit badass and Lincoln was a professional baseball player."

"They golf, Cam." He flips off the ignition and looks at me. A huge, shaky sigh of relief pushes past my lips as I see the hint of playfulness in his eyes. "I'm pretty sure golfing removes any badges of bad-assery they may have."

"Whatever you say," I grin. "But don't get Ford on the ground. I've seen him in action."

"I'm sure," he teases.

"Hey, just offering you a little insight. Take it or leave it."

When he doesn't answer, I look at him. Studying his profile, I can't believe how good-looking he is. Even though I've seen him a thousand times, it catches me off-guard.

His skin is the perfect tan, the scruff on his cheeks makes my fingers itch to touch it. There's a little bend in his nose. He says it's from a right hand in a boxing match when he was a teenager. On anyone else, it would look like it needs fixed. On him, it's sexy.

He takes a breath, holds it, and looks at me. Sucking in a breath of my own, I give him a smile—a real one.

"There we go," he says, twisting his lips to hide a smile.

"What?"

"I've missed that smile." He reaches out and brushes a strand of hair out of my face. "You look really pretty today. I don't think I told you that."

"You didn't. You were too busy being mad at me."

That does it. He grins at me, the sexy one that melts me from the inside out.

"Are you still mad at me?"

"Yes," he says instantly, the smile dropping from his cheeks. "I don't like you risking yourself. Not for Nate, not for Ryder, not for anyone. And I'm pretty pissed off no one thought I should know about this."

"Okay, you're mad. What does that mean?" I ask, the shakiness in my voice back.

"I don't know," he says sadly. "Let's get through this lunch before we try to hash that out."

He hops out of the car and opens my door before I can get my buckle off. Swinging it open and offering me a hand, he pulls me to my feet. We stand only inches away, both fighting our natural inclination to kiss or hug or make contact of some kind.

"You look really nice today," I tell him. "If you weren't mad at me, I might've said you looked super sexy in khakis, but you are mad and I don't want to go thinking those kind of thoughts about you."

"Why not?"

"Because it might be a lonely night tonight."

We turn towards the door, him a step behind me. "You were right about one thing, Cam."

"What's that?"

He steps around me and opens the door to Hillary's House, his brows tugged together. "It may be a lonely night."

TWELVE

DOMINIC

I've driven by this place a hundred times in my life but never stopped. As soon as I step foot in Hillary's House, it's everything I thought it would be—an uppity place that tries so hard not to be. It's like when we go to a fast food place and get the triple burger with bacon and curly fries instead of the burger that costs a buck off the discount menu... only in reverse. It's our way of feeling fancy. This is their way of feeling like an everyday man. Someone just needs to clue them in that the everyday man doesn't walk around in loafers or pearls.

A stillness settles over me, causing my palms that were a little sweaty to dry, as I spot what has to be her brothers at a table in the back. This happens before I walk into the ring. It's a silence that trickles from the top of my head, through my chest, over my gut, and down to my feet. It washes through my veins and allows me to focus on the task, or men, at hand.

Some fighters get amped up, go nuts, before the bell rings. Not me. It's a waste of energy. I need all of mine on the job to be done. Especially today.

Cam gives me a reassuring look as we make our way through the restaurant. There's a sparkle in her eye, one I see often when she talks about her family. It's fascinating. The idea of having a family as close-knit as the Landry's is completely alien to me. She has friends, like Joy, but the stories she shares are always of her sister or one of her brothers or one of their wives.

We approach the table and I set my gaze on the two men. I've seen them before on television for different things, mostly charity events and political campaigns. At the moment, I wish I'd paid more fucking attention.

This is not my element, and it's both of them versus me. If I didn't have this loan bullshit on my mind and all of the related complications, I'd feel better about this.

Ford and Lincoln look enough alike to undeniably be brothers, yet one is wider and blonder and the other leaner and darker. The blond one laughs, shaking his head at the other as we approach.

"Hey, guys," Camilla says. The forced cheeriness goes unmissed by all of us. Their heads whip up, doing a quick fly-by of Cam and then land on me. "Dominic, this is Ford," she says pointing to the lighter-haired one. "And this is Lincoln."

"Hey, Dominic," Ford says, standing. He's about my height and weight with a clean look about him. There's no doubt he's assessing me, but he's classy enough about it. "Nice to meet you, man."

"Same here."

We exchange a firm handshake and courteous, yet guarded nods, as we take our seats. My chest tingles, burning with the anticipation of what's to come. It's the same sensation I experience as I wait for the referee to start a fight. It's the unknown, not sure what will be coming your way but knowing you better be bringing your A-game because your opponent sure as hell is.

Camilla settles in to my right as I finish my introductions. I flash her the best smile I can, maybe for more my own reassurance than hers, before resting my eyes on Lincoln.

He's sitting across from me, a wide smirk on his face. Holding back a chuckle, because that won't get me anywhere, I'd put money that's the exact face that made Nate want to send Lincoln's teeth across the bar.

"Lincoln," I say, extending a hand. "Nice to meet you."

"You too." He shakes my hand, his grip stronger than it needs to be. I return it with as much force as he's giving plus another couple pounds per square inch. The fucker grins. "Dominic, was it?"

"Yeah. Dominic Hughes."

"Where have I heard that name before?"

I shrug, sitting down. "Who knows? It's a small world."

He nods again, this time looking up as the waitress slips between him and his sister. "What can I get y'all?"

"I'll have a water, please, Lola," Ford says. "No lemon."

Cam takes the menus from the raven-haired waitress with a smile and passes them around the table. "Me, too."

"What about you, Linc?"

"Water."

"Make it four," I chime in, watching Lola's eyes glitter as they meet mine.

My stomach twists and turns as I feel the Landry eyes peering at me, waiting for me to fuck up. Lola is attractive. There's no doubt about that. But she's not what's sitting next to me, and anything compared to Cam loses.

"You aren't a Landry," Lola grins.

"No, he isn't," Camilla says with a little more force than necessary. "Lola, this is Dominic. Dom, this is Lola."

We exchange hellos, cut brief by Cam's grabbing my hand under the table and locking our fingers together. I smile at the touch as I watch her place them next to our silverware with a pointed glance Lola's way.

If we were alone and I wasn't trying to keep my head about me, I'd find it incredibly hard not to give her hell about this. My lips would be on her as soon as Lola walks away, the demonstration more of a turn-on than I can muster.

Satisfied that I'm taken, Lola traipses towards the kitchen. Lincoln snickers.

"Is this Swink's version of going caveman?" he cracks. "I think you were almost hateful with that. I kind of like it."

"Hush," she glares at him. Her cheeks go rosy, her hand slowly slipping from mine. "Don't be an ass, Linc."

"That's like asking the sky not to be blue," Ford scoffs.

"Well, fuck you too," Lincoln says, continuing on with some inside joke the three of them laugh at that I don't understand.

Instead, I sit back in my chair in wonderment. It's like being at a table in a foreign land full of customs and exchanges you haven't seen before. It's like Nate and I, but on a whole other level, like what Nate and I and Joey could've been if Joey hadn't been run over, our mother wasn't weak, and our father not a useless son of a bitch.

Cam elbows me in the side, making me jump. "What?" I ask.

"I was just asking you what you do for a living," Ford says.

"Oh, sorry," I say, clearing my throat. "I work for Monstone Repair."

"That's heating and cooling, right?" Ford asks.

"Yeah. That's my nine-to-five," I say, wondering if they even know what that truly is. "I also bartend some at my brother's bar."

Lincoln leans forward, his athletic reflexes on full display. "The Gold Room?"

"Yeah."

"You resemble the guy we met down there. What was his name?" he asks, turning to Ford. "You know who I mean? The guy behind the bar."

"Nate," Ford and I say at the same time.

"That's my brother," I continue. "He said you were in a while back."

Lincoln reclines in his chair, crossing his arms over his chest. He twists his lips before smacking them open. "Dominic, your brother is kind of a dick."

"He can be. But, funnily enough," I say, looking him right in the eye, "he said the same thing about you."

Ford laughs as Lola places glasses of ice water in front of each of us. She then scribbles down our order and leaves again—this time with no ogling.

"I kind of want to revisit this Nate thing," Lincoln says, leaning against the table with his jaw set in stone. The look he gives me ramps my blood pressure. I feel my fingers automatically moving, stretching, readying themselves for a fight should it happen.

"Let's move this conversation along before it becomes a giant pissing match," Cam sighs. "Ford, what did you do today?"

"Not a lot," he says, trying to navigate everything around him. "I worked some. Going golfing after this."

"You golf?" Lincoln asks me.

"Uh, no."

"That's too bad."

"And why is that?"

"I'd love to beat your ass on the golf course," he grins.

"You fight?" I volley back, not about to let him think he got one over on me.

"Fight what?"

"Men."

My response isn't what he expected and it's clear he isn't sure exactly what I mean. "Not in a while."

"Oh my goodness, stop it," Camilla chirps. "Ford, make them stop."

"I kind of want to see where this goes," he laughs.

As they banter back and forth, Lincoln and I don't take our eyes off each other. It's not a two-seconds-away-from-pounding-the-other's-face kind of thing, but rather a don't-push-me-because-I-shove-back kind of thing.

"If you ever want to test that, I train at Percy's downtown. I'd love to do a couple of rounds with ya," I smirk.

"Percy's, huh?" Ford asks.

Before I can respond, Lincoln is cutting in. "I might have to take you up on that."

"Oh, the hell you will," Ford laughs. "I'm not going to save your ass if you walk head-first into a fight club."

Lincoln looks at him like a scorned puppy. "For real? You have to take my balls right here?"

"Danielle took your balls a long time ago," Ford chuckles, clapping him on the shoulder.

"You guys are so embarrassing," Camilla mumbles.

I look over at her. She's shaking her head, watching the salt shaker like it's the most interesting thing in the world. The way her cheeks are a little pink makes me want to reach out and kiss her.

Instead, I reach for her hand beneath the table. Her head turns to mine and a slow, soft smile spreads on her lips as our fingers interlace.

"It's okay," I mouth to her as her brothers banter between themselves.

She gives my hand a squeeze, her dainty palm almost encased by mine. Then, in a flash of movement, her shoulders throw back and she lifts her chin.

"Hey," she projects, her voice clear. "Can you guys hush for just a second?"

My stomach flips as I send her a questioning look. I have no idea what she's doing but she's doing *something*. She drops my hand and sits up in her seat.

"I want to say something," she says, clearing her throat. "I don't think this is particularly any of your business, but Dominic has suggested it's the right thing to do."

"What's wrong, Swink?" Ford asks.

"Nothing is wrong. I just have a little announcement that I want to make and then forget—"

Lincoln's palms smack against the table, the contents shaking at the force. "You're fucking pregnant!" His jaw drops as he looks at Camilla and then, menacingly, at me. "Percy's tomorrow," he growls.

"My Lord, Lincoln," Camilla laughs. "I'm not pregnant."

"Thank fuck," Ford exhales, slumping in his seat. "I was starting to side with Lincoln on this fighting thing."

"Okay, hold up real quick," I cut in. "What if she was pregnant? Would that have been the worst thing to happen?"

"Yes," they say in unison.

"Okay, no," Ford says, giving Lincoln a look to shut up. "It wouldn't have been, and I'm sorry if that sounded really disrespectful to you. That's not how we meant it."

"That's how it sounded," I shoot back.

Ford and Lincoln exchange a look much in the same way Nate and I do, before Ford squares his shoulders to me. "Look, this is really hard for us. Swink is our baby sister, and aside from that one kid with frat boy hair, she's never really brought a guy around us before. We just want what's best for her."

"And don't you think I know what's best for me?" she asks. "I appreciate you guys, Ford. I do. Sincerely. But ..." She looks at me, the vulnerability in her eyes something I can't resist. It's not a sign of weakness this time. It's a need of support, a silent plea to give her a hand.

"I get what you're saying," I say, blowing out a breath. "We're in the same boat. I want what's best for her too."

She takes my hand again, but I don't look her in the eye. I can't. Truth be told, I don't know what's best for her. Not really.

"I can tell you all what's best for me. Right now it's Dominic. Maybe it will be Dominic for a long time, I don't know." She moves her hair to one shoulder and looks at Ford. "I've learned by watching you guys and by going through things myself that you can't predict what's going to happen. Look at you and Ellie."

Ford grins and I wish I knew what they were talking about, but I don't.

"I've let you guys kind of ... guide me for my whole life," she says softly. "I love having four big brothers. I always have. You were rock stars to my friends, and I've always felt safe knowing I had you in my corner. But now I have Dom too."

She squeezes my hand as my heart tries not to choke itself out.

"It was also easier letting you call the shots," she admits. "But I want to start calling them myself."

"What are you saying?" Lincoln asks.

"I'm just saying I want a little freedom from you guys breathing down my neck. I know you do it so I don't mess up, but ... maybe it won't be so bad if I do."

This is the Camilla I know. This is the woman that can fuck me up with a smile or put me in my place with more class and etiquette than I could imagine. She's just that—a woman. Not the little girl they once knew.

It's Ford that breaks the silence. "We all mess up, Camilla. Look at Lincoln."

"Fuck you again," he laughs, and just like that, the tension ebbs from the table. "I get what you're saying. But you need to accept the fact that we'll always be hovering nearby. You're our baby sister."

My hand falls to Camilla's thigh. It lands almost at the bend of her hip, and her foot stops tapping. Her eyes dart to me, her lips falling apart. I give her a wink to help quell the anxiety flooding her pretty blue irises.

"I'll be fine. I need you guys to trust me a little more. Okay?" she asks.

After a few moments, they both nod.

"Good." Heaving a deep breath, one hand clamping down on mine, she blows it out. "Back to what I was saying earlier. In the spirit of this conversation, I don't think this is your business. But Dom says I need to tell you."

They look at me, curious looks painted on their faces. I keep my features blank.

"I loaned Nate ten thousand dollars."

"You did fucking what?" Lincoln barks.

"Lower your voice," Ford warns him, his tone too calm. His gaze rolls to mine like sharpened steel. "Did you know about this?"

I sit up a little taller and ignore the slightly panicked look from

Camilla. "I found out yesterday and I was about as happy about it as you are right now."

"What are you thinking?" Lincoln asks. "Seriously—ten thousand dollars?"

"I was thinking that it's my money and I can do whatever I want with it."

The corner of his eye on me, Ford directs his attention to his sister. "That's true. You can. But that doesn't mean you should go loaning people ten thousand dollars. And I know you know Nate, and it's Dominic's brother—"

"Which only makes it a worse choice," I cut in, throwing up my hands. "I have major issues with the fact that neither one of them told me."

"Can I speak frankly?" Ford asks.

"Yeah, cut the shit."

"Do I need to worry about this?"

"Clearly we fucking do," Lincoln shoots off, shaking his head.

"No, you don't have to fucking worry," I say, turning my heated glare on Lincoln. "My brother is a stand-up guy."

"We've met," Lincoln deadpans.

"Exactly why he told me not to even come here today," I reply.

Cam's linen napkin goes sailing on the table. We all look at her and almost see smoke coming out of her diamond-studded ears. "I'm not listening to any more of this."

"We're just making sure—"

"Ford, enough." She scoots her chair back, knocking my hand off her leg in the process. "I've never once given you crap about any of your life choices, even when I was a teenager and watched you make a slew of bad ones. I'm not asking you to approve mine, so if that's what the two of you are thinking," she says, looking from one to the other, "you can get that out of your head right now. I'm allowing you to meet Dom out of respect for you. I would appreciate some respect of my choices back."

My jaw drops. If we weren't sitting here, I would pick her up and swing her around for finally having a backbone. It's obvious this is a new thing for them. The look on Lincoln's face is priceless—brows shot to the ceiling, jaw hanging open like mine. Ford is more reserved, but there's no mistake he's trying to wrap his head around this too.

I place my hand on her thigh again, but she knocks it away.

"And as far as the money goes, it was from *my* account. It cost you guys *nothing*. If I come to you broke and crying, you can shove it all in my face—but only then. I won't listen to it before." She looks at me. "And not from you either, Dominic."

Ford whistles through his teeth, letting his fork hit the table. "Well, okay then."

"I loaned that money to someone I trust, to the father of a little boy that reminds me a lot of Huxley, and I won't feel bad about that. Going forward, I won't ask any of you," she looks at me, "including you, Dom, what I can or can't do with anything—money or otherwise."

No one says a word, not even to Lola when she comes by to check on us. I give her a little wave, letting her know everything is fine and to encourage her to leave. After a couple of long minutes, I take a drink.

"I know what this must look like," I say. "She's dating a guy that works on air conditioners for a living. I don't eat at places like this or golf or belong to a country club somewhere. You gotta be thinking she's lost her damn mind forking over that kind of money to Nate. You have to."

"I'm not saying we don't," Lincoln admits.

I look at my girl. Her skin is flushed, her eyes crystal clear, looking more beautiful than ever. I give her a reassuring smile and her shoulders sag at the gesture. Leaning forward, she presses a kiss to my cheek.

"I don't want my family," I tell them, "right or wrong, to come between yours. So I give you both my word, man-to-man, that she will be paid back."

Ford pauses, looks me over, then smiles. He extends a hand and we shake again. This seems good enough for Lincoln as well. He takes a big bite of his burger.

"How old is your nephew?" he asks with a mouth full of meat.

"Four."

"The loan. What's it for?" Ford asks, cutting into his chicken breast.

"He's redoing The Gold Room. Wanting to make it less ..."

"Seedy?" Lincoln offers, taking another bite of his burger. "No offense."

"None taken. It's really just basic things that should've been done decades ago. Paint. New flooring. New seal on the roof. Things like that."

"How long has he owned that place?" Ford asks.

"A while." I pick up a fry and drop it. They're using forks for fries. Shoving my hands under the table, I feel my face flush. "Nate got into it originally for a fuck fest, I think. Then he got married for a few years and they had Ryder. Now it's just the two of them, he's seeing things a little different."

"Kids will do that to you," Lincoln nods.

"You know," Ford says, taking a sip of his water, "I know a guy that does flooring that's affordable. The guy was in the service with me, but is damn smart, hard worker, and is just getting started. I could hook you up if you are interested. No pressure."

"That'd be great," I say, feeling thrown off-balance. "Thanks."

Lincoln takes another bite. "What's Troy's brother do, Ford?"

"Yeah. Travis is a roofer, I think. I'll ask and send that to you too if it would help."

Camilla beams, the smile on her face the widest I've ever seen it. "I love this, you guys."

"What?" Lincoln asks.

"Not you talking with your mouthful," Cam groans. "Mom would kill you right now."

"Mom's not here."

Cam rolls her eyes. "You're disgusting."

He makes a point of swallowing, much to Camilla's disgust, before looking at me. "Tell us about yourself, Dom."

"Dom?" Cam laughs.

"You call him that."

"I'm also having se—"

"Easy," Ford warns, making us all laugh. "We don't hate him now. Don't push your luck."

The table bursts with laughter, Camilla leaning her head on my shoulder. I lay my arm along the back of her chair. My tattoos peek out from beneath the rolled-up sleeves of my shirt, the edge of a cross that I had inked to remember Joey visible.

Something about the moment stills time. The voices around me are muffled as I feel trapped somehow in this weird spot mentally— thinking about Joey, how he had Nate's laugh and our mother's need to please everyone. If he were an adult, I wonder how he'd fit in this situation. Probably better than me.

I look up to see two women sitting at the table across the aisle from us. They're decked out in bright dresses and huge, tacky neck- laces. They smile politely at Ford, and I wait for them to also look my way. I hope they don't.

Their smiles falter, slipping from their faces when they see me with Camilla. It's almost a look of horror before they recover when Cam sits up, posture perfect, and addresses them.

"Good afternoon, Paulina. Raquel. How are you this afternoon?" she says, going into what I call pageant mode. It's so not the Camilla I know. And it's not one I particularly like.

"So, back to this thing about your brother calling me a dick ..." Lincoln's words draw my attention away from his sister. When I look at him, he's grinning. "Tell him I paid for the entire bottle of Patrón and we only drank half. He owes me."

THIRTEEN

CAMILLA

The roar of the engine is the only sound I hear as Dom's car takes the curves leading back to my house. It's been a quiet ride since we left Hillary's House, neither of us saying much.

It's a lot to process. For both of us.

Letting my head roll to the side, I watch Dominic control the car. One hand on the steering wheel, one on the gear shift, his jaw is pulsing like it does when he's working something out in his head.

Why does this have to be so damn hard?

Ford promised to call me later to talk about things. There was an edge to his voice, but I think he was surprised in a good way. He offered again, before we left, to get him info on some contractors to help with The Gold Room and the two of them had an in-depth conversation about fighting styles and things that went way over my head while they ate apple pie.

It was a little more contentious with Lincoln, but it was mostly Linc keeping him on his toes. I'm just not sure how Dominic felt.

"Hey," I say, my voice barely heard over the engine.

He decreases the gas and the rumble softens. "Hey."

"I think things went well. How about you?"

"Yeah, I mean, it didn't go too bad."

"What did you think of them?"

He gives me a weird look and turns his focus back on the road. "Ford was okay. Lincoln ..."

"He's just a big kid," I explain. "He makes a lot of jokes and has this whole Daddy-role thing now that he has a baby. I really think you two could be friends."

His laugh is loud and amused, and I don't know how to take it.

"What?" I ask.

"I think that's a pretty strong, and inaccurate, word."

"You didn't like him?"

"I didn't say that. I just, uh, I'm not sure our personalities mesh well."

Looking away, I watch the marshmallow-like clouds high in the sky as we make our way back through the city. My nerves start to wobble the closer we get to my house. Whether or not to push the conversation more or to let it be is murky. I don't know.

"Who were the two ladies you were talking to?"

"Paulina and Raquel?"

"The two wearing more perfume than a department store," he clarifies.

"That's them," I sigh. "They're friends of my mother's. Raquel is really nice. She's working with Ellie and Danielle on a joint project for helping restock local food pantries. Paulina ..."

"Is she the brunette?" he asks.

"Yeah. She slept with Barrett—"

"Your brother?" he laughs, looking at me quickly.

"Yes, my brother," I say, rolling my eyes. "Probably Graham, too, if I'm guessing. She's married to a friend of my father's but he's about a million years older than her and she's never had any interest in him besides his checkbook."

"So she uses your brothers as her harem."

"Ugh," I groan, crossing my arms. "That whole thing is disgusting to me."

When I don't look at him, he chuckles. When I still don't look at him, he pokes my thigh with the tip of his finger. "Well, I think your mother's friends weren't too entertained with you being with me."

My heart leaps in my chest as I twist in my seat. "What?"

"Both of them looked at me like I was hitting way out of my league."

"To hell with them," I say, trying to simultaneously keep my irritation at a minimum and think back to their reactions. "Did they really? What did they say?"

"Nothing. You know how they roll—they'd never say something publicly. That would hurt their stock. Just, you know, be ready for your mom to get a call about it."

He focuses on the road and makes a valiant attempt at keeping his features void of emotion. But I know him well enough to see it for the façade it is.

The corners of his lips barely turn down, the sadness in his eyes only noticeable if you look for it. Dominic excels at hiding his feelings, and when we first met, I thought maybe he didn't really have deep emotions. Over the weeks and months we've been together, I know differently. I suspect, even, that if he were broken open, maybe he feels them more deeply than most.

My chest squeezes at the signs he's not meaning to give off, and I wish I could get my hands on my mother's friends and straight tell them what I think of them. How dare they make Dominic feel any which way? They don't even know him.

I touch his arm, letting my hand lie gently on the curve of his bicep. It's as if the contact releases some of his tension because I can actually feel him relax.

"I'm sorry they looked at you that way," I whisper.

"Don't worry about it. Women like that—if I wasn't with you, they'd be asking for me to be their dirty little secret." He watches for my reaction. "When I go to houses like that—"

"Like mine?"

"Like yours," he concedes, "those women like the tattooed, blue-collar asshole. We're what they're not supposed to have. I'm exactly what their missionary-style, four-inch-cocked husbands are not."

"Dom." His name is a sentence, not a question or the start to anything more. I remove my hand slowly.

"So it's nothing for you to apologize for. If I wasn't sitting with you, it would've been a different ballgame."

There's so much I want to discuss, so many directions I want to go with this, that I can't pick one. I just sit, buckled in my seat, and wish there was a way to strap in my thoughts too.

"For the record," he says, smirking, "the brunette has fucked Ford too."

"How do you know that?"

He just laughs.

"Is that what you think of me?" I ask guardedly. "That I'm with you because I shouldn't be?"

He takes a moment to respond and with each passing second, my anxiety grows. "Maybe."

"Really? That's offensive, Dominic."

"That's the truth." He bites his lip as he waits for the guard at the gate of my subdivision to let us in. "Do I think that's what got your attention at the start? Yeah. Absolutely."

The gate moves up and he eases the car through. "Is that why you're still here? No."

"I hate that you think I'm so shallow."

"I didn't say that. I said you wanted me at first because you shouldn't. The same way you always want a pint of butter pecan ice cream that you lament you shouldn't eat because of the calories. Then we buy it and you eat a couple of spoonfuls and then you're done because it's not really what you wanted. You wanted the lemon sorbet. You just were proving to yourself you had choices and could go off-script."

"So you're the butter pecan ice cream?" I ask, trying to follow along.

"Yes. I was at first. Now, maybe, I'm ... those little chocolate cookies you keep in the back of your cabinet behind the cereal."

"Wait," I laugh. "I thought we were talking ice cream."

"We were, but let's broaden it to food."

"Fine. Keep going. This is interesting."

He whips the car into my driveway, but not without a quick squeal of the tires that he knows pisses off my neighbor. The black marks in the maintained streets are *undesirable*, the guy two houses down calls it.

Turning off the Camaro, he faces me. "I'm the cookies you love, but don't want to love. That's why you keep them behind the cereal. The cereal is a good choice, full of fiber and all that bullshit you look at on the label. I'm the snack full of preservatives, fake colors," he says, nodding towards his tattoos, "and cooked in some cancer-filled oils. I'll be the death of you one day. You know it. You just can't quite say no when it's in front of you."

"Okay," I chuckle, waving my hands in the air, "while that is a very thought-provoking analogy there, Waylor's Cookies, you're wrong."

"I don't think so." He hops out and races to my side. The door is opened, letting in the warm afternoon breeze. Lending me a hand, he helps me out and closes the door behind me. "Again, you look very pretty today."

"Is the cookie conversation over?"

"Yes." He pulls me into his chest, wrapping his arms around my back.

I snuggle into the soft fabric of his shirt, breathing him in and shoving off the ice cream discussion to be analyzed later.

"You know," he says, his chest moving with each breath, "I could never be like your brothers."

"How do you mean?"

"How do I not mean?" His voice sounds hollow, almost third-person, and it glues me in place. "They're so laidback. Like they have nothing to do, nothing to worry about. Like they pick their battles, not the other way around."

"We all pick our battles, don't we?"

"Not where I'm from," he admits. "Sometimes battles pick us. Sometimes our lives don't come with trust funds and fairy godmothers."

Pushing off, I look at him. "I can't help I have a trust fund. Just like you can't help you don't."

"I know," he says, brushing a strand of hair out of my face. "I'm just saying today was really eye-opening for me."

My spirits sink like a weight as I watch him search for his next words. There are a million I could come back at him with, but I don't. I'm too afraid to.

"There will be a day when someone like Lincoln or Ford catches your eye, a quality lemon sorbet," he grins sadly, "and you'll wonder what the hell you're doing with the butter pecan."

"I wonder what I'm doing with you every day," I say, trying to get playful Dom back and failing. "But every day, there's no one else I want to listen to telling me about leg kicks or air conditioner units or bringing me Chinese at eleven at night when I just make an off-handed comment that I could really go for some General Tso's."

His eyes lock with mine. "I gotta go." He kisses my forehead and starts around the car.

"You don't want to come in?"

"I gotta watch Ryder for a while today," he says as he reaches the driver's side door. "Nate has to work and Chrissy bailed or something. I don't know. I don't want in the middle of their shit."

I wait for him to invite me to come over. I've helped watch Ryder before. After a few solid, uncomfortable seconds, it's obvious no invitation is coming.

If I gave in to my emotions, I'd start crying. Being in limbo is the worst feeling in the world and that's where we are—in limbo. We've never been an official item, yet ... we have. I don't even know if we are that unlabeled item now.

Demanding things from Dominic gets you one thing—the opposite of what you want. So I can't just ask him what he's thinking or feeling. Even if I did, by the look in his eye, I'm not sure he even knows.

"Okay," I say, heading to my door. "I'll talk to you later."

He waits until I get the door open and the security system off. Tossing my purse on the settee inside, I turn to face him through the doorway.

"Thanks for going with me today."

He bows his head for a moment. "This is going to sound really weird, and I don't want you to think about it too much, but ... thanks for introducing me to your family."

I flip him a half-smile that's immediately returned. "I thought you didn't like my brothers."

With a wink that makes me laugh, he climbs in the car. "I don't."

I watch him zip out of the driveway, listening to the long bark of his tires, and wish I were in there with him.

FOURTEEN

DOMINIC

"Hey." I give a quick nod to Nate as I enter the kitchen. Throwing my keys on the counter, I peel off my shirt. "Where's Ryder?"

"Asleep."

Wadding the shirt up, I toss it next to my keys. It lands half-draped over a bunch of bananas. "Has he been asleep long?"

"No. Just laid him down."

"Good. I'll grab a shower then."

It would be easier for the both of us if I would just do what I said. Just turn around and go to the shower and when I came back, he would be gone.

Tension was high last night, and while we managed a few words, it's Nate that I'm most pissed off at. He knows it. He's been smart and avoided me for the most part. Until now.

Now he stands next to the refrigerator, his Gold Room shirt on, hat pulled down low on his forehead, keys in hand. He's ready to walk out the door I just walked in. But he doesn't move.

"How'd it go with the Landry's?" he asks.

"A lot more complicated, thanks to you."

"I'm sorry. Again, Dom, I'm sorry."

"Again, Nate, fuck off."

He hangs his head, taking off his hat and letting his hand fall to his side. Maybe I'm tired of expending the energy to be mad or maybe I'm just exhausted from the last twenty-four hours. Either way, I blow out a breath that catches his attention.

"Just pay her back. Every fucking penny plus interest."

"I will," he promises. "You know I will."

"Yeah, I know you will."

He extends his hand, and when I take it, pulls me into a one-arm hug. "I am sorry. If I fuck up your relationship with Cam, I'll never forgive myself."

"Nah, I think I'm capable of doing that on my own."

"So, how'd it go? For real."

I inhale slowly, the air crackling as it seeps into my lungs. Thinking back on the day, I don't even know where to start. "I mean, her brothers were okay. Ford's a decent guy. He's gonna send us some numbers for contractors he does business with for the renovations, actually."

"Really? Do they know about the money?"

"Yeah. It's weird. I know," I say, scratching my head.

"Ford. He's the bigger one? Military-looking motherfucker?"

"Yeah."

"He's the one that threatened me," Nate grins. "He's the only one I probably could hang out with."

"We're so fucked up," I laugh. "I thought the same thing."

We exchange a look that goes beyond a smile. It reassures me, somehow, that I have someone on my side just because.

"Now Lincoln," I continue, "kind of an asshole."

"He played for the Arrows, right?"

I nod. "He was decent. I mean, I didn't knock him out or anything, although I was considering it might come to that a time or two. And," I wink, "he said to tell you that you owe him a half a bottle of Patrón."

"Fuck that," he laughs. He waits as I grab a bottle of water from the fridge and crack open the top before continuing. "So, you and Cam are okay?"

The water is ice cold going down my throat, and at the mention of her name, it splashes into my stomach. I cough, water coming back up. Holding my head over the sink, my eyes searing with tears, I cough until I think I'm going to black out.

Once I'm righted and breathing normally, Nate furrows a brow. "Is that a yes?"

"It's an I don't know," I admit.

"Why do you say that?"

"Do I really need to explain the obvious?"

"No, but you need to explain the stupid."

Rolling my eyes, I place the water on the counter and lean against it. "I've always known she came from a completely different world than we do. Her life is picture-perfect. It's like a fucking movie, man."

"Fast forward to the part where you get to the point."

"The point is," I say, sucking in a breath, "I'm never going to fit into her world and I'll never trust mine with her."

He doesn't respond because I'm right.

"At the risk of sounding like a pussy, I'll admit I hate it. If she were anyone else, *anyone else*, I'd wife her. There wouldn't be a second of hesitation. But she's not just anyone else, and I can't do that to her."

"You make it sound like you're an ape or something."

"I may as well be from the jungle." I lift the bottle again and down the rest of the water, managing to not choke this time. As I lick my lips, cool from the liquid, I toss the plastic into the garbage. "I think I'm going to need something a little stronger tonight."

"Not while you have my kid you don't."

"I forgot about that little shit," I joke. "This blows, you know it?"

"If you believe what you say, it does. I happen to think you're full of crap."

"Oh, really?"

"Yup."

"Look at our mom," I say, going to a place we don't often. "Her parents were decent people. Good people. She got with our sperm donor and look what happened to her. It was like that Jack Nicholson movie where he's not crazy, but they make him believe it and he kind of is at the end."

"But—"

"Or Keeley," I say, wincing as his features drop. "She was a hell of a mom to Ryder and a good wife to you. She loved you and that kid. Then she got hanging around with Bond's ex-wife, took the needle in her vein, and was dead in six months."

Nate runs his hand over his face, still not completely over the death of his ex-wife. They'd divorced when he found out she was hooked on heroin and he got custody of Ryder. He loved her, even then. There's no doubt he always will.

"I can't let that happen to Cam," I say quietly. "She has the world, Nate. Everything anyone could ever want, she has it. The only direction she can go is down and she can go so fucking far down if she turns the wrong way that ..."

My head shakes side to side, my eyes forcing closed not wanting to imagine Camilla as anything but how she is right now. Happy. Bright. Lively.

"I'm afraid I can't protect her from all that shit, Nate."

He looks at me with the pity that I'll only take from him. I'll take it from him because he understands my plight. He's been there. He knows the anguish even more than I do. "Yeah, I see what you're saying."

"Cam's a hard girl to distance yourself from," I grin. "I tell myself if I'd realized it when I met her, I would've stayed away. But I know that's a lie. There's nothing in the world that would've stopped me from seeing her, just like I'm having an impossible time telling myself to stop seeing her now."

"Do you have to though? I mean, it's not about money, and she's not some chick from the bar or whatever. She has a house. A gate. Security if she wants it. She can kind of take care of herself."

"Then what good am I? Why would she keep me around if I can't even protect her?"

"The dick?"

"This isn't funny," I say, but find myself laughing anyway.

"To answer your question," he says, making his way to the door, "you could love her. And be there for her. And support her. That's what I think about when I think about the good times with Keeley. That's what I miss. I miss seeing her eyes light up when I'd bring her home little gifts or the way she'd look at me like nothing else mattered. Like we were a team. We'd talk about what we wanted in life and how we were going to get it and dream and plot and plan and laugh at how dumb we were."

With a little smile, he opens the door. "I gotta go or I'm going to be late. Be home later."

"See ya."

The door snaps shut and I'm left standing in the kitchen. The picture is crooked on the wall where Nate tried to rehang it after my tantrum yesterday. The picture itself is one from my grandmother's kitchen. It hung in there my entire life. It reminds me of ham loaf and mashed potatoes and Gospel songs on the radio while we ate with plastic silverware in front of the television.

With a sad smile, I head down the hallway to check on Ryder.

FIFTEEN

CAMILLA

"Those are super cute." Joy points at my new yoga pants and smiles. "Where'd you get them?"

"Halcyon," I say in reference to Ellie's store. "She has a new line in and they're amazing. I love them. She has these in green too."

"I might run by there tomorrow. Cute workout clothes make me want to wear them which, in turn, gets me off my butt and into the gym. Sometimes."

We go back to stretching after our yoga routine. I planned on skipping today, but after yesterday, my body needed the release.

I kept my phone in my pocket all evening yesterday and even took it into the bathroom while I soaked in the tub just so I wouldn't miss his call in case one came through. I warred with myself whether or not to just call him but decided he might need the space after dealing with my brothers. Maybe I needed a little time, too, to let things marinate.

"So," Mallory says, plopping down beside us, "Sienna said Ford and Linc met your mystery man yesterday."

I eye my sister as she sits in between Mallory and I. "Yes. They met Dominic."

"Oh, he has a name," Mallory teases. "You know, I feel like I'm ostracized from information because of Graham."

"You know, you feel right," I laugh.

"Okay, but you guys directed me to him," she protests. "It isn't fair that I don't get to be one of the girls."

"Whoa!" Joy says, cutting in. "Did you say Dom had lunch with your brothers?" Her eyes are wide, her jaw hanging open. "I know none of you want to hear this, but that's like alpha heaven right there —no offense, Mal."

"That's gross," Sienna flinches. "Except for the Dom part. I'll agree with you there."

"Hey!" I laugh.

We break into a fit of laughter, each of us mentally erasing a different part of that statement. It's Mallory that brings us back to topic.

"So," she says, "this non-info thing. It's not fair. It's not like Graham is going to marry me or something."

She rolls her eyes and tries to make it seem offhanded, but it's not. There's a pain on her face that Sienna and I both pick up on.

"What's going on with G?" Sienna asks.

"Nothing. Absolutely nothing." Mallory frowns. "I've left every possible hint that something needs to happen. There's a bridal maga-zine on the coffee table. I've been talking about flowers and good months for weddings. And ... nothing." She worries her lip between her two bottom teeth. "Look, I know in the grand scheme of things we haven't dated that long. I get it. But, hell, I live with the man. I can't as much as look at another guy without him taking me home and ..."

"Yeah, just trail off right there," I wince.

"No. Don't. I'll take details," Joy jokes as Sienna elbows her.

"We're together. I can't imagine not being with him, and I don't think he has plans to not be with me," Mallory laments.

"He definitely doesn't," Sienna agrees. "It's Graham, Mal. Every-thing has to go on his time. At his pace."

"On his schedule," I add. "Maybe he's scared. He's never really done the serious girlfriend thing before."

"Maybe he doesn't want that with me," she says. "I see everyone in your family getting married, having babies, and I just want to be a part of that. I watch Dani with Ryan and I get ..."

"Baby fever?" Joy offers.

"Yeah. That."

"I think the Landry boys do that to everyone. Sorry. Again, no offense," Joy adds.

"None taken," Mallory sighs. "I know he loves me. He bought this place for me. We're married in every way that counts ..."

"Except for the one that does," I finish. "I'm sorry, Mal. Want me to talk to him?"

"No," she says, getting up. "I don't. I just need to stop feeling sorry for myself and enjoy what I have." She flashes us a smile that's only mildly happier than her frown. "I have another class to teach. Talk to you guys later."

"I have to go too," Joy says. "I need a shower after all that visualizing."

"You're so gross," I say as she and Sienna trade goodbyes. Once she's gone, my twin looks at me.

"What are you doing today?" she asks.

Pulling my legs together like a butterfly, I shrug. "I don't know. I need to go by Dom's in a little bit and grab my laptop. I left it over there and I need it to send a few emails about the charity thing coming up."

"How'd it go yesterday? You didn't call so I was afraid to ask."

"The actual meal didn't go too bad ..."

"What's wrong, Swink?"

"I don't know. I just ... Dom said some things that bothered me."

"What about?"

I look at my sister. Her eyes reflect my concern. "A lot of things. Me. Him. Us."

"You didn't break up because you're not in bed crying."

"No," I chuckle. "We didn't. I don't think. I mean, we didn't talk much when he did call because he had Ryder and was distracted. But he seemed fairly normal and insinuated he'd see me today."

We exchange a look.

"Let me give you a ride over there," she offers. "That way if things aren't all abs and awesome, I can take you home. And if they are, I can leave you and you can figure out how to get home on your own."

Standing up, I laugh. "Abs and awesome?"

She stands too and tosses an arm over my shoulder. "Are there two better words to describe Dominic?"

As we head into the sunshine and towards her SUV, I concede. "No, I guess not."

***

MY KNOCK IS LIGHT, not sure if Ryder is awake or asleep, and also because I'm a little less enthusiastic about being here than I was. Dom's car isn't outside. That was a little deflating. I shot him a text that I would be here, but didn't hear back.

As I'm ready to tell Sienna we should just go, the door flies open. Nate is on the other side, his face breaking into a smile as he sees us. "It's not every day you open the door and see not one but two beautiful women on your doorstep."

"How are you?" I grin.

"Good. You?"

"Decent. I left my laptop in Dom's room. Can I grab it?"

"Sure. Come on in." He pulls open the door and lets me and Sienna inside. "Dominic's at the gym. He's been there for a few hours, so he should be back if you want to wait."

I wrinkle my nose. "Should I?"

"What she means," Sienna says, "is give us the dirt, Nate. What's he saying that she isn't supposed to know?"

Nate belly laughs and I see Sienna's gaze go to the sliver of abs that's visible as his shirt slides up. "Just get to the point, Sienna."

"It's how I roll," she shrugs. "So spill."

"He's not saying much."

"And you lie."

"He's my *brother*," he emphasizes. "If Priss told you shit, would you tell me?"

"No."

"And you expect me to tell you stuff?"

"Yes," she sighs dramatically. "The bro code isn't the same as the sister code. You still have to tell us stuff."

Nate looks at me, shaking his head. "How do you deal with this?"

Laughing, I plop down on the sofa. The cushions squeak as they sink into the old springs beneath them.

"Oh!" Nate says, "Check this out."

He grabs a set of papers from the kitchen and spreads them on the coffee table in front of me. Sienna sits beside me and we take in a bunch of paint samples, light fixture images, and flooring options.

"Nate, if you didn't know, I love design," Sienna squeals, sorting through the items like a kid in a candy store.

"That's what I heard," he says. "I like this one for the floor. It's durable and—"

"And keeping it looking nice will be a disaster," Sienna says, tossing it to the side. "Now this one is durable and would be easy to keep clean."

"But how are you ever going to match what's already there with that feel?" I ask. "Unless you're changing the trim and bar and all that, it'll look crappy. Even with paint, the styles don't match."

My sister's gaze flies to mine, her eyes shining. "You *are* good at this."

"She's good at a lot of things."

Our heads twist to the side to see Dominic standing in the doorway. Dressed in red mesh shorts and a sweaty white t-shirt, the sight of him alone makes my entire body clench.

His hair is a mess, his cheeks still red from the workout. Not to mention he's wearing yesterday's stubble like it's a high-fashion accessory.

"We didn't hear you come in," Nate says. "I was showing the girls the stuff for the bar."

Dom's Adam's apple bobs. "Cam, why don't you come here for a minute?" He shoves off the doorway and heads down the hall.

"Go on," Sienna whispers. I can barely hear her over the blood rushing by my eardrums. "I'll stay out here with Nate."

Forcing a swallow of my own, I head down the hall and find Dominic sitting on his bed. I step inside the small room and close the door behind me. My feet stop just a few inches from the threshold as I try to make sense of the look on his face.

He doesn't smile, doesn't glare. Gives me nothing to base a decision off of.

"Are you okay, babe?" I ask softly.

"Come here."

The gravel in his tone skirts over my skin as I take the three steps to the bed. His arms are around me, his cheek pressing into my stomach before I can even get situated in front of him.

He holds me tight, almost knocking me off-balance. I rest my arms on his shoulders, cradling the back of his head as he nuzzles against me.

Instead of talking, I run my hands down his back until I hit a spot that makes him wince. As he pulls back, I catch a flash of pain in his eyes.

"What happened?" I ask, moving around him. Climbing on the bed, I lift the edge of his shirt. There's an angry, red burst on the right side of his back, halfway between his shoulder and hip. "I'll grab some ice."

He looks at me over his shoulder, his blue eyes clear. "Just stay with me. Tell me about your day."

The simplicity of his request both worries me and comforts me. Before I answer, I help him lie back, probably more help than he needs, and prop his side up with a pillow. He grins the whole time as he tells me it's unnecessary.

"I don't care if it's necessary," I groan. "Let me make myself feel better about this."

Once he's settled, I lie next to him. "You smell like sweat."

"You like it and you know it."

"I didn't say I don't," I smile. "I was just pointing it out."

"What did you do today?"

"Went to yoga. Talked to Mallory and Joy for a little while and then came by here to grab my laptop."

He runs a finger down the centerline of my face. "You didn't come here to see me?"

"I hoped you were here," I admit. "But you didn't answer my text so I wasn't sure."

"I was training. My fight is coming up and the guy I'm going to fight has a helluva ground game."

"I have no idea what that means."

He grins. "I know you don't. Keep it that way."

"But I want to know. I want to understand you. What those things mean, why you like fighting."

"I don't think you can understand it. You're not cut from that cloth."

There's a finality in his voice, one that tells me he's made up his mind. Before, it was more open-ended. Until today, there was a little window of opportunity that was left dangling out there for another time and place. That's closed.

"I could learn that cloth," I offer.

He kisses me simply, easily, just a sweet gesture that turns me to mush. "You'll be happy to hear that I think this is my last fight."

"I am happy to hear that. But what changed your mind?"

"My body isn't cut out for it anymore," he says, curling his nose. "It hurts when you get hit."

"I thought you didn't let them hit you."

"I don't. Not on purpose," he laughs. "My reflexes are starting to catch up with my age and fighting is a young man's sport."

"Quit now. Don't get hit anymore."

"I can't. I need this payday."

The thought of him taking abuse for money makes me physically ill. "Dom, if it's about money, I—"

"Don't." His eyes back up his insistence, the combination chilling me. "Don't do that."

"Do what?"

"What you were just about to do. I'll take care of myself."

"I don't understand you."

"Tell me something I don't already know."

The wall between us is back up. I can feel the gate locking in place. Reaching out, I touch his arm. Tracing the tattoo of the cross for Joey, I try not to lose the easiness between us, but it's already gone.

My phone rings in my pocket and I fall on my back and pull it out. "Hey, G," I say, looking at the ceiling.

"Where are you?"

"Does it matter?"

"No, actually, it doesn't. What matters is that I'm going to arrive at your house in about thirty minutes and I need you to be there. Can you do that?"

I look at Dom. His eyes are closed, his breathing even. "Yeah, I can do that."

"See you then."

The line clicks dead. Putting it back in my pocket, I roll over and press a kiss to Dom's cheek.

"Where are you going?" he asks sleepily.

"I need to go home and take care of a few things. Do you need anything?"

"A kiss."

I lower the few inches to his sweet lips and let my own pucker against them. He moves his mouth against mine—slow, steady, and sinful. When I pull back, breathless, his eyes are open. He doesn't smile. "Call me later, Cam?"

"Will you answer?"

"Yeah."

His eyes close again as I climb off the bed. I get to the door but stop and look at him. "Dom?"

"Yeah?"

"I miss you."

"You're with me."

"You know what I mean."

He looks at me and nods. "I miss you too."

SIXTEEN

CAMILLA

I don't even love wine, but I take a gulp anyway. It's strong and bitter, and I realize I should've checked to see if wine expires before taking as large of a drink as I did. This bottle has been in my refrigerator since Sienna came back home for Barrett's campaign. That's been ... a long time.

"Ugh," I grimace but take another sip anyway. I don't know what's up with Graham, but after everything else, I need a little fortification.

On cue, the doorbell rings. Wine glass in hand, another drink tumbling down my throat, I spy G on the other side and pull it open.

His look is lethal. I almost drop the glass.

"What's wrong?" I stutter, watching him charge by. "Graham?"

Sitting my wine glass on the entry table, I latch the door and turn on my heel. He's glowering at me from the other end of the foyer.

I've never seen my brother, any of them, so angry. Ever. His eyes are narrowed, wickedly so, as he heaves air in and out of his body. "Just saw Ford," he says, his words measured. "He said he had lunch with you and Lincoln yesterday."

"Yes," I say, equally measured. It's suddenly all clear why he's so angry. Ford told him he met Dom. Thinking fast, I decide to go on the defensive. "And with Dominic."

He smiles, but there's no kindness to it. No amusement. "And Dominic. So, tell me, Camilla, what do you know about Dominic?"

"All I need to." When his eyes narrow even more, I see where this is going. Storming by him, I don't even look his way. "You can see yourself out."

"I'm not done here yet," he barks after me.

"I am."

My steps smack off the tile as I enter the kitchen and position myself as far away from my brother as I can. Knowing this is about Dominic changes everything.

I generally listen to G. I value his opinion, but I won't stand in my own house and listen to him take his opinions on a man he's never met and twist them all around and throw them at me.

My blood boils, my own eyes narrowing as he stands across the room. "What do you want, Graham?"

"Let's start with this: I had breakfast with our mother this morning."

"Good for you."

"She said Paulina called her last night."

"Fuck Paulina," I say with more emphasis than I even intended.

He lifts a brow.

"Yeah, Graham. *Fuck Paulina*," I hiss, watching him absorb a very un-Camilla-like display. "Oh, wait, you already did."

His eyes darken, making him look more like my father than I've ever realized. "Choose your words wisely, Camilla."

"The same goes for you."

"What's gotten into you?" he growls. "Is this what he's is doing to you? Making you some crazed lunatic?"

"This is a crazed lunatic?" I laugh. "Really? It seems to me that being accosted in my own home and standing up for myself is a little less lunatic-y than barging into your sister's house and making her feel like some kind of criminal for nothing."

His lips twist together, dismissing me. "I want you to take a good look at yourself in the mirror, little sister, and see if you like what you see."

Imagining what Graham is seeing causes me to smile. It's something he's never seen before. It's something I've never felt before. Determination.

I've fought with Lincoln before and sparred with Ford, but never Graham. He's always been so much older than me that our conversations have always been logical, even-footed. Him the older brother and me the younger, more submissive sister. Not today.

Today it doesn't matter if I make him mad. I don't care if he thinks I'm an idiot or calls me foolish. I have absolutely no need to humor him or try to see things from his perspective because he is wrong. On so many levels.

"Dom has made me see things differently," I admit. "It's making me see people differently."

"Is that right?"

"It's absolutely right."

He grabs the back of a barstool at the island and squeezes the top. "Are you aware that your ... what is he? Your boyfriend?"

"He's whatever I want him to be."

"Of course he is," he scoffs. "I'm sure he's a modern day Romeo."

Heaving a deep breath, I look him in the eye. "Graham, I'm trying very, very hard to remember that you're my brother and all this probably, hopefully, comes from a good place. You're making it extremely difficult."

He considers this. Shifting his weight to the other leg, his eyes never leave mine. "Ford says he thinks it's serious between the two of you."

"Did Ford tell you that they got along? That they had a decent conversation and that he was helping him out with a few things?"

"I also talked to Lincoln."

"Oh, yes, by all means, listen to Lincoln for the first time in your life," I laugh, which only makes Graham's anger return. "You should listen to him, actually. You want to know why?"

"I bet you're going to tell me."

"Because at least Lincoln had the guts and class to meet him and decide for himself. You haven't bothered to do anything but listen to what you *don't* want to hear!"

"Oh, I'm sorry. Forgive me for not wanting to hear that he's cocky—"

"Lincoln," I say, letting him know I know where he heard that.

"Unable to take care of you—"

"Ford," I sigh.

"And looks like, and I quote, 'a man that just walked out of a federal prison,'" Graham concludes.

"Paulina. Maybe Raquel," I sigh dramatically. "Did they also mention that he's smart, has a day job, a night job, and a part-time job," I say, counting the fighting as a part-time gig. "Did they mention that he makes me feel special? That he's as overprotective in a lot of ways as you are," I glare, "or that he's never been in prison but might just end up there if he heard how you're talking to me right now?"

Graham rolls his eyes, making a show of his annoyance. "Are you aware Dominic is Nolan's nephew?"

I nod, taking a long, strangled breath. "Yes. I am aware of that."

"And you're still seeing him?"

"Is that a rhetorical question?"

He roughs his hands through his picture-perfect hair, mussing it all up. He looks around the kitchen like he's trying to find a way to talk sense into me or something equally as dramatic. I would laugh if we weren't discussing this particular topic.

"Cam," he begins, "I'm a reasonable person. It may not seem like it right now, but I am. That being said, do you have any idea what this is going to do to Barrett?"

"I know he doesn't like Nolan and I get it. But—"

"Doesn't like Nolan?" he says incredulously. "That man tried to ruin Barrett's career. He almost got Alison assaulted, do you remember that? Nolan almost destroyed Barrett's ... *everything* ... and here you are—"

"Here I am what?" I power back. "Maybe falling in love with someone that had an asshole of a father that was brothers with another asshole? How is that Dominic's fault, G?"

"How are you going to explain this to Barrett?"

"You were aware that Paulina screwed Barrett and, most likely Ford, and you still slept with her. Nobody was worried about that. I'm not sure why we all care who I'm fucking."

His eyes narrow, his knuckles turning white. He's ready to fire back at me, but I don't give him the chance.

"You need to be a little less worried about what I'm doing and more about what you are. I talked to Mallory today. You do realize you're on the verge of messing that all up, right? Or we're not allowed to talk about that? Just who I'm sleeping with?"

The flinch is obvious, his hand dropping from the chair.

"Yes, Graham, I do know that he's Nolan's nephew. I also know how genetics work and that you don't get to pick who you're related to. If that were the case, I would opt out of sharing any DNA with you right now."

He takes that hit, tugging at the collar of his white button-down shirt. His cufflinks twinkle in the light cast from the chandelier over his head. There are lines on his face I haven't noticed before—deep, worrisome etches in his skin. If I wasn't so mad at him, I'd ask him how he was feeling. But I don't because I am still angry.

"I also know about the loan," he states.

"Good for you."

"Cam, please tell me you understand why this is concerning. Please tell me you haven't lost all of your mind."

"I get it. I'm not stupid. It's a lot of money to be loaning someone that looks like he ... what did you say? Walked out of prison? Something like that?"

Looking at the ceiling, he sighs.

"What is this, Graham? Is this about the money? About social status? Did it offend you somehow that Mom's friends saw me with someone not in a Brooks Brother's suit? Did that somehow take down our Landry brand?"

He shoots me a glare.

"Because if that's the case, if that's what we've been relegated to, I'm not sure I fit in here anymore."

"Of course that's not it," he mutters. "I'm just ... I'm trying to control what's going on here."

"Let me give you a piece of advice for a change. Go home. Find Mallory. Worry about that relationship and not mine. Trust me when I tell you that your efforts will be much more appreciated and are much more necessary in your own house."

He shakes his head. "I take it you're going to continue seeing him."

It's not the words so much that pierce me. It's more the tone, the dismissive nature of them that zip right through me like a hot knife.

"Get out of my house."

He doesn't move.

"I'm not joking, Graham. Get out of my house now."

"Swink ..."

"No," I say, shaking my head and feeling my hands start to tremble. "Leave. You aren't welcome here."

He holds my gaze before turning to go. He gets to the door and yanks it open. When he turns, I see fire in his eyes. "When you wise up, you know where to find me to get you out of whatever mess he gets you in."

The door closes. I wait a few seconds to make sure he's gone before bursting into tears.

SEVENTEEN

DOMINIC

The house is quiet. Nate is at the bar and Chrissy came by and took Ryder a little while ago. It's just me, a beer that is the temperature of piss, and a muted television.

Everything hurts. My body. My head. My heart. It all aches like a motherfucker.

My legs stretch in front of me as I sit on the sofa, my eyes watching but not seeing the talking head on the news. There's some story on about a family that had something tragic happen but are now all smiles, holding hands, all that shit. Shit I've never had.

Shit I'll never have.

Not the way I want it.

I'm tired. The thought of getting up in the morning and going to work and then to the gym and then home to *this*, makes me want to close my eyes and just sleep. There's no point to it. No point to any of it.

Yesterday was supposed to be a way to make some inroads with the Landry's. I figured it was probably for naught and that's why I refused for so long.

Then things changed.

I don't know when it happened, but it did. She became not just a girl I was fucking but someone I looked forward to seeing at the end of the day. I made sure there was sorbet, something I didn't even know existed before her, in my freezer. It was her voice I wanted to hear before I laid down.

Cam makes me feel things I haven't felt before. Give a fuck about things I didn't know I could care about. Like the fact that she made it home at the end of the night or had enough cold medicine when she wasn't feeling good.

When things got to this point, I don't know. But when she asked me to meet her brother and I could see that it mattered to her ... I felt like *I* mattered to her.

That's why they say feelings are dangerous. They take a quick fuck and turn it into visions of something a year, two years, ten years later. The shit that's on the television right now.

I click it off and down the rest of the lukewarm brew.

My eyes start to close when a knock at the door brings them open. Wincing as I get to my feet, I set the bottle down and get to the entry. Looking through the hole, my heart almost stops beating.

I can't get it open fast enough.

Her face is streaked with mascara, her beautiful sky-blue eyes watery and puffy. It takes one look, not even a question, before she lunges forward and wraps her arms around my waist.

"What the hell happened to you?" I ask, pulling her inside and shutting the door. My heart thunders in my chest as I try to see her face. "Are you okay?"

"Yes." She nuzzles against me, her words muffled by my shirt.

Scooping her up, her legs hanging off one of my arms as my other cradles her back, I carry her to the sofa. As I sit, I place her on my lap. "Okay. What's going on? Why are you crying?"

She takes a deep breath and it shakes as she comes down from the crying high. A quick, easy smile that touches her eyes settles some of my nerves. "I don't want to talk about it, Dom."

"I really don't care if you want to talk about it," I laugh. "We're going to talk about it." Gathering her hair and twisting it together, I place it over one shoulder. "Tell me. Did I do something? I mean, I probably did, but ..."

"It wasn't you."

My features fall. This changes things. "Okay. Who did?"

"Graham," she whispers.

"Your brother? He made you cry?"

"Yes."

I move in my seat, finding it impossible to get comfortable. She tries to climb off my lap, but I keep her in place. I need her here. With me. On me.

"I threw Graham out of my house," she says quietly without looking at me.

"Why?"

Her shoulders rise and fall. "He just ... he was being irrational."

I watch her face. There's a sorrow there that burns me to the core, and suddenly, I get it. "It was because of me."

"Dom ..." she pleads.

I'm right. "What did he say?"

"Nothing. Just that he'd talked to Ford and Lincoln and either put it together or someone told him, I don't know, but he found out you're Nolan's nephew."

"Of course he did," I mutter, feeling my head begin to pound. "I'm sorry."

"What are you sorry for?" She tries to cup my face with her hands, but I shake them away. "Dom, listen to me, it's not your fault."

"I know it isn't my fault I'm related to Nolan. Clearly. But I'm sorry I put you in this position."

Lifting her off my lap, I stand up and head to the center of the room. Pacing a circle, I feel my soul start to splinter.

"I told him to leave," she says, a tear trickling down her cheek. "I told him I won't put up with it."

"But he's right."

"About what?"

"About everything he said," I admit, feeling my spirit begin to wane. "And everything he might not have."

She gets to her feet, both cheeks now damp. "He's not right. About any of it," she sniffles. "You've been telling me to stand up for myself and think for myself, Dominic."

"I have. But, Cam, this isn't a fight you have to take, babe," I sigh. "This is your family. Yes, you need boundaries with them. Yes, you need to tell them to mind their own business and you need to step out of their shadow and show them who you really are and what you're capable of. But, Cam ..." I shake my head. *"That's your family."*

"I thought you hated my brothers."

"It doesn't matter what I think about them. You need them. You can't let some asshole like me get in between you."

"I need them?" she asks, her brows lifted. "You know what I *need*, Dominic?"

My breath still in my chest, my hands nearly shaking at my sides. I wait for her next words, unable to look away.

"*I need you*," she whispers.

With those three little words, she takes the few steps between us and wraps her arms around my waist. I hold her tight, squeezing her against me for dear life as I struggle to maintain enough oxygen flow to stay cognizant.

No one has needed me before. Not in the way she just looked at me. Women have needed me for an orgasm or a safety net or something to do on a Friday night. There's never been a female that's looked at *me*, the me under the ink and the game, and said they wanted that.

There aren't words available to give her because I'm not sure what to say to that. My mouth feels dry, cottony, but there's a warmth flooding me that I'd prefer stick around a while.

Cam melts into my chest, her fingers pressing against my back as she clings on to me as if she's afraid I'll reject her. That's my fault too.

"I won't come between you and your brothers," I say, stroking the back of her head. "You can't let a guy like me ruin that."

"A guy like you?" She pulls back so I can see her face. "I just defended you to the smartest man I know—no offense."

"None taken, I don't think. Well, maybe not."

She grins. "You're definitely the hottest."

"That makes me feel a little better."

"And the sexiest."

"That also helps," I smile.

"And the sweetest."

"That's a lie," I laugh, watching her gorgeous smile reflect back at me.

She lifts a hand and touches my cheek. "You're not going to come between me and my brothers. They might be mad and throw a fit, but if they want to act like children, that's their wives' problem. Not mine."

"The last thing I want to do is cause you any problems. I look at you and think all I'll ever be able to do is fuck you up, and I'd kill myself before I let that happen."

"I know," she says, her eyes twinkling. "That's why I trust you."

"Tell me one thing," I say. "Did Graham hurt you?"

"Just my feelings. And not even really those. But I might've hurt his," she says, pondering my question. "I wonder how he'll feel about that in the morning?"

Chuckling, I scoop her up as she yelps and head down the hallway. "If you want me to do a little meet-and-greet with Graham, now's the time to tell me," I say, kicking the door to my bedroom open. "You have about twenty seconds and then I'm going to make sure neither of us thinks about him again for a very, very long time."

Her arms around my neck, she beams. "Who are you talking about?"

Tossing her on the bed, I'm on top of her before she can react.

***

Camilla

I tip my face up to meet his stare. The teasing smirk drifts away, and in its place, a soft, sweet gaze moves in. Where his playfulness sends an ache through my core, this side of him melts it.

My hands rest on the back of his neck, the heat of his skin radiating through my palms. I work my fingers into the ends of his hair and then up higher, playing with the messy strands that have, undoubtedly, had his own hands in them not too long ago.

He looks down at me like he's never seen me before. Like if he takes his eyes off me, I might disappear.

"Dom," I whisper.

"Yeah, sweetheart?"

"I meant what I said."

He knows what I mean. I see the shock blitz across his features before he lets it go. "That you hurt your brother's feelings?"

Mocking the look on his face, I let my knees fall to the sides. He misses no opportunity to occupy the space between us.

"No," I say. "I meant it when I said I needed you."

His eyes search mine, watching for a sign that I'm kidding. He should know I'm not. Not about this.

Pressing his rock-hard length against the inside of my thigh, he grins. "You need this?"

"I do," I admit, shifting myself so his sweatpants-covered cock is rubbing along my yoga pants-covered vagina. "But I also need this," I say, tapping lightly against his temple. "And this." I lay my palm flat against his chest.

My heart is racing and I know he can hear it. That or at least the way my breath is almost stuttering as I struggle to stay composed long enough to hear his reaction. It's a gamble to say this, I know, but I've played a lot of proverbial poker lately. May as well play one more hand.

"I just want you to know how I feel, in case there was any doubt," I say. "You—"

His lips fall to mine, halting the rest of my words. There's a tenderness to the kiss, an almost reverence, that has me closing my eyes and letting him lead me wherever he chooses.

Our tongues lap and swirl against one another, the heat of his body sending my own into the stratosphere. His hand lifts the hem of my shirt and pulls down my bra cup, palming my breast with his calloused hand.

When he pulls back, his short, sharp breaths matching my own, he stares at me with a look I can't quite place.

"If anyone ever hurts you, physically or otherwise, whether that's me or someone else, I'll stop it," he promises. "All you have to do is tell me. You know that, right?"

"Of course I know that."

He forces a swallow. "I don't know what to do with you and I don't know what to do without you. It fucks with me, Cam."

"Well," I say despite a sandpapery throat. "I know what you can do with me."

"Oh, I can do that," he grins wickedly. "That's never a problem."

"Then what's stopping you?"

I watch as he strips himself of his shirt, an inch of chiseled perfection visible at a time. His chest is dotted with various tattoos, some he'll talk about and some he won't. The broadness of his shoulders is my favorite part of his whole body. Layers of intricate muscle placed in perfect symmetry, descending on one side to the absurdly sexy stomach, and on the other, a back that was built to perfection.

He hops off the bed, his eyes still on me, as he slips off his sweatpants. They fall down his powerful legs before he kicks them off and stands completely naked in front of me.

My legs clench together at the sight of him, the throb strumming into a pace that I almost can't manage.

"I'm going to give you a tip," I say.

"I thought I was giving you the tip?"

My giggle makes him grin. "You better be planning on giving me more than the tip, Hughes."

"Oh, baby. You're going to get it all."

"Good. Now that's settled, back to the other tip." I study his handsome face. "If we ever get in a fight, which I'm sure we will, all you have to do to fix it is get naked. I can think of nothing else when you are standing there like that."

"Noted."

He crawls back on the bed, the mattress dipping with his weight. His thumbs hook into the waistband of my pants and he yanks them down my legs and casts them to the side. His gaze falls on my panty-less state as his tongue darts to his lips, leaving a glistening trail along the ridge of his mouth.

I sit up and have my shirt and bra discarded in a matter of seconds. My chest heaving, my body begging, I fall back to the pillows, letting my legs fall to the sides, and wait for him.

"If you ever want to distract me, lie in my bed like that," he groans, his cock in his hand as he takes in the sight of me. "There's nothing more beautiful than you, naked, in *my* fucking bed."

I only close my eyes for a half a second when they fly back open to the most glorious feeling in the world. Looking down, his face positioned between my legs, he grins before sliding his tongue straight up the center of my pussy.

"Oh, shit," I moan, feeling him part me with his mouth. "God, Dom."

His teeth bite lightly on my clit, making me shudder. I grasp wildly until my hands are buried in his hair, tugging as bolts of sensations rip through me.

"You like that?" he asks, his lips moving against the sensitive flesh. He licks through my middle again.

"Yes," I moan, throwing my head back into the pillow.

He fills me with one, then two, fingers and moves them in, out, front to back. His tongue explores my sex, not missing a spot, marking my body as his with a flick of his mouth. Finally, just as my muscles begin to quiver, he removes his fingers in one deft movement.

He's grinning when my eyes open to see him watching me. "You were almost there, huh?"

"I hate you," I grimace, letting my bottom lip pout out.

He kisses his way from my inner thigh, up my stomach, over each breast—spending a few seconds on each beaded nipple—up my throat, over my jaw. His tongue dips into my mouth, lapping against my own.

Positioning himself between my legs, I feel him hard against my opening. My ankles lock at the small of his back and I push not-so-gently.

He grins against my mouth. "You want my cock?"

"You want my pussy?"

"Oh, dirty girl," he teases, rocking his hips against me. I moan at the contact, which only widens his smile. "You know I want you. I always want you."

"And I always want you. You just wanted me to say it."

"So?"

I reach up to meet his mouth, capturing it with mine. His cock pushes into me, filling me with one long thrust.

"Ah," I moan into his mouth before losing all train of thought that doesn't have to do with me, Dom, and this bed.

EIGHTEEN

CAMILLA

It's not quite midnight but it feels both much later and much earlier. I sit in the middle of Dom's bed, dressed only in one of his t-shirts, and watch the small television that hangs on the opposing wall. The screen is a little off color-wise and it drives me crazy, but I don't dare say anything. And I dare even less to buy him a new one. I'll just wait for his birthday.

He comes in the room, wearing nothing but a pair of briefs. In each hand is a plate and on each plate is a sandwich. "Dinner is served."

"You look pretty proud of that ..." I take the plate. "Peanut butter and jelly."

"It's all we have. Ryder loves this shit." He takes a big bite, a glob of grape jelly falling to the plate. "Not bad. The key to a great pb&j is the ratio of peanut butter to jelly. You gotta get it just right."

"Is that so?" I giggle, biting into it. It's so thick it sticks to the top of my mouth. "I think you're a little heavy on the peanut butter."

The words are practically indecipherable around the food in my mouth and we burst out laughing at the same time. He hands me a drink, flinching as he moves.

With a furrowed brow, I get the sandwich to go down and take a drink. "What's wrong?"

"What do you mean?" he asks.

"You're wincing again."

"Just my ribs. Still sore as shit."

"Come here." I put my plate to the side and pat the blankets. He sits and I lift his shirt to see a purplish bruise marring his skin. "Dom, baby, that doesn't look good."

"It doesn't feel good either," he says, pressing on it with his hand. "It relieves some of the pressure when I do that."

"You need a wrap. Do you have one?"

"Somewhere probably."

"What kind of an answer is that?"

"An honest one?" He looks at me over his shoulder. "You're really cute when you're worried about me."

"Then I must be cute all the damn time," I say, getting off the bed. "Follow me."

He does what I ask, his hand still on his side. "Where are we going?"

"To the bath."

I expect an objection, but don't get one and that pleasantly surprises me. I was ready for a fight.

We enter his bathroom and I try not to be heartbroken by the sorry state of the amenities. The flooring is a mess of ripped linoleum and shittier linoleum from God knows when. The sink sits on a wobbly cabinet with pressed-board doors and chrome-plated hinges. I lean into the tub, a shallow box that would never fit Dom's body, and put the stopper in the hole. The water comes on, the pipes squealing in distress behind the paneling.

"Do you have bubble bath?" I ask.

He makes a face and disappears in the hall. He comes back with a bright pink bottle with a cartoon character on it. "This is Ryder's. It's all we've got."

"Good enough," I say, taking the bottle and lumping in a lot of the bubble-gum looking liquid. Immediately, I'm taken back to child-hood and the garden tub in Mom's bathroom that Sienna and I used to love to take baths in.

Testing the water, it's perfect.

"You. In," I say, nodding to the tub.

"I just got a shower."

"And now you're getting a bath."

He nods, trying to act serious, but fails when the corners of his lips upturn. He drops his briefs and steps out of them and into the water. As he sits in the tub, his legs bent in a manner that can't be comfortable, my heart hurts. Shaking it off, I squeeze myself in between the toilet and the tub.

Pooling water in my hands, I let it fall over his shoulders and down his back. Bits of the bubbles cling to his skin. Another splash ripples down his body, caressing the ridges of his muscles.

"Is that too hot?" I ask.

"No," he breathes. "It feels really good."

Gripping each shoulder with one of my hands, I knead them back and forth. He hisses as I work out the tension that's caused his body to be so rigid. Eventually, I move both hands to one side and massage until it's more pliable. Then I move to the other.

"That feels really good," he says, halfway grimacing as I work a knot lodged near his neck. "That spot right there has hurt forever."

"Why didn't you tell me?"

He doesn't answer, just bares more of his neck for my access.

"I want you to tell me things, Dom."

"I'm not going to burden you with my shit."

"It's not a burden," I sigh. "It's a burden that you *don't* tell me. It makes me feel ..."

"What?"

I shrug, moving my hands down his spine. "It makes me feel like we're never going to get *there*, you know?"

"I'm trying."

"I know you are." I press a kiss to the center of his back, resting my cheek against the warmth of his skin. "I'm trying too."

We sit like that, the only sound coming from the droplets of water from the leaky faucet splashing into the tub. His heartbeat strums steadily, and I close my eyes and just feel the two of us.

"It should always feel like this," I whisper. Pressing another kiss to the same spot, I pull back. "I like taking care of you. I want to take care of you."

"I'm not a baby."

"No, you're not. You're most definitely a man," I tease, poking him in the side. "But that doesn't mean you don't need babied a little, and I can't do that when you won't let me. It makes me feel like I'm not a part of your whole life. Like there are pieces of you I can't know. Does that sound dumb?"

"No." He looks at me, his eyes wide. "I know what you mean. I feel like that with you."

"But I tell you everything you ask. I let you see all the parts of me. The silly me, the smart me, the sassy me."

"The sexy you."

"Whatever," I say, rolling my eyes. "You're so great at helping me and talking me through things and doting on me. But you won't let me take care of you like you do me. That's not fair to either of us."

There's a shake in his next breath that ignites a spark inside him. I can see it cautiously ripple across his face. "I didn't realize I was doing that, exactly."

"You are," I say, touching my lips to his. "Maybe I'm not super supportive of the fighting thing. It's hard to be when I know things like this wallop of a bruise are going to show up."

"Do you have something in your life that, when you do it, you could forget about everything else and just kind of zone out in that space?"

Instantly, I think of the designs Sienna has been showing me and the plans for Nate's bar. I could play with those things for hours on end and never grow tired. I think, too, of certain charities that I love and could spend all day plotting for ways to help them.

"Maybe," I say.

"That's what fighting is for me. I go to the gym, pound the bag, concentrate on my footwork. You can't fight and think about anything else. You have to focus on what you're doing or you'll get hurt."

"I think you need to focus more," I say, running water down his bruise.

He holds his breath. "Want me to tell you a story?"

"Yes," I reply immediately. "I do. Bathtime Storytime with Dominic Hughes. Sign me up."

He shakes his head, but I can see he's already working on what he's going to say. "Okay, when I was twelve, I skipped school," he blows out a breath that has more emotion in the waves than I care to acknowledge. "I had a black eye from an impact with my dad's right elbow in a futile effort to save my mother from his left fist. I didn't want to make up a bullshit answer and I was just really fucking mad, to be honest. The other kids didn't come banged up and I didn't want to either. It was embarrassing."

I fight back the tears wetting my eyes because I know if he sees them, he'll stop talking. I focus on keeping his back showered with warm, sudsy water because that is something I can control.

"So I was just hanging out around town, just kind of walking around, messing around in some parks when this guy comes up and sits next to me on this bench. I remember the bench was red, down by the minor league baseball stadium, and faced the little tributary that runs down to the ocean. So he just sits next to me—no book, no magazine, no phone or anything. Nothing."

"What did he want?" I ask.

"He sits there a while until I start to get up thinking this guy's a creep, you know? Then he says his name is Jerry Percy. I tell him I'm Dominic and he asks why I'm not in school. I tell him I skipped, that he could call my parents or the school but neither of them would care so not to waste his time."

I have to close my eyes to keep from crying at the thought of a little Dom sitting and feeling so alone. My throat squeezes so tight that I can't answer or show I'm invested in the conversation. It's impossible.

"He gets up," Dom continues, "and I think he's going to go call the cops or something, but he comes back with a bag. He sits again and pulls out a sandwich. It's ham and tomatoes and lettuce and I don't remember what else, I guess it doesn't matter, and he handed it to me. Said his wife always packed him more than he could eat anyway." He smiles sadly. "I ate the fuck out of that. Then he gave me a baggie of chips and a soda, and by this time, he could've kidnapped me and I would've gone willingly," he chuckles. "So when he asked if I wanted to hang out at his gym for the rest of the afternoon, I said I did."

"Percy's," I whisper. "That's your gym now."

"That's my gym now."

I have so many more questions, but I'm afraid to ask.

Before I can respond, we hear the front door opening and Ryder's cries as Nate carries him past the bathroom and into their bedroom at the end of the hall.

We both exhale and then chuckle at our simultaneous reaction.

"Guess there goes your night cap, unless you can do it without screaming this time," he winks.

"When is he moving out again?" I pout. "I should've made that a condition of my loan."

"You're a sucky loan shark."

"I can't be good at everything." I stand, grabbing a towel off the makeshift rack and handing it to him.

He stands and dries himself off quickly before wrapping it around his waist. Before he steps out of the tub, he takes a deep breath. "Hey, you want to go stay the night at your house tonight?"

"You mean you'll stay? With me? At my house?"

"That's what I said, isn't it?"

"Yeah, I think so," I stammer. "I mean, yeah. Yes. Yes, I want you to come stay at my house tonight."

He laughs at my reaction, stepping onto the linoleum. Bending so our noses are touching he whispers, "Then let's get our shit and go before I make you start screaming right here."

NINETEEN

DOMINIC

There's something to be said for calculating the thread count in your sheets. That and sleeping in the bed of a beautiful woman.

The room glows, the all-white décor almost blinding, as I open my eyes. My body feels rested, lots of the aches I wake up with daily in my legs and hips aren't as noticeable, and I wonder vaguely if maybe that means I'm dead. Then I look to my right and see Camilla asleep next to me and realize if I'm dead, I'm okay with that.

Last night wasn't the best sleep I've ever had, but it wasn't the worst. Once we got here late and fucked ourselves senseless, I had a hard time falling asleep. It was well past three before my eyes finally shut, but they did. They don't always.

Cam's on her side, facing me. Her hair is a wild mess against the pristine sheets. I glance at the clock, then back to her. Then back to the clock. Then to the ceiling.

Before I can talk myself out of it, I count to three and then turn to my side. Running a fingertip from her forehead down the side of her face, her neck, and over her shoulder, she wakes up under my touch.

Her lashes flutter as she opens her eyes. "Hey," she says, her sleepy voice killing me.

"Good morning."

"No breakfast in bed?"

"I'm not much of a cook," I admit. "But I promise to buy you breakfast if you get up and come with me."

"What time is it?"

"It's early."

She yawns. "Like five o'clock early or like ten o'clock early?"

"Ten isn't early, babe."

"It is to me," she yawns again.

"It's six."

"Where do you have to be at six in the morning on a weekend?"

"I don't have to be anywhere. I have somewhere I want to be and I want you to be there with me."

She looks up at me with one eye, the other buried in the sheets. "What if I remind you I'm naked? Would that keep you in bed?"

"Nope," I say, springing off the mattress. My feet hit the soft carpeting and I swear I sink a couple of inches. "Get your fine ass up, Miss Landry. The world awaits."

"The world can wait."

***

"STAY RIGHT HERE." I leave Cam just inside the door and jog across the mats. Flipping on the switch, I wait for the hum of the halogen lights and watch them flicker to life high above our heads. "Welcome to Percy's."

"I can't believe you brought me here," she squeals. Almost bouncing on her toes, she claps her hands in front of her as I return. "So this is where you train?"

"This is it. Not super fancy or any of that, but it works."

"It's amazing." She looks around the room, to the section with heavy bags and then on to the speed bags. I think her eyes will pop out of her head when she sees the ring in the back. "There. You fight in there."

"Yup. That's where I go at it with Bond."

She rests her gaze back on me like a little kid at Christmas. "Teach me something, Dom."

"What?" I laugh.

"Come on! Teach me something. Please?"

"What do you want to learn?"

"Hell if I know," she giggles. "Teach me how to throw a punch. Or a kick. Or toss someone over my back like they do in the movies." She makes her hands into fists and rolls them around like the fighters did in old blockbusters.

"Okay, killer. Let's slow down," I laugh, leading her through the gym. "One thing at a time."

"I'm an all-or-nothin' kind of girl."

"Is that so?"

"It is today."

I set my bag on the floor and look for a pair of gloves. I know Percy has extra ones in the back, but I don't want to go get them. Finding them in the bottom, I stand up to see her circling a heavy bag the wrong way. She throws a couple of punches, terribly, then a kick that almost lands her on her ass.

"We've found the thing you aren't good at," I crack, tossing her the gloves. "Put these on before you wreck your manicure."

"I'm so proud of you," she nods, obviously humoring me. "You knew the word 'manicure.' I feel strangely accomplished."

"You would."

"What is a manicure called if it's on your toes?"

"A ... toe-icure? A foot-icure?"

She giggles as I help her into the gloves. "No. 'Ped' is Latin for foot. So it's pedicure."

"Thanks for that bit of trivia I'll never need."

"Could be a Jeopardy question one day," she teases. "Better bank that information."

"It's right here," I say, tapping my temple. "Now let's teach you something you can actually use. Let me see your jab."

She sticks her left arm out.

"No, you're right-handed. You'll jab with your right, not your left."

She repeats the same movement with her other hand.

"Whatever you think you know from doing those aerobic videos, forget it. Forget it all," I tell her, shaking my head. "It's like this."

I demonstrate a few jabs on the bag, popping the leather with my fist over and over. I follow it with a cross a time or two, just so she can see it in order. When I stop and look at her, she's watching me with a smile. "Did you get that?" I ask.

"I got that you look hot as hell doing it."

I look at the ceiling. "Did you see the mechanics of the punch?"

"I saw the way your back ripples," she says, moseying my way. "And the way your legs flex and—"

"So you got nothing."

"I got nothing." She stands on her tiptoes and I bend so she can kiss me. "Can I see it again? One more time. I'll try to watch your arms this time."

We spend over an hour throwing punches, stealing kisses, and learning how to turn your hips over for a roundhouse kick. By the time we're done, we're lying on the mats catching our breath.

She turns her head and faces me. "This was fun."

"Really? You liked it?"

"The boxing was fun. It's a good workout."

I nod in agreement.

"But I really liked being here with you. In your space, you know?"

Rolling onto my side, I move my hand so I'm touching her. "I'm trying to figure out how I can show you I want you to be a part of my life but do it in a way where I don't worry about you."

"This place is harmless, Dom."

"Right now," I agree. "But when it's open, there are people in here that aren't savory. Take Gary, the guy from some place in Texas that no one can find on a map. The guy is flat-out weird, Cam. Serial killer material."

"Oh, he is not."

"He is too! Weird as fuck. Then there's Noah, the kid that snorts more shit up his nose than I care to know. And Bond, the asshole I only tolerate because he's a good sparring partner." I play with a lock of her hair, twirling it around my finger. "I don't want to risk you to any of them. I won't. I just have to figure out safe ways to incorporate you into this. Okay?"

"Okay." She leans forward and presses a sweet, sweaty kiss to my lips. "Now, since you're all give-y today, I have a question. A request."

My stomach churns at the look in her eye. "What?"

"Will you go to the charity event with me this week that I've been planning?"

"No."

"Come on, Dom," she whines, rolling onto her back again. "It's just for an evening. It won't be fun, I won't lie, but I really want to take you with me. Don't you want to see what I've been working on?"

"I'm proud of you, whatever you've done. But ..." I imagine seeing the two wenches from the restaurant there and being under their scrutiny. "It's not my thing."

"You brought me here. I want to bring you there."

"You took me to Hillary's. Same difference."

"No, it isn't. Not at all."

"Then I can't imagine the excitement I'd have at a charity ball," I deadpan.

She gives me the best glare she can muster, which isn't much. "Will you at least think about it?"

"You think about this," I say, getting to my feet and looking down at her. "You consider what it might be like if I got my hands on Graham. Then ask me again to accompany you if you think that's a great choice. In the meantime, I'll be in the ring if you care to join me."

I walk away, hearing her scramble to her feet behind me. "No one is here, right?"

"Nada."

"You know what we could do ..."

I grin, knowing exactly what she's thinking and start peeling my shirt off.

TWENTY

CAMILLA

"I can handle this," I laugh. The wind blows through my hair, the sunshine warm on my face as I look up at Dom. "I've babysat kids before."

"Alone?"

"Yes."

"When?"

Crossing my arms over my chest, I see his attention switch direction and land on my cleavage. I squeeze a little tighter than necessary and watch his pupils widen just a bit.

"Do you want to go to the gym today? Or stay home and play with Ryder?" I ask.

"Gym."

"Then get your ass out of here," I say, swatting him on the behind as I step to the side. "Ryder! Don't go down the slide headfirst, okay?"

"Okay!"

He repositions himself at the top of the slide and scoots down the metal incline and into a pit of sand below. Picking himself up, he goes right back around to do it again with the biggest smile on his face.

The playground behind their apartment complex is minimal at

best. A slide, a broken teeter-totter, a little dinosaur that just bobs back and forth, and a couple of swings are it. Ryder knows no difference. This is his favorite place in the world.

"What are you going to do all afternoon?" Dom asks, coming up behind me and folding me into his chest. His chin rests on my shoulder as we watch his nephew.

"This, probably. I, um ..." I force a swallow, a little nervous and a little embarrassed about my next sentence. "I brought some designs that Sienna has for the company she's thinking about launching with a friend in Illinois. She asked me to take a look at them for some reason, but I don't know why—"

"Because you're smart."

My cheeks heat and it has nothing to do with the sun.

"I heard your suggestions for The Gold Room. Have you ever thought of doing something with design? Maybe interior design or something? Your house is beautiful."

"Thanks," I blush.

"You should, Cam. I think you'd be great at it."

"Really?"

"Yes, really," he laughs, kissing the top of my head.

"Well, I've strangely enjoyed it. And, this might sound dumb, but I've been thinking about how to use design and combine it with volunteer work and scholarships and stuff to see if I can come up with a way to make a difference somehow."

"That," he says, kissing me sweetly, "is an awesome idea. I love it."

My grin causes my cheeks to ache.

"I want to talk about this more. But right now, I need to go. Bond's probably already waiting."

I bite my tongue and don't say the words that come so naturally— the question about why he's doing it or why he can't just stop. While I don't understand the answers, I know what they are. And I know this is important to him. So instead of going there, I smile. "Have fun. Be safe."

"*Oh,*" he teases, backing away slowly. "I like this new Camilla. Where'd she come from?"

"Don't push it."

"You sure you don't want to talk me out of it? Remind me how bad it's going to hurt later?"

"Nope," I say. "I'm going to go to the pharmacy and buy adult bubble bath and ice packs and ace bandages. If I have to worry about you getting hurt, you have to deal with me fawning all over you when you get home."

He doesn't say anything, but he doesn't have to. His smile as wide as his shoulders says it all. With a little wave and a shout of goodbye to Ryder, he's in his car and pulling out of the parking lot in a minute.

The Camaro rips around the corner and is out of sight. I stand watching where he was parked, reveling in the easiness of things right now. Over the past few days, since the fight with Graham and Dom's revelation about his teenage years, things have been a little different. Less complicated. A touch closer. More intimate.

We aren't there, yet, not to the place where I feel like we've crossed the hurdles and are on solid ground. There's still so much to work through. But progress is progress.

I turn to watch Ryder struggle to get in the swing. "Let me help you, buddy," I say, crossing the curb and padding through the grass. I get him situated and then pull the swing back and let him go free.

"Higher, Camilla!"

His laugh pierces the air, a stark contrast to the rather dismal surroundings. He's making the best of what he has.

"You're an inspiration, Ryder. You know that?"

"What's a spiration?"

"An in-spiration," I say, slowing the word down, "means that you inspire me."

"I don't understand what that means."

"That's okay. It's a good thing."

He pumps his legs back and forth, the tail of his superhero cape floating behind him. "You know what else is a good thing, Camilla?"

"What's that?"

"Little brothers!"

"What do you know about little brothers?"

"Well, Chrissy's sister has two little boys and they get to play together all the time. I told Daddy I need a little brother. Chrissy said I should tell him so I did."

"I bet she did," I say, laughing. "But a little brother would need a mommy, Ry, and I don't think your daddy has picked one yet."

"You could be my mommy."

"Oh, well ..." I say, realizing what I just walked into. "I'm not your daddy's girlfriend. I'm your Uncle Dom's. So I could be your aunt, but not your mommy. Although, any woman that gets to spend time with you is a lucky ducky."

He grins at me, his eyes sparkling like Dom's. "You make me happy."

"You make me happy too, little guy." I slow him down until his miniature cowboy boots drag the dirt. "I have an idea."

"What's that?"

"Instead of spending the day here, why don't we go to my house?"

"Could we?" he asks, jumping off the swing.

"Absolutely. Let me check with your daddy first."

***

"I COULD'VE BROUGHT HIM HOME," I tell Nate as he comes through the door. "It would've been no big deal."

"I'd hate for you to have to get out and lug him around, especially if he's asleep."

"He passed out a few hours ago." I tuck my legs under me on the sofa and watch Nate take in my living room. "I think I wore him out. We played at your apartment, then I took him down to Marcone Park and fed the ducks and got an ice cream, then we watched a movie."

"All in one day? Shit, Priss. He won't want to leave."

Laughing, I pick up my glass of hot tea. "It was fun. When Dom called and told me he had to go do an emergency HVAC job, I tried to get Ryder to take a bath. But he kind of just used my tub as a swimming pool."

"Sounds about right."

The lamps around the room cast a soft light on Nate's features. It mutes the general sternness he projects and makes me wonder how he would've ended up had he not had the upbringing he did.

He's handsome. Not quite as good-looking as Dom, but almost. They're both intelligent and hard workers. I can see them both sitting in suits at a business meeting or on the arm of a woman at one of the fancy dinners my parents attend regularly. The thought makes me smile.

"So," Nate says, clearing his throat, "Dom told me you and one of your brothers had a falling out."

"Yeah." My heart tumbles as Graham is brought up. He hasn't called me and I haven't called him. I pick up my phone at least twice a day and almost give in and reach out and then I remember—I have nothing to apologize for. I put the phone back down.

I hate this between us. It's something I can't shake. Even though I do believe, without a doubt, he means well, I can't act like this is okay because it's not. Graham will never respect me if I let him walk all over me.

"If it's my fault ..."

"It's not your fault," I insist. "It's ... it's the joining of a bunch of different things. Family growing pains, I guess. I don't know."

"I can tell it bothers you."

"Yeah," I rasp. "My family is really close. Like you and Dominic but there are six of us. I've gone this long without talking to one of them lots of times, but never because we're actually mad."

"Can I help somehow?"

I shake my head, putting my tea back on the table. "No. It'll work out."

He looks away and lets out a breath. "Did they not like Dom?"

I know what he's implying, questioning, and I feel terrible that such a thing would cross his mind. "Ford and Lincoln did like him, actually. You know Sienna loves him. I mean, what's not to love?"

"Lots of things," he chuckles. "But he's a good guy. I know you know that."

"I do."

He turns to face me, his eyes pure sincerity. "Dom is the only person in my entire life I can count on. I don't know how much he's told you about parts of our childhood..."

"Enough to understand what you're saying."

"He told you? About ... *that*?"

It's like he can't say the words, and I just want to jump up and hug him tight. But I don't. "He did," I whisper.

He heaves another breath. "He bore the brunt of our dad's problems. He was the one that couldn't ignore it, couldn't stand to see the damage the next morning. Dom feels things more than I do, I guess. Or maybe he paid more attention or was around more because he was younger."

His head hangs. "I should've protected him. That night, I—"

"Nate." I wait for him to look at me. When he does, his eyes about slaughter me. "Nothing that your dad did was your fault. And what happened that night was a terrible accident that neither of you wanted but happened anyway."

"He's never been the same, Priss. There's been a piece of Dominic that's been a little untouchable since that gun went off. Like ... it's like something happened when that trigger was pulled that made him feel ... less. Dirty. He's carried that shit around ever since." He makes sure I'm listening before continuing. "Only recently have I caught glimpses of the brother I used to know."

"Nate ..."

"It's true. As much of a badass as he is, he's been on this mental island since all that went down. But he's starting to let you in."

Tears flood my eyes.

"If you're going to cry, we're done here," he jokes, standing up straight. "Where's my kid?"

"Follow me." I wipe my cheeks dry with the back of my hand and lead Nate down the hallway. I prop the guest room door open.

Nate and I stand in the doorway and watch Ryder curled up in a ball in the center of the bed, snoring softly. A juice box that we picked up at the grocery store is on the bedside table.

"I've never slept that well in my entire life," Nate whispers. "Just look at him."

"He's a sweet boy."

"When I was that age, I'd put a chair in front of my door when I went to bed in case it was the night my father would come for me for my ass-whippin'."

My hand rests on his arm, tears coming back to my eyes again.

"It never happened at night. But I never had a night where I didn't fear it."

"I can't imagine that. I hate you had to go through that."

"I don't." He looks down at me, his eyes a little greener than his brother's. "It made me who I am. It made Dominic who he is too. Do I wonder what it feels like to be Ryder right now? Sure. But the fact that he's not living like that is what's important."

"You're kind of philosophical," I say, trying to break the moment.

He chuckles quietly. "Sure."

"You know what? Why don't you let Ryder just sleep here tonight? I'll feed him some sugary breakfast and bring him home wound for sound in the morning."

"You don't have to do that."

"I know. But let's let him sleep."

Nate searches my eyes, looking for something he must find because he eventually nods and pulls the door closed. As we make our way back down the hallway, he starts laughing.

"What?" I ask.

"Nothing. Just thank you."

"For what?"

He stops in the center of the foyer. "For taking care of Dom. Me. Ryder. Just promise me that even if Dom fucks this whole thing up, you won't write off me and the kid."

I laugh and open the front door. "I have a feeling there's not much your brother can do to fuck it up that bad."

"Call me if you need anything," he says, stepping out on the porch. "And thanks again."

"Any time."

He does what Dom does—waits for me to lock the door before going to his truck. I head back to the sofa and curl up with my tea and a heart that's fuller than I ever could've imagined.

TWENTY-ONE

DOMINIC

"She should be here any time," Nate says, rinsing off his plate. "She sent me a text a little bit ago and asked if he was allergic to strawberries. Does she overthink everything?"

"Yes," I laugh, tossing an almond in my mouth.

"She's a good girl, Dom. I just wish that brother of hers would stop being a dick."

"Graham?" I ask, sitting up.

"Yeah. I asked her about it last night and could tell it really bothers her."

He keeps talking, but my head is out of the conversation. This issue has been gnawing at me since the night she came here crying. I go back and forth from wanting to slice his fucking throat to telling her to give in and call him—a very un-me kind of thing to do.

I just hate knowing she's thinking about it when she gazes into the distance or his name comes up in conversation. To know it's my fault.

"Are you working today?" he asks.

"Nah, they cancelled my schedule today because I was tied up on that job all night last night."

"Got ya. I'm gonna grab a shower before Chrissy gets here to get Ry." Nate takes off around the corner and leaves me alone with my thoughts.

My phone is in front of me. I spin it around in a circle, my fingers sliding up and down the smooth glass.

Do I or don't I? That is the question.

The sound of my foot tapping against the floor starts to bother me so I stand, grab the phone before I can stop myself, and hit call on the number I looked up earlier.

As it rings, I pace. And as a cheery voice answers, "Landry Holdings," the sound of her name is washed out by the tumble of white noise over my eardrums.

"Is Graham Landry in?" I ask.

"He is. May I ask who is calling, please?"

"Dominic Hughes."

"One moment, please."

I look at the screen. How I've only been on here for forty-two seconds is beyond me. It feels like an eternity already.

"This is Graham." His voice is curt, cool, just as I expected it to be.

"This is Dominic," I say, "but your secretary probably told you that."

"She did. She's efficient. Now, to what do I owe the pleasure of this call?"

"Look, you don't know me and I don't know you. I'm sure we've both drawn conclusions based on what little information we have about the other. But that doesn't seem fair."

"I don't know," he contends. "I'm pretty safe in my assumptions."

"I bet you are. I'm also pretty safe in mine."

"And what would those tell you, Dominic?"

"That you care about your sister as much as I would care about mine, if I had one. But you took a well-placed concern and ran with it in the wrong direction and now your sister won't talk to you."

"How is that any of your business?"

"If she's hurt, it's my business."

The line trembles with the banter, each of us flexing our proverbial muscle through the line. I hear him breathing. I'm sure he can hear mine as I await his reply.

"What do you want from her, Dominic?" he sighs. "Can you just wrap up whatever game you have going on and do it with someone else?"

"Yeah, I could. If that's what it was."

"Don't tell me you're in love with her," he scoffs. "I don't want to hear that."

"You don't have to hear that. You didn't have to take my call either, but you did. That tells me no matter how much of an asshole you are, how much you posture up right now, you know—*you know* this thing between your sister and I isn't just going to go away. And while that probably scares the fuck out of you, it shouldn't."

"You're right," he says, the sound of a chair squeaking in the background. "It does. I don't know what your intentions are. The reports I'm getting aren't stellar, if you know what I mean."

"That surprises me."

"That people are balking a little at you?"

"Oh, no," I laugh, "not that. I'm used to that. Lived it my whole life and I'd probably be a little disappointed if anyone just gave me a gold star. What surprises me is a man of your caliber putting that much stock in other people's opinions. I know you didn't get to where you are today—sitting in that big corner office overlooking downtown Savannah—by listening to everyone else."

The chair squeaks again. "Maybe I underestimated you."

"I guarantee you did. But just so we're on the same page going forward, because there will be a forward, I don't want her money. I don't want her things. I would destroy anyone that hurts her, including Nolan if I ever see that piece of shit again. I want nothing from Cam, only that she's happy. Right now she's not ... and that's your fault."

He sighs, blowing out a breath.

"Call her," I demand. "You can hate me all you want; I really don't give a fuck. But she's your sister and she needs you as much as she needs me. Fix this. Soon."

I'm taken aback when he laughs. "You are not what I expected."

"Imagine that."

"I have a call coming in that I have to take, but this has been an eye-opening experience. Thanks for the call."

"No problem."

I slide the phone back on the table just as the doorbell rings. Taking the few steps from the table to the door, I can hear Ryder jabbering before I even get it open.

"Dom!" he shouts, giving me a high-five as he races by me. "Where's Daddy?"

"The shower," I laugh, watching him fly down the hallway. It's then that I set my sights on her. "How are you?"

She doesn't answer with words, just a long, leisurely kiss.

"That good, huh?" I say against her lips.

She giggles, pulling back. "I missed you last night."

"I spent the night with two seventy-year-olds reminding me how much they were sweating every six-point-two seconds," I groan. "It was not fun."

"It sounds horrible."

"So what are you doing today?" I ask, shutting the door.

She wrinkles her nose. "I have the charity event at Picante. Remember?"

"That's right," I say, although I didn't remember it was tonight specifically. "Are you excited?"

"I'd be more excited if you would come with me."

"I do make things fun." Hearing her laugh behind me, I head into the kitchen. "How was Ryder last night?"

"Fun," she says like it amazes her. "We colored pictures of lizards and it's safe to say I still have my coloring skills."

"Never know when you'll need those," I wink.

Her cheeks blush as she looks down. "I've been thinking about getting with Mom and seeing about putting something together for small business owners. Something that would help them spruce up their storefronts or something. I think it would be fun and could really help people out."

"Really?"

She nods, still not looking at me. "Do you think that's a good idea?"

I lift her chin with my fingertip. "I think whatever you want to do is a good idea. And, yes, I think you need to do something that makes you happy. Besides me."

"You make me happy."

"I hope so."

Our lips touch, sweetly at first, but as her hands scoot under the hem of my shirt and roam the ridges of my back, her lips part. I deepen the kiss, craving the taste of her.

Lifting her, I sit her on the counter. Her legs wrap around my waist. "If you won't go with me tonight, will you at least stay with me after?"

"I want to say no just to get you going," I say, kissing up the side of her neck, "but I can't even pretend I don't want you."

"Is that a yes?" she moans.

"Uncle Dom," Ryder says, coming from nowhere. "Are you kissing Cam?"

My head drops to Cam's shoulder as I move my hips so he doesn't see the outline of my cock in my shorts.

Cam giggles. "Ryder, if you were a superhero, you would totally be the invisible one."

"We're gonna put a bell on ya, kid," I mutter.

Camilla swats at my shoulder as she jumps off the counter. "I need to go anyway. I have to run by the Farm and pick up my dress for tonight. They delivered it there rather than to my house for whatever reason." She looks at me and cocks a brow. "Was that a yes?"

"You know it was."

Blowing me a kiss, she heads to the door. "I'll see you boys later. Behave."

The door closes and Ryder looks at me. "She's the best."

"Yeah," I smile. "She is, isn't she?"

TWENTY-TWO

CAMILLA

"Hello, Camilla."

"Oh!" I say, my hand falling on my chest. "I didn't see you, Rose. You scared me."

The sweet lady smiles at me from behind the desk in the living room at the Farm. Her hair is piled in some chignon from decades gone by, her pearls shining in the late morning sunlight.

"I'm sorry. I didn't mean to," she says.

"Oh, I know. I didn't realize Barrett was back in town."

"Yes," Barrett's personal secretary says. "We came in for the event this evening. Alison was not about to miss it."

It makes me proud that my sister-in-law, the pregnant wife of the Governor, for heaven's sake, supports my function to this degree. "She's awesome."

"I agree, Camilla. She's made my job a whole lot easier."

"I bet she has," I laugh. "So where are they?"

"They took the golf cart down to the lake so Huxley can fish for a little bit. Alison didn't feel like walking and Barrett wasn't leaving her behind."

"I didn't see their car."

"Troy took it to town to run a few errands and grab some lunch. Do you want something, dear? I could have him pick some up for you."

"No, thank you though. I just came for my dress. Have you seen it today?"

"Yes, actually. It's in the hall closet by the bathroom."

"Thanks, Rose!" I meander through the Farm, not going straight to the closet but stopping in the living room first. It's quiet, unlike most times I'm here.

The walls are sprinkled with pictures of us throughout the years. There are goofy pictures of Lincoln and Sienna at a car wash one summer and of me in my cheerleading outfit from high school. Those are mixed with images of Ford graduating from military school and Barrett taking the oath of office. It's a wall of memories, one that makes me a little nostalgic.

We've spent so many hours, days, years here together celebrating good times and convening for the bad ones. Tears from joy and sadness have been shed, screams for wonderful announcements and terrible declarations have been heard by these walls. No matter what, we've done it together. As a family.

My heart twists in my chest, tears dotting my eyes, when I turn to see Graham and Lincoln watching me from the back porch. Turning away, I refuse to let Graham see me weak. But, in typical G fashion, he's in the door and in front of me before I have a chance to flee.

"What's wrong?" he asks, any traces of his recent venom gone.

"Nothing," I sniffle. "I was just thinking about all the things we've done in this room. Ford's wedding, Barrett's election celebration. Our sixteenth birthday party."

"I had fun that night!" Lincoln chimes in from the porch. "Taylor Thompson. Wowza."

Graham and I chuckle ... until we look at each other. Our grins falter.

"Look, Swink," he says, clearing his throat. "I want to talk to you for a minute."

"We've been through this."

"Cam, I'm sorry."

Squinting, making sure it's Graham I'm seeing in front of me and not Barrett, I shake my head. "What?"

"Come on," he chuckles. "Don't make me say it again. It hurt enough the first time."

"What are you sorry for?"

"Does it matter?"

"Absolutely."

Shoving his hand in his pockets, he sighs. "I'm sorry for acting like a dick."

"Because ..." I lead him on.

"Because someone pointed out today that it's really stupid to make judgements on people based on someone else's opinion."

"That's true. So what were you doing? Basing it off of Linc's?"

"Don't throw me in this!" Lincoln shouts.

"Will you butt out?" Graham shouts back. Shaking his head, he focuses on me once more. "I need to trust that you know what you're doing. You've never given me a reason to doubt your judgement—not really."

"Oh, give me one bad decision I've made."

He crooks a brow. "Ten grand ring a bell?"

"That hasn't been proved to be a bad decision. Just like the idea of you proposing to Mallory hasn't been proven to be a bad one." I crook a brow back. "Catch my drift?"

"Don't change the subject. You're an adult and I need to give you the benefit of the doubt. Just be smart about things, Cam. Please. And if you need anything, whether you're mad at me or not, call me."

His features soften and I feel my anger wane. "Thanks, G. But I think I'll call Dom now. Maybe I've outgrown you."

"I wish Lincoln would," he groans.

"Not a chance!" our brother shouts from the porch again.

Graham and I laugh before he pulls me into a hug and all is right in my world.

***

Dominic

"It's busy in here tonight." Joe stumbles through the door of The Gold Room and takes his usual seat on the end. He smells a little like urine and a lot like whiskey and I wonder which bar he hit up on the way here. "Do I got room on my tab for somethin' to eat?"

"I'll check." I head to the back, without checking his tab, and grab the hamburger I made for myself before we got busy. "Here you go," I say, sliding the plate to him.

He doesn't say thank you, doesn't acknowledge me in any way, just scoops up the sandwich with both hands and eats nearly half of it before I can look away.

"Where's Nate?" Billy calls from the other end.

"He'll be here in a second."

"Gotcha."

I lean on the bar and watch the television that hangs overhead. It's covering the Landry Charity Gala at Picante. The anchor is talking about how charities get so much more attention, and money, when the Landry's are attached to them.

They have a mini-red carpet set up leading into the hotel lobby. Baseball players, a B-level movie star, and a few musicians have all been interviewed before they disappear through the doors.

I've seen this before. It's not unusual. The Landry's are well-known for their charity work. But now that I know Camilla and know she's there ... it's weird.

"What are you thinkin' about, baby?"

I look up to see an older woman, leather skin and bright red lips, leaning towards me. Her tits are resting on the bar, laying it out there that if I want it, I can have it.

"Just wondering what it's like up there tonight," I say truthfully, nodding to the cameras.

"Fancy clothes, fancy cars. More money than they know what to do with so they give it away."

"I suppose you're right."

"Of course I'm right," she breathes. "They're a whole different level than us."

I'm on the verge of admitting how right she is when my phone buzzes on the shelf below me. I see Cam's name on the screen.

"Do you need anything or can I take this call?" I ask her. "It's important."

"Oh, take it," she says, waving a hand through the air. "I got nowhere to be."

Swiping the screen and heading into the back, I feel my heartbeat soar. "Hey," I say once I can hear.

"Hey." Her voice is sweet, but missing the warmth I usually hear. "Where are you?"

"I had to fill in for Nate for a little bit."

"So you're at the bar?"

"Yeah." I hear her sadness and want desperately to make it leave. "Hey, your brother's buddy Travis called today."

"Troy's brother?"

"Yeah, that one. He's coming by tomorrow to look at some stuff for Nate. He's a cool guy."

"Travis and Troy are both awesome. I knew you'd like him."

"So what are you doing?" I ask like I have no idea.

"Well, I'm in the car on my way to Picante," she sighs. "I wish you were here."

"It's on T.V.," I tell her. "I've been waiting to see you."

"They're supposed to interview me when I get there. I hate that part of it."

I laugh, picking up a glass and putting it in the sink. "You're famous."

"Hardly," she groans. "We're pulling up. I'll see you after?"

"Let me know when you're home and I'll come over," I promise. "Have fun tonight."

"I'll miss you."

"You, too, Cam."

She's gone before I even get it all said. With a frown that I hate wearing, I tuck my phone in the pocket of my jeans and head back to the front.

"Can I get a Jack and Coke?" someone shouts right away.

I make the drink and deliver it to a man next to Billy. When I look up, I see her on the screen.

She's breathtakingly gorgeous in a light yellow dress that sits off her shoulders. Her hair is pulled up, diamonds in her ears, and her make-up so minimal, if she has any on at all, that she looks like an angel.

"She's pretty, all right," Red Lips says, sidling up to the bar again. She sighs a rough, smoker's cough. "I wonder what it's like to be one of them."

"I have no idea," I say, fascinated by Camilla. She smiling, not looking at all like the mellow woman I just talked to on the phone. She laughs, teasing the interviewer, before posing for a few pictures and disappearing inside the hotel.

"I'll never know," Red Lips admits. "Hell, you could dress me up in one of those dresses and dot me with diamonds and I'd still look like a poser. You can take the girl out of the trailer park but you can't take the trailer park out of the girl."

She laughs at her joke, repeating it to the guy that joins her at the bar. He laughs too.

I, on the other hand, do not. Not because she isn't funny. Because she's right.

TWENTY-THREE

CAMILLA

"Are you tired of smiling yet?" Sienna whispers in my ear. "My cheeks ache."

"Mine too. And my feet hurt."

My twin sister, sheathed in a navy blue strapless dress, stands with me in the back corner of the room. "At least we're at the point where they're drinking enough to want to talk to themselves and not us."

"Excellent point," I laugh.

"Who has an excellent point?"

We look over to see Mallory and Ellie headed our way. Ellie's stomach is just starting to be noticeably more round than usual, but only if you're looking for it.

"Ellie, you are beyond adorable," I say.

"She is, isn't she?" Mallory adds.

"Trust me, this doesn't feel adorable," she groans, her hand resting on her belly. "I've been sick for weeks straight. I'm over it. Can I have this baby yet?"

We laugh as she slumps into a chair and looks at us in defeat. "I'm not kidding, guys. I'm exhausted."

"Just sit there and I'll grab you some water. Okay?" Sienna asks.

Ellie looks grateful and Sienna takes that for a yes and disappears into the crowd. I feel Mallory's eyes on me.

"What?" I ask, giving her a look.

"I just want to say I'm thrilled you and Graham made up," she says. "He was *this close* to being thrown out of his own house."

"You should've. He deserved it," I huff. "But he acted like a man today and apologized, so I forgave him."

She pulls her brows together. "You know why he apologized, right?"

"Don't tell me you made him."

"No, not me." She flashes me a mischievous grin. "Dominic."

"What?" I gasp. "What are you talking about?"

"Dominic called Graham."

"When?"

"This morning. Graham let the cat out of the bag on the way over."

"Oh, my God," I breathe, only imagining that conversation. "Did he give you details?"

"No. Just that Dominic made some valid points and ... I think he made an impression on your brother, Cam."

Burying my face in my hands, not even bothering to worry my make-up will smudge, I wonder just what transpired and why no one bothered to tell me. "You know," I say, dropping my hands, "Graham just went off. I've never seen him that mad and I get why. I do. But it was still so ... weird."

"He's been that way recently," she says, her voice dropping. "I don't know what's wrong with him. He's rash, temperamental, not the Graham I know. I'm worried about him."

"You have no idea what's wrong?"

"None." She looks down, inspecting her perfect manicure. "Maybe he's trying to figure a way out."

"Out of what? A business deal?"

"Me."

The one-word answer is enough to have me reaching for her.

"Don't hug me or I'll cry," she laughs, batting my hands away playfully. "Besides, it makes me feel all dramatic and I hate dramatic."

"Since when?"

She just laughs in response. "I'm being dumb. I know. He probably has something going on at work and doesn't want to weigh me down with it. I just need to be patient. This, too, shall pass."

"I'm sure you're right."

Looking up, I see Graham watching us from the other side of the room. He looks distinguished with his silver tie and perfect posture, holding a glass of something dark in his hand.

I flash him a look of shame and he holds his palms out as if to say, "What?" I huff a breath and look back to Mallory. "It'll be fine. Like you said, just give him some time."

"Where's Dominic?" she asks, not-so-smoothly changing topics.

"He didn't want to come."

"That's too bad. We all want to meet him."

"Are we talking about Dominic?" Alison says from beside me. She leans forward, kissing my cheek, before pulling back and grimacing. "This pregnancy thing is for young people."

"Like you're old," I laugh.

"Much older than I was when I had Huxley," she admits. "Ellie? Care for some company?"

"Please," she says, opening her eyes. "I think I just fell asleep."

"Welcome to my world, sister."

Sienna comes back with two bottles of water, one for Ellie and one for Alison. Mallory and I chat for a while about yoga and pizza, our two favorite things, before Huxley appears at our side.

"Miss Camilla," he says, bowing. "My father would like to speak with you about an urgent matter."

"Is that so?" I grin. "You are too cute in that suit, Mr. Huxley."

"It's Mr. Landry," he winks, "and let's use 'handsome,' please. 'Cute' is for kids."

"Oh," I say, making a face at his mother. "Handsome. Yes, Mr. Landry. Please lead me to your father."

He offers his elbow, making me giggle. I take it and we wind through the room until we're in a smaller room to the side. Barrett and Graham are chatting in the middle of the space.

"Oh, I get both of you?" I sigh, rolling my eyes. "Thanks for the escort, Hux."

"No problem."

I hear the door swing closed behind me as I look at my two oldest brothers. "What can I do for the two of you?"

It's a rhetorical question. The look on Graham's face tells me exactly what this is about. I shoot him a look and brace myself for another onslaught.

"Easy, Swink," Barrett laughs, setting his glass on a table. "You're getting that killer look in your eye I've been hearing about."

I shoot another blast of it towards Graham for good measure. They both laugh, which only puts me more on edge.

"Look, before you two go—"

"Cam," Barrett interjects. "Wait a second." He walks towards me and stops a few feet in front of where I'm standing. "I know about Dominic. I know about Nolan."

"He can't help who he's related to. Look," I say, almost frantically, "I know Nolan tried to bomb you, Barrett, and I hate him for that. But Dom—"

"Stop," he laughs.

My shoulder slump as I heave in a breath and watch my brother's face.

"Graham and I have been talking about it. I'll admit, I was pissed off at first. But then, you know what?"

"What?"

"I remembered back when I started dating Alison and how annoyed I was at everyone saying she was wrong for me because of what it could do to my campaign. How her background looked crappy, because it did, and how she was a single mother and all that. I remember thinking, 'Why doesn't anyone care if I'm happy?' I almost lost her because of that."

"That's the same thing I'm thinking," I say, looking over his shoulder at Graham before resting my eyes on Barrett again.

"If he turns out to be like Nolan, we'll kill him."

"Barrett!"

"I'm kidding."

"I'm not," Graham says, causing Barrett to shake his head. "And don't think we don't know about what happened to his father. We do. Nick Parker found out for us."

"You hired a private investigator?" I ask, my jaw dropping. "That's too far, G. Too far."

"Hey, that was Dad's directive," Graham says, holding up his hands. "He trumped me on that."

"Oh, shit," I say, looking at the ceiling and fake crying.

Barrett laughs, moving away and picking up his drink again. "I'll handle the old man. He's mellowing out in his old age. I think you'll be fine."

"Mellowing out?" I ask. "Maybe to you! He's as uptight as ever with me and Sienna."

"He remembered when that happened," Graham says, coming forward. "I guess Nolan had talked about what an asshole his brother was—Dominic's dad. He said it was better off that he was dead."

"But Dom has to live with that," I point out. "You think that's easy for him?"

"It couldn't be," Barrett admits. "But Dad will be fine. I got you on this."

"Why are you so supportive?"

He shrugs. "Maybe *I'm* mellowing out in my old age. Maybe I know how it feels to be in your situation. Either way, I want you happy, Swink, and everyone I've talked to says you're happier than you've ever been. Except for Graham. He says you're meaner," he winks.

My heart leaps with joy, tears wetting my eyes. "I am happy, Barrett. I really am. And I'm only mean to G when he deserves it."

Before he can say a word, Huxley is opening the door. "Hey, Dad. Mom wants you."

"The boss needs me," he says, shaking my shoulder as he walks by.

It's just Graham and I, both fighting a smile. "I heard Dom called you."

"Mallory has a big mouth."

"That she does. She also told me you've been acting weird. Like, weirder than normal."

He blows out a breath, leaning on one of the round tables in the room. He starts to talk, then stops.

"Spill it, G. What's going on?"

"Lots of decisions to be made."

I bite the side of my cheek, trying not to smile. "The answer is yes."

"What answer?"

"The answer to the question you're thinking."

"How do you know what I'm thinking."

"Because you're my big brother and I spent my entire childhood observing you. Granted, back then it was so I could use that information to my advantage. It's just handy now too sometimes."

"You're too much," he scoffs, shoving off the table.

I shrug. "Okay, so you aren't wondering whether you'd make a good husband? You aren't curious, at least a little bit, whether it's too early to marry Mallory or if you should wait and be really, really sure? Because this definitely goes against the plan you made when you were ten years old," I say, rolling my eyes.

He doesn't flinch.

"You are," I say, wagging a finger at him. "You're thinking both of those things and the answer to the first is yes, even though you're a dick, and the answer to the second is no, because you'll never be more sure than you are right now."

"She leaves her clothes on the floor."

"Pick them up."

"She doesn't rinse the plates before putting them in the dishwasher."

"Does the world come crashing down?"

"She wants a puppy."

"Oh, I'm with you on this one," I laugh. "Puppies are a lot of work."

He cracks a grin. "I just worry ... what if I can't handle it? What if we go into this with different expectations and all of a sudden realize it's wrong?"

"That's impossible," I scoff, heading to the door.

"How do you figure?"

"You love her, right?"

"Right."

"Then how can it ever be wrong?"

He opens the door for me. "Not bad, little sister. Not bad."

TWENTY-FOUR

CAMILLA

"No, no more champagne," I say, waving off the proffered glass. "Really. I've had enough."

The server gives up and heads across the room to my mother and her friends. I watch him offer Paulina a drink and she takes it. Of course she does. I hope she chokes.

I turn to head to the patio for fresh air when I nearly bump into Daphne and Barron Monroe. Our parents have been acquaintances forever, although I don't quite have an affinity for Daphne. She's Barrett's age, while Barron went to school with Sienna and I. He's handsome, smart, wealthy ... and he knows it.

"Careful," he says, steadying me by the elbow. He flashes me his best smile—the panty-dropper as Sienna calls it. "How are you tonight, Camilla?"

"I'm good. Tired," I admit. "Have you two enjoyed your evening?"

"Yes, thank you for the invitation," Daphne says. Or I think she says. It's a bit of a slur. "I'm going to the patio, Bar-ron. Find me later?"

"Of course."

She leaves us, wobbling on her heels.

"My sister could use a lesson or two from you about class," Barron says, pulling out a chair. When I don't sit, he cocks his head to the side. "You said you were tired."

I didn't plan on sitting, but it suddenly feels like an excellent idea. My feet almost sing as I sit and give them some relief. Barron sits across from me, looking all dapper in his black suit and yellow tie.

"Look," he laughs, "we match."

"You have good taste."

"You are lovely tonight, Camilla. But, then again, you always are."

"Thank you," I blush. "You look handsome, per usual."

"So," he says, getting settled in his chair, "what are you doing next weekend?"

"Random," I laugh. "I have no idea. Why?"

He considers my question, his long, thick lashes on display as he narrows his eyes. "I have a proposition."

"Okay. Shoot."

"I have to go to Paris for a few days. It's a long flight and I'll have some time off to explore the city, and you know, I was thinking it would be fun to do that with you."

My mouth hangs open as I try to process this out-of-left-field offer. "Um, Barron, I'm honored you'd like to take me to Paris with you. But the answer is no."

"No? Come on, Camilla. Who doesn't like Paris?"

"I love Paris," I laugh. "That's not the issue."

His charm seeps away as his lips form a thin line. "What's the issue?"

"I'm in a relationship."

His eyes roll in his head. "Oh, yes. I've heard about your plumber boyfriend. I just didn't expect you'd sink that low."

"He's not a plumber," I fire back, my chest rising and falling much more sharply than before.

"Does it matter what we call him?" he laughs. "What are you

doing with him anyway, Camilla? You're the talk of the country club and are making a complete ass out of yourself."

My chair shoots back as I get to my feet. Leaning forward, my hands planting on the table, I get just inches from his face. "You are the one making a total ass out of yourself. Dominic may not belong to the country club, but he would never talk to me like this."

"So he's a civilized barbarian?"

"No, that's me. He would knock your teeth out right now if he were here. I'm the one that will smile politely and ensure everyone at your beloved country club knows that you've been screwing the manager since we were fifteen."

"Why would you do that?" he growls, getting to his feet.

"Because I think you love her. Because I think you'll get kicked out of your precious little club and I think that would be amusing. Does it matter? The fact is, if you want to mess with someone I care about, all's fair."

"Is there a problem here?"

I whirl around to see my father standing behind me.

"Everything is fine, Daddy."

"Mr. Landry," Barron gushes, ignoring me, "how are you? It's so nice to see you this evening." He extends a hand which my father takes. "How's business?"

"My business is fine, thank you for asking." He gives Barron a nasty look and ushers me away. "What did that little son of a bitch say to you?"

"Nothing."

He chuckles as we stop walking. I look up into his face, a mixture of my brothers. His hair has some grey to it now and the lines in his face are deeper and heavier.

"You are just like your mother."

"How do you figure?" I grin.

He doesn't answer, just laughs. "Speaking of which, here comes the devil."

Our mother arrives and my father kisses her on the cheek. He whispers something in her ear and takes off across the room toward Graham.

"This turned out excellent, don't you think?" she asks, surveying the room.

"Yeah. Absolutely."

"What's wrong, dear?"

"It's been a long week," I admit. "And then I just had Barron Monroe come up to me and ... let's say I said everything I wanted to say with a smile."

"As long as you maintained the smile," she winks. "How are things with you? You know your siblings talk ..."

"Too much," I sigh. "I guess you know about Dominic."

"I'd love to meet him."

I look at her and force a swallow. "I know Paulina and Raquel saw us at lunch the other day, and according to Graham, didn't say very nice things about him."

She considers her words, looking anywhere but at me while she does it. Finally, after I'm about ready to burst into tears, she focuses on me. "We live in a very idyllic world, Camilla Jane. We are blessed that we can avoid a lot of common struggles in life. Now, I could go on and on about why that's true, about how hard our families have worked and planned and saved, but I don't think that's necessary."

"No, it's not. I get it," I say, thinking back to all the ways those things were reiterated to us growing up.

"It's very easy," Mom continues, "to forget what it's like for other people. When we are sitting in a beautiful home, wearing expensive clothes, eating whatever we'd like, it's easy to look at those struggling in different ways—because we all struggle, Camilla, and pass judgement."

"I think your friends pass judgement incredibly easy."

"That they do," she sighs. "They're spared in a lot of ways by the exclusivity of our world. If Paulina or Raquel had to wear their sins and mistakes on their clothes, sort of like the way Dominic may display some of the things in his life unwittingly, let's just say they'd be a lot less judge-y."

My bottom lip trembles and I let her pull me into a tight embrace.

"I told both of them that. I explained that if you were happy and healthy and he treated you right, I couldn't care less about anything else. We then had a quiet conversation about how I'm more concerned about you not sporting black eyes than I am about you wearing diamonds." She pulls away and wipes away a fallen tear from my cheek. "Don't spend a minute worrying about them, Camilla. They were probably jealous, if I can read between the lines."

Giggling, I dab beneath my eyes and breathe a little easier than I have for a while.

"Can I meet him?" she asks.

"That's probably not going to happen too soon. He and Graham aren't really seeing eye-to-eye, although I think they've called a truce."

She places her hand on my shoulder and looks me in the eye. "I raised your brothers to be the men they are. I'm proud of them. Immensely. But sometimes they can get a little ..."

"Overbearing?"

"Yes. Probably so." She takes her hand away and plays with her pearls. "I'm going to tell you the same thing I've told each of your siblings when they've come to me for advice. As long as you're happy, we'll adapt. And if you are happy, if you can't imagine them never lighting up your phone again, you need to hold on to that. It's precious."

"It's not that easy with him," I voice. "He doesn't feel comfortable in places like this. So much of what I do, he doesn't want a part of. And he doesn't want me to be a part of his either."

"Sounds like your father," she laughs.

"Daddy? How?"

"When we started dating, the man wouldn't let me near a campaign meeting," she sighs, rolling her eyes. "He said it was no place for a woman like me. Even though I came from that kind of world, as you know, my father being as much of a business man and statesman as his, he tried to shelter me from the ins-and-outs that he saw that maybe I didn't. It caused some conflict."

"How did you fix it?"

Her smile lights up the room. "Well, first of all, I tried to remember that it came from a good place. Would I have wanted him to show no regard for my safety? No. Of course not. Then I showed him how strong I was. I learned about campaigns, I brought tea and water into the strategy rooms and didn't flinch. I showed him if this was what he was going to do, which I knew when I started dating him, that I was going to do it too. At least in a support role. Because that's what makes a relationship, Camilla. The support. The shoulder. The ear that listens. That's where the love and respect and true collaboration lie. Not in anything else."

I glance at the clock on the wall. "Mom, would it be terrible if I left early tonight?"

"Typically, yes. You know I think we should be the last to leave."

My heart sinks.

"But," she whispers, "I heard you had a sore throat and just couldn't take it anymore."

I kiss her cheek. "Thanks, Mom."

"Get out of here before your daddy sees you."

TWENTY-FIVE

CAMILLA

He's not answering his phone, so that means he's at the gym. It's the only time he doesn't answer me or at least quick-text me back.

Still in my yellow dress and heels, I navigate my car onto the dimly-lit road that leads to Percy's. There are people on the street corners, looking at me like they'll stick a gun in my window if I slow down too much. So I don't. Actually, I get a little heavy on the accelerator.

A calendar flips through my head and I realize Dom fights in a couple of days. He's stopped talking about it, other than to infer he's generically training. There are no reports of the date or his opponent or what tactics he's going to use or how much he hates Bond. He's just slowed down from any casual mention at all.

If he's going to fight, I'm going to be there with my pom-poms in the air. Maybe I can get Ford to teach me a thing or two before then. Just the basics, like Mom said.

I pull to the curb and cut the lights and ignition and scan the parking lot for any creepers. It's not well-lit but it's better than the roads. There are lights on inside and my car is parked next to his. There's one other small compact car by the door.

Hopping out and dashing to the front as best I can in heels, praying it's unlocked, I pull it open.

There are no chimes like at a regular business to alert the workers someone has walked in. Some of the lights that hang from the ceiling are on and some off, making the room a bit moody.

Glancing around, I don't see signs of anyone. I don't hear anything either. I'm about ready to call out his name when I see a shadow in the ring in the back.

With a wide smile, I dart in that direction but slow when it's not Dom's voice I hear. Instead, I hear one I vaguely remember.

"Does that feel better?" It's a woman's voice that's cooing through the room. It's *her* voice, Red's, the one from The Gold Room the day I walked into Nate's office and saw her sitting with Dominic.

My blood turns to ice. Suddenly, I can hear everything, see everything, almost taste the feeling in the room.

Her giggle cuts through me like a chainsaw. "Hold still and I'll put some of this on it."

"There's no way to get it on where it hurts with the bandage."

"Should I take it back off? Man, I'm bad at this nursing thing."

"Yes, you are," he laughs.

The warmth of his chuckle, the easiness of it ringing through the air, pelts me. I almost gasp.

"Bond gets you with that hook every time," she says. "Have you thought about throwing a left hook on the inside when he throws wide?"

"Yeah, I have. I'm impressed, Hannah."

"Well, don't be," she flirts. "I heard Percy telling someone a few days ago. I just borrowed the lingo."

"Well, he told me that too. Apparently I should remember it more often."

She giggles again and I want to puke.

My stomach sinks that she knows this part of him, that he's impressed by her knowledge of whatever it is they're talking about. Fighting. Punching. Things that are foreign and beyond me.

Then she giggles a third time and I realize I may have more of a fighter in me than I expect. I want to place a punch right in the middle of her face. My hands clenched at my sides, my nails pressing into my palms, I step farther in the room so I can see them.

She's sitting in the middle of the ring next to him. A bandage is wrapped around his chest, and by the way it's fastened, I can tell he didn't put it on. Someone else did. *She* did.

I take a deep breath and know I'm probably not going to handle this with a smile.

"Hey, Dom," I say as sweetly as I can manage.

I've never seen someone's head whip around so quickly. His eyes are wide as he struggles to his feet, grimacing in pain. I don't look at Red, but she's looking at me. Her smirk smacks the side of my face, her taunt, also inaudible, is there. I feel it.

"What are you doing here?" Dom asks, babying his side.

"I left the event early. Maybe, *again*, I should've called."

My teeth grind against each other, my hands trembling at the fury of imagining her hands on my man.

"You know what? I'm sorry," I say, "I did call. That's how I knew you were here. You didn't answer."

"He was training," Red interjects, looking at me like I'm an annoyance.

"You—" I start, but Dom cuts me off.

"Hannah, thanks for your help tonight."

"Anything for you." Her eyes are on mine as she places her hand on his shoulder and lets it fall down his arm. "Need anything else, *Dom?*"

"You have about three seconds to get away from him," I seethe.

"And what are you going to do about it?"

"She's not going to do anything about it. Just go, Hannah. Okay?"

She stands in front of him, her hands on her hips. "I still have this cream ..."

"I swear to God ..." My body quakes as I look at Dominic.

"You," she says as she climbs out the ring a safe distance away from me, "need to leave him alone. He's injured and has a fight in a couple of days. Don't be fucking his head all up."

"Hannah, enough," Dom orders, his voice gravelly.

"You need to leave him alone," I glare.

"Why? Because you're his little goody-two-shoe girlfriend and you said so? Let me give you a little piece of advice. If you gave a fuck, you'd have been here timing his rounds and wrapping his hands and not off posing for pictures like the mindless idiot you are."

"Excuse me?" I start around the ring but am stopped when Dom's voice booms through the room.

"Hannah. Enough," he growls. "You wanna play a little game, that's fine. Cam is smart enough to see it for what it is. But if you're going to tread into disrespecting her, calling her names, that's a level you don't want to get to. Trust me."

She rolls her eyes. "Put a show on now for the girlfriend. Fine. See you later."

I stand on one side of the ropes, Dom on the other, while Hannah whistles and rummages around up front taking her sweet time. A couple of long minutes later, the door slams. And we're alone.

Just having her gone dissolves some of the fire, but in its place, is a singe of hurt.

Maybe some of what she said is true. Maybe he thinks that too.

"What are you doing here, Cam?"

"I'd ask you the same thing but I'm not sure I want the answer."

He blows out a breath like the fate of the entire world lies in it. "You know I don't want you here. Not at night and not alone."

I don't respond.

"Oh, stop it," he sighs.

"Stop it? Really? You're going to say that to me when I walk in here and see *that*? Her touching you and cooing like a baby? It's ..." I force a smile. "It's beyond frustrating."

"I needed help with the bandage," he sighs. "She was the only person here."

"Conveniently."

"Whatever, Cam. I'm banged up here. Forgive me for taking care of myself. Isn't it you that's always preaching that?"

"Yes," I gulp.

My insecurities flare and I know it's an ugly reaction. It's one I'm not used to, poise and confidence coming fairly easy to me. But now neither are really present.

"Let's say you walked in to Mallory's yoga studio one night," I say, my voice starting to shake, "and I'm there, alone, with Barron Monroe."

"Who the fuck is he?"

"Just a guy I've known my whole life," I shrug.

His jaw pulses as he envisions this situation.

"Let's say Barron is helping me with a pulled muscle. It's just some muscle rub on the back of my thigh—where I can't reach. No big deal." I let that sink in. "How's that working for you?"

"I'd break every bone in his fucking body," he seethes.

"Oh, but Dom," I say innocently. "I couldn't reach."

His eyes narrow as his chest rises and falls.

"That is the equivalent of what I just walked into only I didn't throw in how I didn't want you there—right or wrong," I add as he starts to object. "It's about how it makes me feel, Dominic."

His head drops forward. "I just feel sorry for Hannah. She's not a lot different than me, really."

"I beg to differ."

"But you don't know her. Not that I think you could be friends because I don't," he grins. "But I can't just be hateful to her, Cam. I don't have it in me. But that doesn't mean I want her or think of her in any way other than a girl that really has nothing to go on."

His face falls, his jaw loosening up, and he sits back down on the mat. "I saw you on television. I thought you looked beautiful. But I see you now and realize ... you're even prettier in person."

"Don't change the subject."

"I'm not. Well, maybe I am," he mutters. "Nothing happened with Hannah, Cam. Nothing will ever, ever happen with her. She legit helped me fasten this thing around my waist because I might've cracked a rib tonight. I don't know. It just hurts."

"You can't fight with a cracked rib."

"I've fought with cracked ribs before."

"If it splits and punctures one of your organs, you could die."

He almost smiles. "I could. But I won't."

"You don't know that."

His arms are draped over his bent legs, his black mesh shorts riding up on his thighs. He looks so long and lean and sweaty and sexy, and I wish I could pretend I didn't see Hannah touching him. I wish I could erase it from my mind.

"How did the event go?" he asks quietly.

"Fine. Raised a lot of money. Goal achieved."

"That's great."

"Then why don't I feel better about it?"

"Get up here," he grins, patting the mat next to him.

A part of me screams to stay the course, be mad, keep the distance, but for my good and his, I need to touch him. To make sure he's okay.

My heels are off and I'm slipping under the ropes before I can heed the devil on my shoulder's warning. Sitting next to him, I lay my head on his shoulder. "I'm still very, very angry," I warn. He pulls me closer and I take a deep breath. "I have something to tell you."

"What?"

"It doesn't matter one way or the other, really, but I'd want you to tell me."

"Cam ..."

"Barron Monroe asked me to Paris tonight."

"Paris as in France?"

"Yes."

"Some asshole asked you to Paris?"

"Yes."

He shakes his head like he can't believe it. "I'll kill him."

Shrugging, I blow out a breath. "You could've been there. Bet he wouldn't have asked me then."

"I definitely don't think those are my people. I think they're the kind of people that get my kind of people sent to prison."

"Well, I think that about your kind of people."

"What?"

"I have a thing against trashy gym whores that put their hands on my man, okay?"

"It wasn't like that, Cam."

"It was enough like that that I want to break her in half."

He bursts out laughing, pulling my head into his chest. It's damp with sweat and probably ruining my make-up, but I don't care. As a matter of fact, I cuddle as close to him as I can and breathe him in, touching his back lightly until he jumps from pain.

"I'm not kidding," I say. "I have moves now, remember?"

"Oh, I remember," he chuckles. "You better work on that before you go throwing punches."

"I hate her."

He looks me over. "She's not bad. She's just ... different."

"She's a whore."

"Maybe she is. She's been fucking Nate off and on, so you could ask him his opinion. I don't know. You know why? Because I *don't care*." He stands and offers me a hand. When I place one in his, he pulls me to my feet. "The only girl I care about is standing in a beautiful yellow dress right in front of me. And despite the fact that I am semi-annoyed that she can't listen to save her soul and showed up here at ten at night alone, she's all that matters to me."

"Really?" I say, fighting the corners of my lips from tugging up just yet.

"What else would matter?"

"Dom, seriously, she better never touch you again. I mean it. I'll go crazy. Rich girl crazy. We have tons of avenues of destruction at our hands."

"Noted." He bends down and puts his lips on mine. I don't kiss him back at first, trying to hold out long enough to make my point. Then his tongue licks along my bottom lip and I can't help but return the gesture. "Now that's settled—"

"Oh, it's not settled," I resist. "I hate her. You have to understand the depths to which I'd like to see her eaten by a host of fire ants."

His laugh washes over me and makes me smile even though I don't feel like it. "Fire ants?"

"It's all I could come up with."

He moves to the side and winces, almost dropping to his knees in pain. "Fuck."

"What can I do for you, Dom?" I say, rushing to his side.

Sucking in a breath, he stands back up slowly. "Nothing," he hisses. "I just have to wait 'til it goes away."

"You can't fight like this. You could get seriously injured. This is no joke."

"I'm fighting. That's the end of it."

Taking a deep breath, I try to remember I'm playing the role of supportive girlfriend, not naysaying nag. But when his face pales and he doubles over again, gripping his side, a gleam of sweat dotting his forehead, I can't help but want to protect him.

"Dom, I'm serious. There's no reason for you to risk this. You have to think about your health here."

"I have to think about paying my rent that just went up. I have to think about buying groceries and feeding Ryder until Nate gets himself back together. I have to think about making sure The Gold Room doesn't go to the tax sale this year and sock a little away to buy a few things for Christmas. This is my way of not having to do it again.

"This money is my rainy day fund, Cam. Without it, I'm more paycheck-to-paycheck than I already am. I've counted on this for years now, like a bonus I get every six months or something. Don't think I don't know I can't keep doing it ..." He looks at the floor, embarrassment written all over his face.

Instantly, I feel bad. "I'm sorry. I didn't realize ..."

"It's hard for you to think about things like this. It must be. You were just at a place where people were giving their money away, offering trips to Paris. I'm destroying myself so I can keep a roof over my head if I get laid off at some point." He smiles a broken, wobbly smile. "I don't blame you for thinking the way you do. You're right, actually. But sometimes being right doesn't fix things."

"Can I at least come watch you?" I ask, my hand on his forearm on his Joey tattoo. "Let me be there. I want to be."

"There's no way." His response is immediate and with a flourish of finality.

"Why?"

"Imagine the wildest, most about it people you can think of. Now put them all together in a room where the purpose *is* fighting. What do you think you have?"

When I don't answer, he does it for me.

"Mayhem. You have mayhem."

As if the conversation is over, he climbs out of the ring, taking a few seconds to recover from the movement in his ribs. He helps me out, kisses my forehead, and after I slip on my heels, he leads me out the door.

TWENTY-SIX

DOMINIC

Dominic

She comes out of her bathroom wrapped up in a giant white towel. Another is wound around her head like a turban. She smells fresh and clean and looks like my Cam all stripped of the fancy shit that I love, but that's not her.

She's this: simple and sweet and innocent. She's everything I'm not and I want to protect that about her. Yet just by being with me, it brings out things in her that shouldn't be.

Hateful, like she was tonight when she saw me with Hannah. Damn, that makes a man feel good to see his woman want him, only for her, that bad. But she shouldn't even fuck with the idea of being second to someone else. Not even for a moment. It's impossible.

Careless, like she is when she shows up in places she shouldn't be.

Conflicted with her family because they think she can do better.

Sitting on the edge of her bed, I look up at her. I know I'm switching into fight mode. It happens a day or two before fight night every time. I'm touchy, cross, more than a little ill-tempered. It's exacerbated by the text that sits on her phone a few inches away—a text that offers all the things I can't provide.

"What's wrong with you?" she asks, going into her closet. She rummages around and comes out a few minutes later in the yellow number I love for bed.

"You got a text," I tell her as she climbs onto the bed. I don't move, just sit facing the doorway. "I was lying there and it went off. Thought it was mine and picked it up."

I give her time to read it, process what I've seen, before I look at her. "I don't care who that bastard is, I'm going to dismantle him."

"He couldn't whip his way out of a wet paper bag," Camilla sighs, sinking back in her pillows. "So if that makes you feel more like a man, go for it. Just know if I wanted to beat him up, I probably could."

"That was Barron, wasn't it?"

"Yes."

Exhaling a long, shaky breath, I look at the doorway again. "He really asked you to Paris." It's not a question, although I questioned it before. I know it's true because I read the text. "Some dumb shit asked you to another country."

I could never take her to another country. I can barely take her out of this county. Who is she hanging out with where invitations to France are tossed casually around and why did this Barron Monroe think she was fair game?

"As you can see, I told him no. Which is more, I might add, than you told Red."

"Damn it, Cam," I growl. "I needed the help."

"She looked handy all right."

I twist around the best I can. "I've known her for years."

"I've known Barron since we wore diapers. Does that make a difference to you? Barron also didn't touch me tonight—"

"You better hope he didn't," I say through clenched teeth, the mere thought of it making me want to come unglued as I turn to look at her.

There's a shift between us that wasn't there before tonight. I don't know what caused it or how to fix it, only that I won't be sleeping and I won't be saying anything that will be helpful tomorrow. And by the look on her face, she won't either.

Standing, I grab my shirt off the floor and pull it over my head.

"Where are you going?" she asks.

"Home. I have a bunch of shit to do and I'm not going to sleep anyway."

She sits up, her gown barely covering the tops of her breasts. "I'm sorry, not about Barron because I can't help that. But I am sorry about the Red stuff. I need to let it go."

"Yes, you do." I bend over and give her a simple kiss. "I'll call you tomorrow."

She starts to say something, but I keep walking. It's probably better than me sticking around. We're both irritable and it'll end in a fight. There are no two ways about it.

***

Camilla

"Here they are in green," I say, holding up a pair of yoga pants. "I think she said she has them in a grey now too."

Joy and I search the racks of Halcyon, looking through Ellie's new arrivals. Her business is really picking up, and she and her business partner, Violet, have hired a couple of people to help them. They especially need it now that Ellie's going to be a mama.

"I didn't know you were here," Ellie squeals, coming around the corner from the back. "Why didn't you tell me you were stopping in?"

"It was a last-minute decision," I tell her. "We were having lunch down the street and decided to come in for yoga pants."

"I love hers," Joy gushes. "I need them in every color."

"There are a bunch in the back that we haven't put out yet. Let me go see what's back there."

She disappears, leaving the two of us milling around with a few other customers.

"How are things with Dominic?" Joy asks.

"Good."

"And the lie detector reads that's a lie."

"It's not a lie. They aren't bad. They're just ... not as great as they have been."

"What's going on?"

I shrug again, flipping through a rack of shirts. "I'm mad that this little gym rat keeps hitting on him. He's mad that Barron asked me to Paris."

"Barron Monroe? Ew."

"I know," I sigh. "I'd never go. But it's enough to make Dom frustrated and ready to kill."

"Pardon me for saying this but that would be ... *oh my God.*" Her eyes bug out as she looks over my shoulder. Just as quickly, she goes back to the rack of clothes. "Who in the hell is that?"

Looking back, I laugh. "Hey, Nate!"

"What's up, Priss?"

"You know him?" Joy hisses. "Introduce me."

"Nate, this is my friend Joy," I say as he gets closer. "Joy, this is Dom's brother, Nate."

He stutter-steps as he takes her in, a slow grin splitting his cheeks. "Nice to meet you, Joy."

"Same here. I've heard a lot about you."

"Is that so?"

"Not really," she giggles. "But isn't that what people are supposed to say?"

"Excuse me for butting in," I say, laughing. "What on Earth brings you here, Mr. Hughes?"

"I saw your car and knew this was your family's place. It's driving me crazy hanging on to this check and I wanted to give it to you and not be responsible for it anymore." He takes an envelope from his pocket and extends it to me. "Thank you again, Cam."

I take the envelope, but he pulls me into an unexpected hug before I get my arm back. "You are a great friend," he whispers in my ear. "And you'd be an even better one if you told me Joy doesn't have a boyfriend. Not that I really give a shit, but I need to know which angle to come at it."

Laughing, I pull back and shake my head. "Free," I mouth, watching his eyes light up.

"Joy, do you have any plans for this evening?" he asks, jumping right to the point.

"No. And if I did, it would be nothing I can't move around."

He grins. She swoons. I can't help but giggle.

"Would there be any chance we could hook up and grab some dinner or something?"

"I'd love that."

I leave them standing by the yoga pants and make a beeline for Ellie as she comes back into the room. "I love watching love," I sing-song.

"What did you do now?" she asks.

"I didn't do anything. Fate just swung by and—voila! Dates are being made."

"Nice," Ellie giggles.

Nate says something and Joy throws her head back and laughs. His face is lit up like I've never seen it and it warms my heart for them both. They exchange numbers and Nate heads for the door, stopping short of leaving.

"I'll be right back," I tell Ellie. Making my way across the store, he waits for me. "How'd that go?"

"Lord, she's beautiful. And funny. We're going to dinner at six."

"She'll love you."

"Hey, take it easy," he jokes. "I'm just looking for a lay."

"You are not, asshole. You need a good girl to settle you down, and Joy might be the one to do it."

"Maybe. Maybe not. We'll see."

"Yes, we will." I toe at the rug. "So, how's Dom today?"

"You haven't heard from him?"

I look at the ground, my heart sinking with it. "He's irritated with me. I'm irritated with him. I don't think we're in full-blown avoidance, but the communication isn't flowing either."

"I heard about Hannah," he cringes.

"I hate her."

"I won't fuck her anymore, just for you."

"You're such a jerk," I say, but can't help but laugh. "But Dom?"

He shrugs. "He's good. A little grouchy, but he usually is before a fight. And with that rib ..."

"He shouldn't be fighting, Nate."

"I agree, but he's going to regardless of what we say, so it's always better just to support him and try to help him not get hurt."

"Is that what you suggest I do? Just support him?"

"Always, Priss. Always." He looks at his watch. "I gotta go. I have a few errands to run and then I take over for Liz at the bar. Need anything, call me."

I watch him walk out and jog to his truck. As I watch him climb in, I take my phone out and type a quick text.

ME:I MISS YOU.

DOM:GOING INTO GYM. Talk soon.

TWENTY-SEVEN

DOMINIC

"What the hell is this?" I breathe in the steam radiating off the tea in the china cup in front of me.

"Chamomile." Cam places another bag in a cup that matches mine, all dainty and painted in light pink flower petals, and then pours water on top. "It helps sore muscles, spasms, and inflammation."

"So does whiskey," I offer, taking a sip. It's grassy and flowery and nothing I'll hopefully ever drink again. "Not bad."

"I don't care whether you like it or not, I want you to drink it."

She sits at the table across from me and watches me. I don't know what to say, the weirdness between us from the whole Hannah and Barron bullshit still fresh and heavy. It's stupid. I know it and she probably does too. If I was in this situation with anyone else, it would be so much easier. I'd just walk away.

Fact of the matter is that I'm in this situation with *her*, Camilla Landry, the woman that is the epitome of what they call a "catch." She's the catch of a lifetime, the best thing in the world you could possibly haul in. But then I look at the line I reeled her in with, the boat I'm captaining, and I have to consider that I'm a jackass for doing this to her.

"I can feel it healing me already," I joke, needing to dissipate the stress in the room somehow.

She smiles proudly. "See? I fixed you." She knows I'm kidding, but is playing along with the same need to stop the tension.

It's been two days since the charity event. I don't know why we aren't communicating, but we aren't. Part of it is this upcoming fight —both because she doesn't want me to do it and because I'm focusing on it just to keep from getting hurt. It's the nature of the sport.

"You'll be interested to know," I say, setting the teacup down, "that Nate called off seeing Chrissy tonight. And he told Hannah he was busy."

"Really?"

"He's been very ... *joyful*," I wink.

"Ah," she squeals. "This makes me so happy!"

"She seems nice and I think Nate likes her. At least enough to want to see her again tomorrow night."

"Did he tell you he paid me back?"

"Yeah," I say, taking another sip of the tea. "Did you tell your brothers to fuck off?"

She grins, pulling her legs up on the chair. "I did, actually. I just sent them a group text and told them I had the money so they could stop being worried about me being scammed."

I shake my head, my annoyance rising. "Maybe they'll see us for what we are and not what they think we are."

"I think you're wrong about them."

"Oh, really?" I laugh.

"Yeah, really. I talked to my mom about Paulina and Raquel." She bites her lip to keep from smiling. "She said they were jealous."

"Of course they were. Have you seen me?"

"Oh my God," she laughs. "You sound like Lincoln."

"Don't do that to me."

She laughs again.

"I've missed that," I admit.

"What?"

"That sound. Your laugh," I sigh. "Right now, you look carefree and happy. Like you used to."

Naturally, the look falls from her face at the mention. Her feet go back to the floor and her forehead mars with evidence of how complicated things have gotten.

"What's wrong between us, Dom?" She looks at her teacup, twirling it around on the table. "I hate this."

"I hate this too. I hate it most because I'm the cause of your missing smile."

She frowns, then catches herself and leans forward. "It's not you, Dominic."

"Really? What else is it?"

"It's fighting. And Red," she snarls, then grins so I know she's not completely serious. "It's my brothers and charity events and self-absorbed heirs that invite me to Paris."

"I'm still busting his ass."

She rolls her eyes. "I want things fixed. We have to figure out how to navigate all of this before it causes real problems."

"Can we fix it at all? I mean, really, Cam. How much of this will just keep coming back over and over again because of who we are and what we do?"

"You aren't fighting after this though, right?"

"No," I concede, "but I'll still go down there and train. It's my therapy, and God knows I need therapy. I'm tight with Percy; he's like family to me. You're still going to do charity work because that's who you are. It's ... us, Cam, that's the problem. Not something we can just say we won't do anymore."

Her eyes get watery. I feel like a dick, although I'm trying to be honest. I don't want to hurt her—that would be the last damn thing I do on purpose. But these aren't things we can ignore and we may as well get them out there.

She stands and comes around the table. I scoot back and she

wastes no time sitting on my lap. I rest my head on her shoulder, breathing in her perfume with the scents of the body wash she uses just underneath.

"Tell me we're going to be okay," she demands, swaying slowly back and forth.

"We'll figure it out after the fight." I sit up and touch her cheek. "I can only do one thing at a time and I fight tomorrow. I have to focus on that."

"How are you feeling? Honestly?"

"Better. Not great," I add when she starts to call me out. "But I'll be fine. It's just three rounds."

"Just three rounds," she scoffs.

"Three. Rounds." I take her face in my hands and kiss her, knowing it will be our last kiss before I fight.

Breaking the kiss, I stand and look down at her. "I'll text you tomorrow before I go in the ring. But don't call, okay? I need to get you out of my head or that's all I think about."

"I'm going to be a nervous wreck," she says, wringing her hands.

"Then I'll text you as soon as I win. Promise."

She walks me to the door, that stupid wedge apparent between us.

"Don't forget to text me," she says.

"I won't." I can't help myself. I kiss her again, this time longer and deeper. "Talk to you soon."

"Not soon enough."

TWENTY-EIGHT

DOMINIC

The lockers behind me were once painted black. Before then, they were red. You can tell by the layers of paint peeling away on each and every one of them.

A faucet drips in the shower room next to the locker area I've been put in while I wait my turn in the ring. The room on the other side of the showers is a little nicer and most fighters pick it ... and that's why I pick this one. I'm alone.

Not talking to Camilla last night or all day today seemed like a good idea. But I'm starting to wonder if it was a mistake. I thought I could focus on the fight, but all I've managed is a knot in my stomach that I can't get to go away.

Winning this fight is a must-do. I've trained for it, battered myself for it, and I could use the money. Why I can't block everything else out and feel good about my strategy not only confuses me, it pisses me off.

I trained through the police investigation when I was a kid. I trained through work lay-offs and break-ups with girlfriends and working two jobs. I even managed to focus when I was working towards my HVAC certification. Now, the final fight of my life, and I'm losing my edge.

The crowd roars outside and I hear the announcer over the intercom tell the fans to settle down. It's insane out there, bottles being thrown and brawls starting in the crowd. The energy in this arena, an old warehouse, is all jacked up. That is a distraction in itself.

Voices come down the hall and I listen as they echo. I make out Nate and know it's his fist that slams on the metal door before he opens it.

"Hey," he says, his head sticking in. "How you doin'?"

"Ready to roll."

"Don't sound so enthusiastic." He steps in, but still blocks the door. There's something in his face that causes that knot in my stomach to twist harder. "This will excite you some more. Look what I found."

His arm comes off the doorframe and Camilla walks around the corner. She's working her bottom lip between her teeth as she looks at me with wide, curious eyes.

"What the fuck are you doing here?" I yell, springing to my feet. "Damn it, Camilla! Can't you fucking listen to anything I say?"

"I wasn't going to tell you I was here," she whispers.

"Oh, because that makes it okay. Fuck!" I groan, throwing her what must be a death stare because she flinches, her face paling, but she holds her ground.

She walks to me, her chin up, posture straight, and puts her hand on my arm. I just look at it.

"You do realize I'm expending all the rage I need to be spilling out there, right? When the other guy is trying to kill me?"

"I just wanted to support you."

"You could've done that from home," I seethe.

"Yes, I could've. But I wanted, *needed*, to make sure you're okay."

"There are a thousand people out there just dying to do something stupid tonight and now you are in the mix. How in the hell am I supposed to concentrate when I'm going to be worried about you?"

"How was I supposed to be sitting at home and not worrying about you? Damn it, Dominic! Don't you understand?"

I force a swallow, my eyes trying not to see the emotion in hers.

"This is important to me. *You* are important to me."

"You are important to me too," I gulp. "That's why I don't want you here."

"I'll be fine," she insists. "I'll stay out of the way."

I look at Nate. He understands. He shakes his head in frustration with Camilla, but knows better than to get involved.

"Are you alone?" I ask her.

"Yes."

"Of course you are." Hearing the fight before mine coming to an end, I scramble for a solution. "Nate, get her a seat somewhere high. Out of the way."

"I can take care of myself," she says, narrowing her bright blue eyes.

"Cam, baby, most days I'd say you're right. Tonight, you're wrong." I look at my brother. "Somewhere high."

"I could keep her with me," he offers.

"Fuck, no," I hiss. "The closer you get to the ring, the more shoving and shit happens. Get her out of the way."

"I'm right here," she insists. "Don't talk about me like I'm not here."

"We know you're here. That's the problem." I set my sights back on her. Her attempt at blending in is adorable. Jeans, white sneakers, and a pale purple shirt. "You don't look like the average fight fan."

"Don't be an ass, Dom," she says, fighting the tears in her eyes. "Come on, Nate. Lead me to my seat."

They turn but stop.

"Hey, Dom," Hannah says over the top of their heads. "You about ready to head down to the ring?"

Camilla casts me one final look over her shoulder, a look so full of hurt and anger that I have to close my eyes from seeing it. I know if I don't, I'll be going after her, and I just need to get through this.

When I open them, she's gone.

***

Camilla

"Stay here," Nate tells me, pointing to a seat under a giant American flag. "I'm not kidding, Priss. *Stay here.* I'll come get you when the fight is over."

"I don't need you to come get me."

He looks over his shoulder as Dom's opponent starts towards the ring and then back at me. "I get why you're here. Should you be? No. But I respect that you are, okay? But, listen to me, you should've called me and let me figure this out, not springing it on us."

"I'm going to be fine," I insist. "Make sure *he's* fine. He's the one with busted ribs and an attitude to match a wounded badger."

"That's the plan." He starts down the steps, taking two at a time. He gets to the rail where he has to turn and go down another set of stairs. "Three rounds. Be here when I look up."

"Fine, fine."

I get situated in my seat. There's no one in my immediate vicinity, and as I look around, I'm kind of grateful. The noise in this place, whatever you call it, is incredible. I keep flinching as the crowd roars —I'm not even sure what for most of the time.

Everyone has a drink of some sort, and although I thought smoking was illegal in all public areas, apparently fights are an exception because there's enough smoke in here to give someone cancer.

The longer I sit, the more uncomfortable I feel. Everyone has a pack, a group of people surrounding them. Everyone but me.

Like a tsunami wave that comes from nowhere, I feel every word Dom has said about these things. I must stick out like a sore thumb because Nate found me easily, without even looking, I think. The groups to my right and left have spotted me. The one on my right just kind of snickered and went back to their party. The one on the left seemed more ... interested in me. I focus on the ring in the center of the room, two flights of stairs below, and listen as the announcer calls Dominic's name.

A blast of rock music rips through the building and I see Dom coming up a ramp from the far side. He's shirtless in a pair of dark green shorts, his hands in dark gloves.

The crowd goes wild, definitely louder than they were for his opponent. Every female in the room is whooping and screaming, shouting profanities and lewd suggestions and offers that render me speechless.

I'm on the edge of my seat in every sense of the word. My heart is beating so loud that it nearly drowns out the chaos surrounding me. People are chanting Dom's name, filling in the walkway below to get a better look as he's approved by the referee and enters the ring.

I'm panting, my breath coming in quick, rushed spurts. A burst of activity rumbles from the people to my left, but I can't take my eyes off the ring.

Dom heads to the corner where I see Nate and an older man with "Percy's" written across his shirt in green. The older man is in his face, looking animated, and Dom nods, showing his mouth guard. Then he looks at Nate. Nate points up, at me, and Dom's head turns. Our eyes meet. Even in the midst of all these people in this crazy place, we find each other. I smile at him, holding a hand on my heart. He almost smiles, but not quite. Then he looks away.

They're in the middle of the ring, and before I know what happens, the bell rings.

Everyone is on their feet, yelling, shouting, splashing beer out of cheap plastic cups. There's a flurry of activity from Dom's opponent, but Dom seems to block most of them. Dom fires back with punches of his own, landing a few.

They go round and round, pulling my heart right along with it.

My hands are clenched in front of me as I keep whispering, "Come on, Dom," in repetition.

The clock on the wall starts to wind down and I take a breath of relief. It's a moment too soon.

Dom gets hit by a kick right above his waist on his right side. He drops to one knee.

My heart stops as I spring to my feet, watching as his challenger gears up to take him out.

"No!" I shout, my voice not a drop in the bucket in comparison to the madness around me.

Just as he's within striking distance, the bell rings and the round is over.

I fall back in my chair, landing with a thud. The audience is amped after that display, the close call on Dom, but not me. I can barely breathe.

The stands shift, everyone angling for a better view in expectation of an angsty second round. I, too, head down the steps and stand at the railing. My fingers twist around the rusty metal pole, my eyes glued on Dom in the corner.

He's bleeding from a cut above his left eye. The older man has a giant cotton swab held to it as he yells in Dom's face. Dom turns my way and I see the panic on his face.

He reaches for Nate and they exchange a few words. I realize— they can't see me. I'm not where I'm supposed to be.

Hurrying back to my seat, I trip and fall onto a woman in the aisle on the left.

Her drink, a cheap beer, soaks my shirt. It's the loss of her drink, not the impact, that has her screaming in my face.

I look over my shoulder to the ring just as she plants her hands on my chest and shoves me backwards.

TWENTY-NINE

DOMINIC

"Where the fuck is she?" I shout, panic sitting right in the middle of my throat. "Where is she, Nate?"

I hear Percy tell me to get my head straight, that the bell's gonna ring, but I have to find her.

"Fuck ..."

The way Nate utters that one little word has my gut sinking, my instincts switching gears from self-preservation to protecting Camilla. I follow his gaze to just above the walkway on the second floor. Her purple shirt is all I can see as she goes toppling over two seats.

Nate is gone and I only catch a glimpse of him as he turns a corner at the base of the tunnel to hit the stairs to get to her.

"Cam!" I scream, watching as a black-haired woman stands over her. "Camilla!"

"Fighter, are you ready?"

Ignoring the ref, I look at Percy. "Stall the fight."

"I can't stall the fight. What the hell are you talking about, Hughes?"

The bell goes off behind me as I grab the top rope and begin to climb out of the ring. There's a woman standing over Cam and it's enough to send my adrenaline on an all-time high. I hear the gasps from the crowd, the murmurings, the shouts from the ref to protect myself as I start over the barrier.

Then I feel it. A blast, unchallenged to the side of my face. For a second, I can feel every inch of my face move—my jaw, my nose, my skin. My knees buckle as I'm knocked sideways by the force, my feet slipping, only barely catching me as I take a step to the side to get my balance.

"Come on, Dominic!" Percy shouts.

I look up for Cam, but can't really see. Everything is still blurry from the punch. My head rings, but I'm cognizant enough to know that I'm in trouble.

"Umph," I groan, the wind knocked out of me as a kick, a punch —I'm not sure—rips through my side. My ribs crunch like an accordion, the cartilage separating them smashing.

The pain is blinding. My mouth opens to help my lungs get enough oxygen so I don't pass out. Despite it all, I'm looking up in the stands, trying to focus on Cam.

Getting to my feet, adrenaline tearing through my veins and buffering the intensity of the agony long enough for me to focus, I see Nate with his finger in some guy's face and Cam standing beside him. Watching me.

Movement catches in my peripheral vision and I see my opponent charging in my direction. Knowing I have one good, solid move left in me, I turn my body.

His right arm is pulled back, ready to fire, as he lunges forward. Like a coiled spring, I unleash a left uppercut.

He doesn't see it coming. Doesn't expect it. It gives me a bigger opening and I put every bit of power I can muster into the punch. It hits its target—right under his chin—and he falls backwards, his eyes rolling as he hits the mat.

The bell rings and the ref covers him, waving his arms indicating the fight is over.

Cheers from the crowd filter back into my ears as I look up again, trying to find Cam. Tears stream down her cheeks, Nate at her side. My brother gives me a thumbs-up and I fall to my knees, gripping my side, as the pain becomes unbearable.

My body feels like it's splitting in two, like something inside is definitely wrong. I sway, searching desperately for something to hold on to so I don't pass out.

My arm is lifted by the ref and I'm declared the winner, but it's all secondary to staying conscious. My vision goes in and out.

A smile starts spreading across her cheeks, then falls just as quickly.

A pair of hands are on my shoulders, a lock of bright red hair swishes in front of me. "Dom, are you okay? Where do you hurt?"

I angle around Hannah, my heart racing now for another reason altogether.

My gaze meets Cam's, her smile faltering further as she looks from me, to Hannah, and back to me.

"Move, Hannah," I growl, shuffling to my feet. I wave off the medic as I watch Nate walk a couple of steps behind as Cam makes her way to the stairs.

***

Camilla

"Slow down, Miss," A man with a stethoscope admonishes me as I run by him down the drab hallway. I burst through the door to the locker room, my eyes scanning the rows of lockers until they fall on him.

He's slumped against the wall, his eyes closed, his skin ashen.

"Dom," I blurt, rushing to him. I kneel in front of him, touching his cheek. "Are you okay?"

His eyes flutter open. The blues are full of pain, but when they land on me, the corners of his lips struggle to lift. "Cam." His face twists in pain. "I don't know whether to kiss you or kill you."

"I'm so sorry," I say, my voice at the point of breaking. Seeing him like this, so not like Dom, is something I can barely accept. And to know that my presence helped put him in this situation is unbearable. "I'm so, so sorry."

I'm not sure if he's punishing me by not responding or if he doesn't know what to say. Either way, it hurts my heart. Guilt swamps me as I take him in and my heart shatters into a hundred thousand pieces.

"I shouldn't have come," I say, the words toppling from my lips. "I just wanted to show you I cared, that I supported what you were doing." Tears flow down my cheeks. "I didn't realize ..."

"I told you."

"I know you did," I sniffle. "I know and I should've listened."

He exhales sharply. "This place is no place for you, Cam. You could've gotten killed."

"Well, you know what? This place isn't a place for you either."

"This is what I am, Camilla. This is my version of a charity event."

The fact that he says my full name, something he very rarely does, is not lost on me. I fall back on my heels and look at him through the hot liquid pouring from my eyes.

There's a sadness soaked into his eyes, the way he's sitting, so pitiful, so painful, that I want to break out into a sob right before wrapping him in my arms and taking him home. With me.

"This is not what you are," I insist. "I understand you love to fight. It's weird to me, but I get it. What I don't get is that you would fight for money, that you think it's okay to put yourself in danger like this."

I reach out and touch his cheek. His skin is moist, cool, not like I expect.

"Dom, you are worth so much more than whatever prize money you'll win tonight. Don't you see? Your life is worth way more than that. Your health, your happiness. I ... I need you and I need you to be healthy and happy. You deserve that. You are so, so much more than all of this."

He chuckles and I hear the exhaustion in his voice.

"Let me take you home and put you to bed," I say, offering him my hand. Instead, he looks over my shoulder. I follow his gaze and see Nate and Red.

"What's she still doing here?" Red barks.

Dom starts to say something, but I turn and block his line of sight.

"The question is, what are *you* still doing here?" My hands fly to my hips as I stand as tall as I can. "Get your ass out of this room. You aren't welcome here."

"Well, it isn't your room, is it? Percy paid the fee. I'm an employee. So maybe you need to—"

"Shut the hell up." I take a step to her, looking at Nate in case I get myself in deeper than I can dig out. "Wasn't one Hughes brother enough? Sorry, Nate," I add as an aside, making him chuckle.

Red's jaw drops. "Excuse me?"

"Let me make this crystal clear for you. Get out. Leave Dominic alone. Find another man to throw yourself at, but this time, try to find one that isn't taken, okay?"

Her eyes narrow as she comes towards me. Nate puts a hand in between us.

"Hey," he says, looking at Red. "Time to go."

"Are you blinded by her money too?"

"Go, Hannah."

"Y'all are fucking crazy," she growls.

"Nah, we're being pretty restrained, I'd say," Nate tells her. "If you want to be pissed, be pissed. But keep Cam out of it."

"Oh, protect her," Red glares. "I don't get it. I don't."

"You don't have to get it," Nate tells her. "But that doesn't change the way it is."

She leaves with a direct glare at me as she goes.

"Nate, give us a second, okay?" Dom breaks the quiet.

"I'll grab the car and be around back so we can get you out of here. Sure you don't want to go to the hospital?"

"If it's broken ribs, there isn't shit they can do. I'm not paying that bill."

Walking to Dom again, I feel a shift in the air. A shiver runs down my spine as I take in the look he's giving me.

"Sit down with me for a minute," he says softly.

I do, placing my hand over his. It's cool and damp and makes my stomach churn. "I feel responsible for this. I'm so sorry."

"It's not your fault. It's mine." He heaves a breath, blowing it out slowly. "I should've had you watch from the locker room or at least stood in the tunnel. I just ... I didn't think clearly."

"It's my fault," I assert. "You told me what this was like and I got you hurt ..." My eyes leak again, my heart breaking, the force of which almost knocks my breath away.

"Nate should have the car around in a few minutes. I need to go home and get some meds and try to get some sleep."

"I'll meet you there."

His face is blank. "I, um, I think I should go alone, Cam."

"Why?"

"I have a lot on my mind and I just ... I need some space. I think you do too. You could've gotten hurt worse than me tonight, and by the grace of God you didn't. Think about that, Camilla."

"Don't call me 'Camilla,'" I demand, my breaths turning into hiccups as reality settles on my shoulders.

He hangs his head. It only spirals me harder down, down, down.

"I have thought about it," I say, going back to his point. "I made the decision to come here, and if it was wrong, I'll take the blame. I'll pay my penance. Just don't block me out," I cry.

"I'm not blocking you out. I just ... this was my worst nightmare. At least I got hurt and you didn't."

I can't respond over the lump in my throat. His voice is raspy, but I can't see if he has tears or not through my own. I just sit next to him, breathe him in, and wish for the love of God I'd listened and not come to this stupid fight.

"Can I come see you tomorrow?" I ask, almost a plead. "In the morning?"

He looks away and doesn't respond. Nate comes in and helps him to his feet and they quietly ignore me.

I watch them through the fog, the two men I care about blurring together. Dom finally looks at me.

"Percy is outside. He'll help me, and Nate will make sure you get to your car, all right?"

"Dom, wait. I ..."

He takes my hand and guides me closer. He presses a soft, simple kiss to my cheek. "Go straight home."

"But Dom!"

With a sad smile, he hobbles out the door.

THIRTY

CAMILLA

"Here." Sienna hands me a saucer of cucumber slices. "Put these on your eyes."

"I don't want to put them on my eyes," I pout, taking the dish and setting it on the table beside the porch swing. Tugging the blanket up around my chin, I stare at the lake.

The Farm is the only place I have no memories of Dominic, and it's where I want to be. It's my happy place, my peaceful place. Sienna picked me up this afternoon and came over with me.

I watch the water glisten and think of Dom and wonder if he's feeling better. I called this morning and he didn't answer. So, I did what any logical person would do: I called Joy and had her call Nate.

Whether or not Nate is mad at me too I haven't figured out. I can't remember much about what he said or did last night. I can't remember anything other than Dominic, and as soon as I remember that, I start to cry.

It's a vicious cycle, one that kept me up all night.

"You need to do something," Sienna sighs, sitting beside me. "Or don't go out in public. I don't want anyone thinking you're me."

"You're mean," I say, feeling like I should laugh but not able to actually do it. "What time is it?"

"Five? Maybe six? You've been like this for hours now. You have to sleep at some point, Swink."

"I can't. I close my eyes and I remember seeing him fall. The guy racing to him and not being able to do anything about it."

The tears come again and I feel so stupid for still crying, for breaking down, but there's nothing I can do to stop it. I'm on a Tilt-a-Whirl of emotion.

"I should've listened to him."

"No, he should've listened to you," she suggests. "You shouldn't have gone by yourself, I'll agree with him on that. That was really stupid. But you just wanted to be there for him. There's nothing wrong with that."

"Tell that to his ribs," I say. "Tell that to him. Tell that to my heart."

"So dramatic."

"I mean it. You know, every time I do something I want to do, someone gets hurt. It gets someone in trouble. I guess this is why our brothers treat me like a child, huh? Maybe I am just a child."

"You aren't a child," she scoffs, rolling her eyes. "You are having disagreements with a very alpha male. On one hand, you want to do the things you've seen our family do your entire life. Helping each other, lending each other a few—or ten thousand—dollars," she cringes. "We support each other. How many baseball games did we miss of Lincoln's?"

"None."

"How many of Ford's baseball, soccer, whatever he was doing that season did we not see?"

"None."

"How many of our things did our parents miss? None. See my point?"

"I guess."

"You're just loving the way you know how to love. It's just, with

Dominic, he does things that aren't as ... normal, maybe, as the rest of the world we're used to. And he loves by keeping you from having to deal with a lot of things that are really present in his reality."

Letting the blanket drop from my chin, I pick up a cucumber slice. "He always says we're too different. That we'll always face these problems. Maybe he's right, Sienna."

"Maybe that's a whole bunch of bullshit."

"What's bullshit?"

I turn to see Ford standing in the doorway.

"I was just coming by to do some fishing and saw your car, Sienna. So," he says, coming out and leaning on the rail, "what's bullshit?" He eyes me suspiciously, his lips set in a thin, grim line.

"Cam thinks she should give up on Dominic because they're not seeing eye-to-eye at the moment."

"It's not that," I say, aggravated at my sister. "I went to Dom's fight last night."

"You did?"

"He told me not to and I did it anyway. I'm fine, let's let that be known before I go on," I say. "Some chick shoved me and Dom got distracted and got hurt."

"Is he okay?" Ford asks.

"Yeah. I think. Maybe a broken rib or something. I don't know because he won't talk to me."

"Because you went?"

"Yeah. I should've listened and I didn't. He's furious ... and he should be," I say, wiping away a tear.

Ford takes me in and then surprises me. He smiles.

"Don't smile," I warn him. "This isn't funny."

"It is, kind of. I'm happy Dominic is standing his ground with you."

"What?"

"I'm just saying it's nice having someone look after you instead of us doing it for a change." Ford stands up and looks at Sienna. "What happened when you moved to LA?"

She groans. "Lincoln went with me to get me settled. Graham called every fucking day, set a limit on my credit card, wouldn't let me even pay my rent. The one night I stayed out to party, they called my landlord. Fucking idiots."

"They did?" I laugh.

"She was nineteen," Ford points out. "Do you guys have any idea how many times we've had to bail Lincoln out of things?"

"Yes," Sienna and I say together. We all laugh.

"What about Barrett? Who do you think did his clean-up? Graham. My point is, we look out for each other. We're all just ... dumb ... in different ways. You haven't moved away or had a serious relationship or anything like that. So maybe it seems like we're over-protective. We spend more time with you."

"Maybe that's the answer." I stand up and look at Sienna. "Are you really going to Illinois?"

"I think so," she says warily. "Why?"

"Maybe I should go with you. I can be your secretary," I offer. "I just know I can't stay here if Dom doesn't want me."

Sienna stands but moves shoulder-to-shoulder with Ford. "You can always go with me. But you need to think about that, Cam. Your life is here."

I gaze back across the lawn again. "Not if he's not with me."

***

Dominic

"Sienna brought me an idea she had for the back of the bar," Nate says, attempting to distract me again. Attempt number eighty million. Fail number eighty million. "Wanna see?"

"No."

"Come on," he sighs, tossing the papers on the coffee table. "At least answer her calls."

I look at the phone and see another missed call from Cam. It's midnight. She's usually in bed by now and I wonder what's keeping her up. I could call her. I could answer hers. But I don't because I'm a dick.

"How are you feeling?" he asks, changing tactics.

"Hurt as fuck."

"Your ribs or heart?'

"Fuck you."

"Good answer," he laughs. "You're right about one thing—you're a dick."

"That's what I was just thinking."

We watch the television, some show about giant fish that scares the beejesus out of Ryder. But he's asleep so we can watch it without worry.

I don't even like this show. It must've come on after whatever I was watching before it. A show I couldn't place if my life depended on it.

"Why are you doing this, Dominic? I know you're irritated at her, but she's a good girl."

"Because she's a good girl. It's better this way."

"Is it?"

"Yeah," I glower. "It is."

"You know what I think? I think you need to get over your fucking self."

"If I wasn't broken in half, I'd get up and beat the shit out of you."

"No, you wouldn't. Because you know, somewhere in that thick skull, I'm right."

"This will end sooner or later, Nate. I'll fail her. I'll get her hurt or blacklisted or something. I can't even take care of her. I'm dead weight."

He sits all nonchalantly out of reach, fiddling with the remote in his hands. "What have you ever failed at? You're a hell of a fighter. The best brother a guy could want. A great uncle, you take care of everyone, work your ass off. How do you justify yourself?"

"Last night."

"Oh, when you were too hard-headed to even allow her to be a part of it? That's on you, asshole. Had you just seen her for what she was trying to do, we could've managed that. But, no, let's be all stupid about it and let it get out of control."

I breathe as deeply as I can without coughing, my temples pulsing. "We're lucky it's me in this shape and not her. It could've been her. Why was she there? Why couldn't she have been ... in Paris," I whisper, feeling my heart sink. "I can't give her what she's used to. I can't begin to give her a life like she deserves."

"Are you talking monetary shit? Because she's got that covered," he laughs. I don't. "People are perfect for each other for different reasons, Dom. It's one person's weakness supplemented by the other's strengths and vice versa. She doesn't need money. She needs ... you."

I imagine her face and miss her so much I could cry. I look at the massive catfish on the television and force a swallow. "What are you? A therapist?'

"A bartender. So, yeah, basically."

My phone rings. I look at Nate.

"Answer it," he insists. "I'll be in my room. Yell if you need help to the car."

"To the car?"

"To go see her," he smiles.

On the third ring, I can't take it and scoop it up. It's not her number and I can't deny that it disappoints me. "Hello?" I ask.

"Dominic?"

"Yeah. Who's this?"

"Hey, this is Ford Landry," he says, sounding surprised.

"Is Cam okay?"

He laughs. "She's fine. She doesn't know I'm calling. I don't sleep a lot, so I was just going to drop you a message for morning."

"I don't sleep either." I struggle to sit up in my chair. "Look, I'm guessing you heard about the fight."

"I did, but I'm not calling about that."

"You aren't?" I ask, surprised.

"No. Mike, a security guy for Landry Security, quit tonight. He's moving back to Utah or someplace and I'm down a guy. I know you're injured at the moment and don't expect an answer right away, but I really think you'd be a great fit."

My mouth drops and I almost drop the phone. "Did Cam put you up to this?"

He laughs again. "No. She doesn't know I'm even thinking about it, actually. According to Sienna, she's been crying for the last twenty-four hours or so."

"That's my fault."

"Then you better fix it."

"The best solution might not be the answer she wants to hear."

"As long as you do what's best for her, that's all I ask, man. And I have a feeling you will."

There's a long silence, both of us letting this conversation sink in. Finally, Ford speaks. "If you aren't interested, that's fine. But if you are and think you and Camilla are going to split, I can assure you that my business and Cam are separate. There wouldn't be an issue." He clears his throat. "She's thinking of moving to Illinois with Sienna anyway."

"She what?" I burst.

"That's what she said. If she can't work it out with you, she's just going to leave."

I shake my head, trying to lift the fog. She's leaving? She can't leave. She can't leave me.

"Let me ask you a question," I say.

"Yeah, sure. Shoot."

"Why do you want to hire me?"

"You're smart. You're fearless. I know you're dependable and a hard worker because I might've checked some references. You're loyal." He takes a deep breath. "I was there last night, Dominic."

"What?" I must've misheard him. "What did you say? You were where last night?"

"Graham and I slipped in the back and watched the fight. We knew Cam was going."

"How did you know?"

"Because that's what we do. She's a Landry. If she loves you, she'll stand behind you one hundred percent. So when we found out you were fighting, there was no doubt she'd go. And we wanted to see what you were made of, to be honest. You're impressive. Very, very impressive."

"You saw what happened?"

"Of course I did. I couldn't imagine being you in there and having Ellie up in the stands like that. I would've died."

"I feel like I did," I wince, getting situated again.

"How are you feeling?"

"Like I almost died," I chuckle, which causes a stabbing sensation to rip through me.

"Get some rest. Think about my offer. Call me when and if you're ready."

"I will. Goodnight."

"Goodnight."

THIRTY-ONE
CAMILLA

"That was amazing, Vivian," Ellie says, rubbing her stomach. "It's safe to say the baby likes your roasted chicken."

"I'm not pregnant and my stomach likes it too," Danielle laughs, giving Ryan a bottle.

"You could be pregnant. Wanna try again?" Lincoln says, wiggling his eyebrows. "We could go for twins this time."

"You can't go for twins," Sienna points out. "And didn't you tell us you were only having one baby after you almost passed out in the delivery room?"

"I did," Lincoln admits, "but it's been awhile. I forgot about how much it hurts."

"Again," Danielle says as we all laugh, "*I* had the baby. Not you."

We're draped around the family room of the Farm. There are so many of us now that Mom had new furniture brought in to hold us all. Even still, Mallory, Huxley, and Graham are sitting at the bar in the kitchen.

Everyone is telling stories, making plans, having a good time like we always do together. I sit next to Sienna on a love seat. She's laughing at something Barrett said, something I missed.

She elbows me in the side. "Hey, you okay?"

"Yeah."

"Heard from Dom today?"

I shake my head, my spirits plummeting even more if it's possible. With each hour that passes that he doesn't call or text me, I feel him drifting away. Joy suggested I just show up at his house, but I'm scared. I don't think I could take the rejection face-to-face, not without the adrenaline of fight night. She's kept me posted on Dom's recovery and that he's looking better and getting around better. He'll go to work tomorrow, and I worry how he'll handle that.

I miss him. Lord, I miss him.

Each morning, I look for his good morning texts. I wait for the mid-afternoon selfie of him at work. At night, I wait for him to check in to see if I made it home or to roll over and see him next to me.

I miss the safety of his arms, the security of his smile. The feeling of having someone to take care of and knowing someone wants to take care of me.

Looking away from my sister, I dab at my eyes. They're still swollen, but no one has asked. I think they know. Dad gave me a pained glance and a longer hug than usual, but that's the only difference from normal.

"Do you remember?" Sienna asks me.

"Remember what?"

"That yoga position we saw in the magazine. Where it was like an adult version of airplane?"

My spirits lift, the fog thinning just a bit as the excitement of our plan kicks in. "Yeah. Did you see that, Mallory?"

"I have no idea what you guys are talking about," she says.

"Come here." Sienna takes my hand and clears Ford from the middle of the floor. She lays on her back and holds her legs up in the air. I put my hands in hers and her feet go to my belly. She winks. "Ready?"

"Yup."

She extends her legs and I hop a little, but instead of balancing at the top, I fall over her head and somersault away. "You're not strong enough, Sienna."

"I am too. Try it again."

"You two are ridiculous," Ford laughs. "Want to try it, Lincoln?"

"Fuck you," Lincoln says. "You'd drop me on purpose."

"Language, Lincoln," Mom warns, leaning her head on Dad's shoulder.

Sienna gets back in position and I jump, but fall intentionally again. "You're too weak. Come here, Mal."

Mallory gets up and joins us on the floor.

"You need to figure this out," I insist. "They said in the magazine it's one of the best moves for mental clarity."

"And soul happiness or something," Sienna adds, ad-libbing her way through this and earning a glare from me.

"Anyway," I say, trying to stay on target, "can you envision what we mean?"

"Kind of."

"Ugh," I say, trying to hide my smile. "G, get down here. I don't think I'm strong enough either."

"I'm not playing yoga games."

"Oh, but you are," I tell him, knowing he'll come. "Mal's been bragging about you."

"You are getting so good," Mallory tells him. She looks surprised when he stands up and takes off his jacket, hanging it on the back of the chair.

"Is G turning into a yogi?" Lincoln teases. "I'll buy you a mat for Christmas."

"Stop it," Dani shushes him. As a response, he takes Ryan from her.

"Lie down," Sienna tells Graham, pointing to the floor.

Graham lies on his back. "Now what?"

"Put your feet on Mal's stomach," I say, moving Mallory so she's in the right spot. "Now hold hands."

Graham pushes up and Mallory is horizontal in the air above Graham.

"I haven't done this since I was a kid," she exclaims. "I didn't think about this as yoga."

The rest of us exchange grins and wait. Graham works one hand free from Mallory's and slips it in his pocket. Mallory is telling a story about yoga class and isn't prepared to look down and see a diamond ring nestled in a pretty blue box.

"Oh my God," she says, forgetting about her story. Her free hand flies to her mouth. She twists on Graham's feet, but he holds her still. "Graham. What the hell?"

"You've come into my life and messed it all up. I mean that," he says softly, making us laugh. "I can't find a thing in my kitchen and my calendar is a mess of pink and yellow highlighters. You make me go out of my mind."

"Don't forget the clothes on the floor," Sienna chimes in.

Mallory's tears drip to Graham's shirt, her hand trembling as she watches him.

"I never thought I'd be able to handle having a life that wasn't in my control," he continues, his voice starting to crack. "But when I look at my life now and imagine it going back to the way it was—organized and clean—I hate it. Because that means you'd be gone."

"Graham ..." she whispers.

"Mallory, will you please do me the honor of being my life?"

"Your life?" she asks, her voice trembling.

"My life. My wife. All of it. Will you?"

"Yes," she says, full-on sobbing. She tries to get down to hug him, but ends up falling ungracefully onto his chest. He holds her to him, whispering things only they can hear in her ear.

My tears stream just as hard as Mallory's. Where her heart is full, mine is so achingly empty.

Sienna puts her arm around me and the contact kills me. I can't take it anymore. I bury my face in her shoulder and let the tears fall.

If I could get up and go to the bathroom without everyone seeing my face, I would. But it's too late.

Barrett stands and puts his arm around Mallory. "You're crazy for putting up with him, Mal, but we love having you in the family. You temper him a little. We're all thankful. Especially Lincoln. Congratulations!"

Everyone descends on the newly engaged couple as they get to their feet, trading hugs and congratulations. Mallory can't stop crying long enough to say anything and she won't let go of Graham's arm. He doesn't seem to mind. He's beaming like the little kid that found the golden egg at Easter.

"Excuse me, Mr. Landry," Troy says from the doorway, his voice only barely heard over the roar of the celebration. Everyone settles and looks at Barrett's right-hand man.

"Since when do you call me Mr. Landry?" Barrett asks. "You want a raise or what?"

Troy laughs. "I'm talking to Mr. Landry. Harris."

"What can I do for you, Troy?" Dad asks.

"There's a visitor here that's not on the gate list. He says he's here to see you."

"What's his name?"

"Dominic Hughes."

I gasp. Everyone looks at me as I sit with eyes the size of saucers, looking at Troy. "Did you say Dominic Hughes?"

"Yes."

Dad's eyes flip to me and then back to Troy. "Let him in, please."

"He's here?" I ask Sienna. My heart flips, my stomach rolling, my hopes spiraling way too high to be safe. "Why is he asking for Dad?"

"I don't know," she tells me. "Guess we'll see soon enough."

My attention fixes on the doorway. Everyone settles down, some refilling their drinks, until Troy comes back in. "Mr. Hughes is here."

My breath is held hostage in my chest as I wait for Dom to come into view. When he does, I just cry.

He's wearing a pair of dark jeans and a light blue shirt that matches his eyes. He has the sleeves rolled up because he hates them cinched around his wrists. The top two buttons are undone on the collar as well for the same reason.

His eyes survey the scene in front of him. I can't imagine what he thinks of us all. He seems a little overwhelmed and a lot nervous as he tucks his hands in his pockets.

Finally, his sight sets on me. A lump spontaneously appears in my throat, my eyes blurry again, as Sienna takes my hand and squeezes it.

"Mr. Landry," Dominic says, walking across the room and extending a hand to my father. "I'm Dominic Hughes."

Dad stands up and shakes his head, not looking nearly as shocked as I would've imagined. "It's nice to meet you."

He moves to my mother, who remains sitting. "It's nice to meet you, Mrs. Landry."

"It's Vivian, dear. But, yes, it's a pleasure to meet you as well."

Alison giggles, looking at me. Barrett glares at her.

Dom nods to Mom, retreating a few feet back closer to the doorway.

With each movement, he flinches. He's trying hard to seem like he's not in pain, but I can tell by the way he favors his side. The way his teeth clench. The way his eyes lack the spark I'm used to seeing.

He takes a deep breath and blows it out. "I didn't expect so many of you," he admits, looking a little bewildered. Finally, he looks at me again.

His eyes soften, his shoulders sag, and I can tell he wants to tell me to, "Come here," like he always does.

"What are you doing here?" I ask softly.

"Good question. A lot of judgements have been passed—from you about me, me about some of you. It's easy to do that, I guess, when you don't really know the other people or anything about them."

"Your brother still owes me a bottle of Patrón," Lincoln says.

"Lincoln, now isn't the time," my father says, bending forward to look at his youngest son. "I'm sorry, Dominic. Go on."

"Yeah, um, you all love her a lot. And I didn't understand that for a long time. Not why you love her—that's obvious," he blushes. "But this big interaction you all have. I just have a brother and it's been the two of us for a long time. This whole thing," he says, moving his arm in a circle indicating us, "is new to me."

"It gets easier," Alison chimes in. "Trust me. I'm not from this sort of family either."

This seems to settle Dom a bit. He looks at me, his eyes completely sober. "I've worried a lot that I wouldn't be able to take care of her. Not like she's used to. I mean, look around. I can't give her these things."

"I'm her father," Dad says calmly. "I'll give her these things. You don't have to worry about that. I've worked my tail off for decades to give my children this. It's your job, if you choose to take it, to give her the things I can't."

Tears trickle down my cheeks as my father stands.

"Son, having a family, whether it's two people or twenty, is a team effort. I couldn't have done it without Vivian. We couldn't have done it without our parents and now without our children, Alison, Danielle, Ellie, Mallory, and even Huxley and Ryan. It's all of us, working together, filling in where the others fall. Take, for instance, Lincoln. I can bail that boy out of all kinds of legal issues, but who is going to make sure his head is on the pillow at night? Who's going to give him children? Who is going to make sure he gets a hair cut—which you need, by the way," Dad says, looking at Linc. "Dani does those things, God love her."

We all laugh while Lincoln just shakes his head, pretending to cover Ryan's ears. "Always me. It's *always* me."

"You're too easy," Ford tells him.

"I don't ask my children to vet their significant others. We have Graham for that," Dad deadpans, making us all laugh. "But I do ask them to pick someone that makes them happy. That puts them first. If they have a skill I can use in the family business, that's a plus," Dad laughs.

"Sir, with all due respect," Dominic begins, "I understand that. But I want to be transparent with you. There are things about me that you might not know, and I ... I don't want any secrets. Before I ask your daughter to forgive all the things I said and implied, I wanted to come to you and lay all this out there. I don't want it coming back to bite me in the ass later."

"Language, Dominic," Mom grins.

His eyes go wide. "I'm sorry."

"Don't be," Lincoln sighs. "I get it all the time."

"Let's hope Dominic is more fearful of me than you are."

"Being that you sign my birthday cards 'Mommy,' there's probably a good chance."

We laugh again, but my eyes are on Dominic.

"I know a lot about you. I knew of your father years back," Dad says, alluding to the accident but not bringing it specifically. "I know of the infamous loan *that was paid back*," he says, emphasizing the last part and looking at Graham. "I also know you're related to Nolan, and for that, I give you my deepest sympathies."

Dom smiles. "And that's all okay with you? If I can get this fixed, I would like to know, for both of us, that we're solid here."

Dad pats him on the back, taking Dom by surprise. "You know what?"

"What?"

"I like you. It took a lot of balls to come in here and say what you said. Whether Camilla takes you back or not, that's up to her. And make no mistake about it, I will always side with my baby girl."

"Yes, sir."

"But I do like you. Ford was talking to me yesterday about maybe hiring you on at Landry Security. I think you'd be a good fit."

I look at Ford who smiles sheepishly back at me. "What's Dad talking about?" I ask Sienna.

"I guess Ford offered Dom a job."

"He did what?"

Ford bites his lip and watches me warily.

"So they didn't tell you Ford and Graham went to the fight ..." She makes a face and scoots away from me.

Ford now looks away, a mischievous smile on his face. Graham won't look at me either, but my anger evaporates when Dominic is suddenly standing in front of me. He holds out his large, calloused hand.

"Want to take a walk?"

Looking up at his handsome face, I see the man I've been falling in love with for months, even if I was scared to admit it to myself. And seeing him here, after everything, is enough to make me fall in love all over again.

"Yes, please."

THIRTY-TWO

CAMILLA

The sun is bright on my face as we take the path off the side of the house and head towards the tree line. My hand is tucked in Dom's and he's holding it like it's his lifeline.

"There's a picnic table just beyond those trees," I say. "We can sit there."

"Okay."

We walk quietly until we're through the trees and at the little wooden table. It has all of our initials carved in it. I sit on one side, Dom sits on the other.

"How do you feel?"

"Better today. How are you?"

"Sad."

He runs his hands down his face. "Cam, I'm sorry."

"I'm sorr—"

"No, baby, listen to me. *I'm sorry*. For a lot of things."

"I went and was told not to. I see why now. I got you hurt. That's really hard to live with."

"Let's forget about that night, okay? If we're going back with twenty-twenty vision, I shouldn't have fought. I was hurt as fuck to start with and was being hard-headed about doing it. It was like I was proving to myself I could. I don't know. It was stupid."

"It was stupid."

He takes my hand and holds it in the center of the table. "Fact of the matter is this: I shouldn't have pushed you away like I did. I was mad. Maybe that was valid. But ... I've never had someone treat me like you do. With respect. With loyalty. You showing up there to support me just blew my mind. I thought I could tell you to stay home and you would. No one has ever cared about me like that."

"Of course I do, Dom. It hurts me when I'm not a part of something you're doing. Like I can't be a part of your life because it's off-limits to me. But then I see Red and she certainly can, and I don't mean to bring her up because I know she's nothing to you, but it makes me jealous that she can have that part of you in any way at all and I can't."

"I guess I always thought you shouldn't or wouldn't really want a part of it. It's a dirty, nasty world. Why would you want to be in it?"

"Because you're in it. And I want to be wherever you are. Don't you see that?"

He rubs a small circle on the back of my hand, a sexy smile drifting across his face. "Come here."

My favorite words fall on my ears, causing a spatter of goose-bumps to dot my skin. I stand and walk around the table to him, sitting next to him but facing the other way.

He takes my hand and laces our fingers together, resting them on his thigh. "Let's do this. For real this time," Dom says. "And by that I mean no excuses. We're all in. If you don't think I'm good enough for you, tell me now. Because once you commit, I'm holding you to it."

"Hold me to it, please." I look at our hands. "And if you think I'm too much of a liability to you, tell me now. Because once I commit, I'm definitely holding you to it."

"Please do."

We exchange smiles, like we used to before the fight, and I feel my insides melt. He leans forward, his lips hovering over mine. His breath is hot and spicy and I can taste the desire in the air.

"Cam?"

"Yeah?"

"Can I tell you one more thing?" he asks, brushing the pad of his thumb over my bottom lip.

"Yeah."

"Make it two."

Laughing, I pull away, squeezing my legs together to dull my pulsing core. "What is it?"

"I cleaned out my locker today at Percy's. I told him I wouldn't be back in, at least not for a long time."

"You didn't have to do that," I tell him.

"I did. It's time to find other coping mechanisms for things. Guess it might have to be your body," he shrugs.

"Oh, darn," I deadpan.

Laughing, he looks at me with that killer smile. "The other thing?"

"Yes?"

He takes a deep breath, the smile on his face the widest I've ever seen it. "I love you, Cam."

"I love you too, Dom."

EPILOGUE

Camilla

One month later ...

"Do you have to go?" I hold my sister in my arms. We've done this before, said goodbye as she heads out on a new adventure, but this time feels different. "Stay here. Please."

"Oh, stop it," Sienna laughs, pulling away. "You can come visit me anytime. The next time Dominic turns into an ass, just hop a plane and come to Illinois."

"I still don't get the whole Illinois thing," Lincoln says. "What do they know about fashion there? Isn't it like cornfields or something?"

"Soybeans, I think," Ford adds. "Either way, get going or you won't make it far by nightfall."

I walk with Sienna to her car. It's loaded down with all the stuff she didn't want to send with the moving truck. Troy and Nate helped get the final few things loaded while Sienna, Joy, and I made a last trip through her house earlier this morning.

Dom watches me from the porch of The Farm. He's talking to Barrett and Huxley about fishing, something I didn't know he knew about. He gives me a sweet smile as I say goodbye to my sister.

Things have been good between us the last few weeks. We're taking it slow, one day at a time, but it feels like we've already been together forever ... it's just different now.

There's no second guessing, no worries about outside influences. The only thing I have to worry about is my mom getting all flustered when Dom's around. She thinks he's the cutest thing she didn't birth since my father.

Joy finishes her goodbye with Sienna and she and Nate take off, leaving our family to have a few moments alone. Mom and Dad go over the last-minute instructions about not talking to strangers, no picking up hitch hikers, and keeping your doors locked.

"It's not like she hasn't done this before," Ford tells Mom. "Let her get out of here."

Mom dabs at her face with a handkerchief. "I hate to see you leave, sweetheart, but I know you have to do what you have to do."

"I'll come back. You know that," Sienna promises.

"Here's a few bucks," Dad says, handing her a wad of cash.

"I have a credit card."

"And she knows how to use it," Graham sighs. He pulls her in for a hug. "I'm heading into the house. Good luck to you. Call if you need anything."

"I will, G," she says, kissing his cheek. "Congrats on the engagement. You should elope to Vegas. I'll be your attendant."

"No Vegas weddings in this family," Mom interjects. "Goodness. Are you trying to kill me?"

Graham laughs, joining Barrett and Dom on the porch. Ford says his goodbye, followed by Lincoln. Before I know it, it's just me and Sienna.

"Once I get settled, we'll make plans to meet up. I heard the boys in Illinois are super cute. You can be my wing girl."

"Dom's totally not going to go for that," I laugh. "But I'm all about coming to see you."

She looks at Dom and gives him a little wave. "He's good for you. I'm proud of you for fighting for what you want."

We hug again. I feel Dom's palm rest on the small of my back as I give my sister a kiss on the cheek.

"I'll miss you," I tell her. "Be careful. Call me a lot."

"I'll miss you too. And call me and keep me posted on everyone. And don't let Graham elope without me. And I want to know any murmurings of baby names from Alison or Ellie. And try to work in Jane, since it's both of our middle names."

Laughing, I watch her get in her car. "I love you, Sienna."

"Love you back, Cam."

"Bye, everyone!" She starts the car and rolls down the window. "If you want a vacation, come see me!"

I lean against Dominic as we watch my twin sister speed off, honking the horn just before she's out of sight.

"How do you feel?" Dom asks me, knowing I've worried about this for weeks.

"A part of me feels like crying. But a bigger part of me knows she's just off for another adventure." I look at him and smile. "She'll be back."

"How do you know?"

"Because we're Landry's. We always come home."

The End

Want to read Sienna Landry's story?
It's available now in CRANK, the first book in
the Gibson Boys Series.

Chapter One is next!

MORE FROM ADRIANA LOCKE

Crank
Chapter One

Walker

"I'm not taking you to the hospital."

Peck teeters on the edge of one of Crave's billiard tables. He sways back and forth, his sneakers squeaking against the cheap wood over the chatter of the patrons of the bar. "You don't think I can land a back flip off here?"

The truth is I'm pretty sure he could. My cousin has the reflexes of a cat. The problem is he also has nine lives, and I'm sure he's used up eight of them already.

"The question isn't if you can land it. It's how bloody the end result would be," I say, taking a sip of beer. "And I'm not trying to splint a head wound. Can you even do that?"

"*You* could. Look at my arm." He holds his left forearm in front of him, his watch catching the light from the new fixtures above. "This is some of your best work."

Memories of splinting Peck's arm with nothing but a belt, a bar towel, and a Playboy rush through my mind, as does loading him into the back of my truck for a quick trip to the emergency room.

"I really think I can do this," Peck insists, working his shoulders back and forth.

Downing another drink, hoping I'm good and hammered before Peck attempts this disaster, I look across the table. My older brother, Lance, is watching me as he brings an Old-Fashioned to his lips. We exchange a look, both of us waiting for Machlan to catch wind of Peck's antics and throw him out of Crave. Again.

"What's the worst that could happen?" Peck asks. "Another broken arm? I mean, I think I can get the rotation fast enough to not land on my head."

"I think it's your turn to take him to the hospital," I tell Lance.

He coughs, choking on his drink. "Yeah, I don't think so."

"Remember how hot that nurse was last time?" Peck asks, wiggling his brows. "Actually, that kind of makes me want to go for it now just in case she's on duty."

"She's not," Lance chimes in. "I think she was fired after the Hospital Administrator found her fuck-foundered in triage three the night of your broken arm."

"Peck! Get your fucking ass down." Machlan's voice rips through the bar, booming over the crowd.

Everyone quiets a few notches, not quite scared of my younger brother, but not willing to test his boundaries either. His reputation as a man you don't want to tangle with without a small army definitely helps his cause when it comes to managing his bar. Peck, on the other hand, just rolls his eyes.

"Just one jump, Mach! One. Uno. I got this." Peck gives Machlan his best shit-eating grin before looking at me and Lance. "If he throws me out, I'll be back in a couple days. Hell, he threw me out on Tuesday and I was back on Thursday for corn hole."

"I think that just means you're in here too much," Lance offers.

Peck starts to respond but his attention is redirected as Molly

McCarter saunters by. The dim lighting does nothing to hide the exaggerated sway of her hips or the way she licks her lips as her sight sets on *me*.

Bracing for what may come out of her mouth, I fill mine with alcohol.

"Hey, Walker," she says, stopping at my chair. Her hands rest along the top rung, her fingertips sliding across the back of my neck. "Hey, Lance."

Lance tips his glass her way.

"I was thinking," she purrs, "my car is way overdue for an oil change. Maybe I could bring it to Crank sometime this week, Walker? Do you think you could *fit it in?*"

"I'm pretty full this week," I lie, ignoring her thinly veiled offer. "See what Peck has available."

A huff whispers through the air and she pivots on her heel. "Thanks anyway."

"I can get you in ..." Peck's voice drowns into the Crave chaos as he follows her towards the bar.

He tails after her, all but drooling, as she slides onto a bar stool. Her gaze flicks to mine, her knees spread just a little farther apart than a lady ever should. Then again, no one has ever called Molly a lady.

"Ever fuck her?" Lance asks, downing the rest of his drink as he turns back to me. "I've been tempted to a couple of times and did get a decent blow job one Halloween when she was dressed up in this nurse outfit."

"What is it with you and nurses?"

"Think about it: they're smart, make good money, work a lot so you have free time, and they're used to getting dirty," he smirks. "It's like a straight shot to my dick."

"And they're good with needles, have access to medicines that can make you lose your mind, and I've never met one who didn't have a warped sense of humor," I counter. "They set off my crazy radar."

Lance laughs. "Did that radar just start working? Because I

distinctly remember you getting balls deep with some psychologi-cally-challenged women. One in particular."

"Are you feeling froggy tonight? Because if you keep that mouth runnin' like that, I'm about to knock those glasses off your face."

I'm kidding. More or less. The problem is Lance knows it.

"Oh, go to Hell," he laughs.

"Already there, brother. Already there."

He takes his glasses off his face and places them on the table. "I usually look at your life and think I'd hate to have it. But after the day I had today, I'd trade you places."

"What? Did the high school kids refuse to learn about the Amer-ican Revolution?" I laugh. "You have such a cush job."

"I'm a professional."

"A professional bullshitter, maybe."

He makes a comeback, but it's swallowed in the roar of the crowd as a popular song blares through the overhead speakers.

Crave, an old brick building along Beecher Street, is longer than it is wide, and pulses with the noise of the crowd and music. Alcohol ads, high school sports schedules, and a giant cork board adorn the walls. The latter is a good read and filled with letters and notes from one townsperson to the next. Affairs have been called out, coon dogs found, marriage proposals made, and entire conversations about who is working what shift at the factory have taken place on that thing. It's been a mainstay of the bar since our uncle founded it almost fifty years ago. When our younger brother, Machlan, took over Crave thanks to Uncle George's failing liver, he extended the wall of cork-boards all the way to the door.

"That's new," Lance says, moving over one seat closer to me. Motioning to the phallic design made up of yellow rubber duck Christmas lights on the wall between the pool tables, he laughs. "Let me guess: that's Peck's handiwork."

"Naturally. Machlan wasn't thrilled, but Peck rallied the masses and they convinced him to keep it."

"It is nicely done," Lance says, chewing on the end of his glasses. "I can see the art in it."

"Fuck. I should've been an artist if that counts as art."

"Apparently things didn't go well with Molly," Lance says, twisting in his chair.

"She's never gonna give Peck a chance."

At the sound of his name, Peck walks through the front door. He stops just inside, the glow from the exit sign giving his mop of blond hair a pinkish hue.

Peck makes a beeline for our table, a look etched in the lines on his face that sends a ripple of concern up my spine. After growing up with him and then working with him for the last few years, I can read him like a book. Something is wrong.

"What's going on?" I ask, scrambling to my feet as he gets closer.

"Walker, man, you need to get outside," Peck says. "Someone just bashed the front of your truck."

"What?" I hiss, sure I misheard him. "Someone did fucking what?"

"Yeah, man. You need to get out there."

Blood ripping through my veins, I plow my way through the bar. Machlan lifts his chin, sensing something is off, but I shake my head as we pass. I know he loves a good fight, but this one is mine.

Lance is on my heels as we make our way through the crowd. "Who did you piss off now?"

"Someone who wants to die, apparently." My fingers flex against the wood of the door, the warm summer air slamming my face as I hit the sidewalk. "You sure you don't want to stay inside? I think getting into a street fight is against your teacher code of conduct."

"Fuck off," Lance chuckles. "I'll have Peck hold my glasses and I'm in."

"You, my brother, are an intelligent heathen."

"I'll take that as a compliment. I think."

The top of my black pickup truck comes into view, sitting

beneath one of the few lamps lining Beecher Street. There are two people standing on the sidewalk next to my truck.

"Do we know them?" I ask Peck through gritted teeth.

"I promise you we've never seen them before."

"So it's not ..." Lance doesn't finish his sentence. "*Holy shit.*"

The two women turn to face us and I think all of our jaws drop. The first is tall with jet black hair and a strong, athletic build. It's the second one who has me struggling to remember why we're out here.

Long, blonde hair with faint streaks of purple and the brightest blue eyes I've ever seen, she assesses me in the hazy streetlight. She doesn't make a show of looking me over like most women do, batting their eyelashes like some damsel in distress. There's something different about her, a quiet confidence that makes her almost unapproachable.

Unapproachable, but still hot as fucking hell.

My gaze drifts down her ample chest, over the white lace fabric of the top that hugs the bends of her body. Cutoff denim jeans cap long, lean legs that only look longer next to the Louisville Slugger half-hidden behind her.

It takes a ton of effort, but my eyes finally tear from her body and to the body of my truck. Sure enough, there's a rip across the grill and a broken headlight that looks an awful lot like a slam from a baseball bat. It's nothing that can't be fixed in my shop, but that's not the point. The point is the disrespect.

"Either of you know what happened?" I ask, leaning against the hood. They remain silent. The only response is a dashed look between them.

Settling my scrutiny on each one individually, watching them squirm, I save the blonde for last.

"Did you see anything?" I ask, turning back to the tall one.

Her weight shifts from one foot to the other as she runs a hand through her shiny hair like we're talking about coffee or having a beer later. "Me? No. I didn't see a thing."

"Really? You were standing out here just now and you didn't see anything?"

"No," she smiles sweetly. "Nothing at all."

Peck steps between us and inspects the damage. When he turns around, he bites the inside of his cheek. "If I were a betting man, Walker, I'd say it looks like someone walloped Daisy with a baseball bat."

The blonde lifts a brow, something on the tip of her tongue that she holds back.

"You got something to say?" I prod.

"You named your truck 'Daisy'?"

Her eyes narrow, almost as if she's taunting me. That she has the guts to challenge me combined with those fucking blue eyes throws me off my game. "I did. Got a problem with that?"

"No. No problem," she says, twisting her lips into an incredibly sexy pout that I want to kiss off her goddamn face. "Just never met a man who named their truck after a flower."

"Me either. Now, before I go calling the Sheriff about this, I'm gonna give you two a moment to consider telling me what happened. And," I say, cutting off the blonde, "I'll give you a piece of information before you decide what to say. Doc Burns' office has cameras installed that will show everything. Just let that sink in a second."

Their eyes go wide as they instinctively move together into a protective huddle. The tall girl points to the blonde who responds with a frantic whisper. She's guilty as hell.

On one hand, I want to break her down and get inside her in ways she's never dreamed. On the other, I can hear my brain issuing an alert to back away slowly.

The longer they confer, the more time I have to watch. The blonde controls the conversation, the other deferring to her as they talk amongst themselves. It's hot as hell.

The light bounces off the wounded plastic of the headlight and draws my attention back to the fact that Daisy is damaged, and in all likelihood, one of these two did it.

"You really calling Kip?" Peck whispers. "He's not gonna do shit about this, you know."

"He might throw them in the back of his cop car and fuck their brains out. Especially the blonde," Lance whistles. "Can you imagine her in handcuffs? *Shit*."

The thought shoots a flame through my veins that catches me off guard. The vision of her bound up with one of these assholes at the helm irks me. Bad. "You two stay out of this. Let me handle it."

The sound of metal pinging against the ground rings through the air. The girls jump, the blonde leaping away from the aluminum bat as it rolls across the sidewalk and lands in the gutter with a flourish. Her eyes snap to mine, guilt etched across her gorgeous face. "It was an accident."

"How, exactly, does a baseball bat accidentally strike the front of my truck?" I ask. "Did it just hop over there and smash itself into my headlight?"

"Well," she gulps. "I ..."

"She was imitating her brother," the dark-headed one says. "So we stop using pronouns, I'm Delaney. This is Sienna."

"I'm Walker. That's Peck and Lance." I rest my attention on Sienna. She's leaned against the grey car, her arms crossed over her chest. "So?"

"I was swinging the bat," she says, "while Delaney puked over there and it slipped out of my hands."

"I think we're gonna have to see your swing," Peck chuckles.

Sienna rolls her eyes. "You do *not* need to see my swing."

Imagining her ass popped out, her body moving for our benefit, seems like a fair trade for the hassle of dealing with this tonight.

"How else do we know it was you? It could've been Delaney and you're just covering for her," I explain, loving the frustration on her beautiful face. "Gonna need to see the swing."

"No."

"Lance, call Sheriff Kooch."

"Wait," Sienna sighs. "It *was* an accident. I can cut you a check for the repairs but please don't call the police. I ... I can't have a record. You don't understand."

Looking away, it takes everything I have not to laugh. The plea in her voice is so damn adorable it almost makes me give in. Yet, she hasn't shown any remorse, and that's something I can't get to sit right.

Swiping the bat out of the gutter, I extend it to her. The air between us heats, our fingers brushing in the exchange. The contact is enough to have her eyes flicking to mine. The light above may be dim, but it's bright enough to see the way her lids hood, her lips part just barely as she pulls her skin from mine.

A zip of energy tumbles through my veins and I remind myself I can't tug on the bat and pull her into me. There's no way I can cover her lips with my own, sliding my tongue across hers, making her attempt at resistance to this proposed swing futile.

Instead, I step back.

"Batter up." Peck motions for her to go. "Let's see it."

"Are you really going to make me do this?"

"Did you really just smash the front of my truck?" I ask. "The answer is the same to both questions, Slugger."

Her eyes narrow, but there's a fire in them that turns me the hell on. She steps away from her friend, zapping all the power I held just a few seconds ago with the flick of her tongue. It darts out, rolling across her bottom lip as the bat comes over her head. Sticking her ass out, bending her knees, her eyes still locked on mine, she slices the bat through the air ... and stops it at the last possible second before impact.

It's everything I thought it would be.

"Any questions, fellas?" she asks, propping it up on one shoulder.

"I have one," I say, forcing a swallow, trying to redirect my thoughts. "If you could stop it that fast, then why the fuck didn't you do that the first time?"

"Very funny." She tosses the bat into the back seat of the car and crosses her arms in front of her again.

"Can I ask why you have a baseball bat to begin with?" Lance asks. "Do you belong to some softball league or something? If so, I just took a huge interest in women's softball."

Sienna laughs as Delaney's face turns red. "Delaney's car is like a scavenger hunt. You can find anything in there. So while she got sick, I just rummaged around in the trunk, found the bat, and fooled around." She looks at me, her eyes softening. "Are you going to be here for a while? I'll go home and get the money. I didn't bring my debit card with me tonight."

It'll cost fifty bucks to fix the damage and about an hour's time. Definitely not worth her going out of her way tonight. But it *is* worth making her come around again and say she's sorry. It might do her some good.

Might not hurt me either.

She clicks her tongue against the roof of her mouth, the motion driving me crazy.

"Come see me Monday morning at Crank. It's two streets over," I say, gesturing to the north, before I can talk sense in to myself.

"Smart," Peck whispers behind me, getting an elbow to the side from Lance.

Her jaw sets, a glimmer of resistance clouding her baby blue eyes. "I have plans Monday. I can try on Tuesday."

The nonchalant attitude cuts through me, like her fuckup is no big deal. I wasn't set on Monday morning, but I am now. "Monday or I call the Sheriff. Your decision, but make it quick. I got shit to do."

"Fine," she huffs. "Monday."

"Fine," I mock. "See you Monday morning."

We start back down the sidewalk, her gaze heavy on my back. I pause at the bumper of their car. "Peck got your license plate number, so don't think about not showing."

"I did not," Peck hisses, catching another elbow from Lance as their car doors open and slam shut.

"What the hell are you going to do with that?" Lance asks once we're out of earshot. "Because I have a list of suggestions if you need them."

As we get farther away, the air clearing of Sienna's perfume, I realize it's not suggestions I need. It's a heavy dose of self-control.

Crank is available now on Amazon, Audible, and in Kindle Unlimited.

ACKNOWLEDGMENTS

MY HUSBAND AND I HAD a friend in high school that gave us a piece of advice that's stuck with me my whole life. He pointed out that when we get ourselves in a pickle, we typically don't hesitate to ask the Creator for help. Then, in a moment of wisdom unusual for a sixteen-year old boy, he asked us to remember to be just as forthcoming with gratitude when things go right.

It's in that vein that I pause first to thank the Creator for this beautiful, chaotic, silly, amazing life I live.

My family is, and has always been, my biggest cheerleaders. There's really not enough words to thank Mr. Locke, the four Little Lockes, my mama, and Peggy and Rob. I love you all so, so very much.

I am nothing without my team. Kari (Kari March Designs), Lisa (Adept Edits), Kylie (Give Me Books), and the team at Red Coat PR —you make this possible. Day after day, release after release, you share your insight, wisdom, time and friendship with me. I want you to know I'll never take it for granted.

I have no clue how I functioned before Tiffany came on board. You, my right hand (and sometimes left), are more than I ever dreamed. Thank you for knowing what I mean when I can't find the words, gently tug me back when I get distracted, write down everything I say and bring it back at just the right time (sometimes months later), and stay on top of everything I can't.

My dear, sweet betas are still here. Trust me when I say, there was a time or ten I thought they'd bail. Many of you have been with me since day one, pre-reading every book I've ever written. Some of you have just come on board and jumped in with your honesty and sharp eyes (and, sometimes, tongues when I need it!). Thank you all for lending your talents to Swink.

Jen C, Jade, Tiffany, Ebbie, and Stephanie keep my groups running, memes coming, stickers posted, steps counted, and lots of laughs rumbling in between. I love you guys.

Susan, Candace, Carleen, and Joy deserve so much more than hugs. You deserve all the happiness in the world. Thank you for sticking by me.

This book wouldn't have happened with you, Mandi Beck. I would've lost my sanity a long time ago. Thanks for being a friend in every way that counts and a few that really shouldn't.

I write the words, you read them, but the bloggers of the world are the part in the middle that gets overlooked. I want to give a huge shout-out to all those men and women that read what they love and shout it from the rooftops. I see you. I appreciate you.

ABOUT THE AUTHOR

USA Today Bestselling author Adriana Locke lives and breathes books. After years of slightly obsessive relationships with the flawed bad boys created by other authors, Adriana created her own.

She resides in the Midwest with her husband, sons, two dogs, two cats, and a bird. She spends a large amount of time playing with her kids, drinking coffee, and cooking. You can find her outside if the weather's nice and there's always a piece of candy in her pocket.

Besides cinnamon gummy bears, boxing, and random quotes, her next favorite thing is chatting with readers. She'd love to hear from you!

www.adrianalocke.com

Made in the USA
Las Vegas, NV
11 March 2021